You know, is it any wonder I haven't been on a date in a year?

"You spend enough time swimming in a cesspool, it starts to just ooze out of you. I'm not good company." Detective Tony Flynn looked Tessa in the eye.

"Well, if you're not, then neither am I," she whispered.

"That I can't imagine. You sweep into your nightclub around midnight, and the place just halts for a second. Like everybody in there takes a breath at the same time at the sight of you."

"I think you're imagining things."

"It's the truth. So, elegant lady of the night, what do you know about evil?"

"Suffice it to say that years ago I was swayed by a man to leave my family, my home, my whole world. And he turned out to be a liar. Beyond that, he was evil. Last night at the club, something happened to convince me that he's still alive…and that he's come back for me…."

Dear Reader,

Enter the high-stakes world of Silhouette Bombshell, where the heroine takes charge and never gives up—whether she's standing up for herself, saving her friends from grave danger or daring to go where no woman has gone before. A Silhouette Bombshell heroine has smarts, persistence and an indomitable spirit, qualities that will get her in and out of trouble in an exciting adventure that will also bring her a man worth having…if she wants him!

Meet Angel Baker, public avenger, twenty-second-century woman and the heroine of *USA TODAY* bestselling author Julie Beard's story, *Kiss of the Blue Dragon*. Angel's job gets personal when her mother is kidnapped, and the search leads Angel into Chicago's criminal underworld, where she crosses paths with one very stubborn detective!

Join the highly trained women of ATHENA FORCE on the hunt for a killer, with *Alias*, by Amy J. Fetzer, the latest in this exhilarating twelve-book continuity series. She's lived a lie for four years to protect her son—but her friend's death brings Darcy Steele out of hiding to find out whom she can trust….

Explore a richly fantastic world in Evelyn Vaughn's *A.K.A. Goddess*, the story of a woman whose special calling pits her against a powerful group of men and their leader, her former lover.

And finally, nights are hot in *Urban Legend* by Erica Orloff. A mysterious nightclub owner stalks her lover's killers while avoiding the sharp eyes of a rugged cop, lest he learn her own dark secret—she's a vampire….

It's a month to sink your teeth into! Please send your comments and suggestions to me c/o Silhouette Books, 233 Broadway, Suite 1001, New York, NY 10279.

Sincerely,

Natashya Wilson

Natashya Wilson
Associate Senior Editor, Silhouette Bombshell

Please address questions and book requests to:
Silhouette Reader Service
U.S.: 3010 Walden Ave., P.O. Box 1325, Buffalo, NY 14269
Canadian: P.O. Box 609, Fort Erie, Ont. L2A 5X3

URBAN LEGEND

ERICA ORLOFF

Published by Silhouette Books
America's Publisher of Contemporary Romance

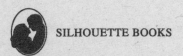

SILHOUETTE BOOKS

ISBN 0-373-51322-4

URBAN LEGEND

www.SilhouetteBombshell.com

Printed in U.S.A.

ERICA ORLOFF

is the author of *Spanish Disco, Diary of a Blues Goddess, Divas Don't Fake It* and *Mafia Chic,* all published by Red Dress Ink. She is the author of *The Roofer,* published by MIRA, and the upcoming Bombshell book *Knockout.* She loves playing poker—a Bombshell trait—and likes her martinis dry. You can visit her on the Web at www.bombshellauthors.com.

With love, to my father, who fueled my imagination with Sherlock Holmes and old Creature Feature movies when I was a kid. And to my mother, who always made sure I had plenty of books.

ACKNOWLEDGMENTS

Special thanks to my agent, Jay Poynor.
My editor, Margaret Marbury.
Donna Hayes, Dianne Moggy and all the terrific people at Bombshell, MIRA and Red Dress Ink, with whom I work and whom I admire. Thank you to the brilliant Pam Morrell, creature-of-the-night expert extraordinaire. Thank you to Cleo Coy, also a vampire fan. To Writer's Cramp—Pam, Jon and Gina. Thank you to Jen Yanchak for sharing her opinions on vampire lore. To Alexa, Nicholas and Isabella. And to J.D. For making me laugh. Occasionally making me cry. And being there…always.

Prologue

Shanghai, 1911

"It is the…boy," Shen had whispered, his voice trembling, his head bowed low to Tessa as she chanted before the small altar of Buddha in the corner of her bedroom. Shen's dark eyes had been shiny with tears.

Tessa had dropped her jade prayer beads to the floor. What she had feared most had come to pass. She extinguished her burning incense, pulled on her cloak and followed Shen through the black night, through the streets of Shanghai into dark alleyways filled with the noises of rough men, barbarians, Mongols, warlords, and drinkers, past houses lit by lanterns, to the opium den, its dim red interior filled with filmy curtains and silk cushions, to where her lover lay, not really a boy, but with a face always childlike and youthful.

Tessa had tried to steel herself for this moment, even as she rushed behind Shen, her black wool cloak up around her face, teeth chattering from nerves. But at the sight of Hsu's face, eyes shut as if just sleeping, she flung herself on the body and kissed his soft cheeks, his eyelids. She would have, in that instant, traded her soul for his, but she knew her soul was worthless to Buddha, to anyone. Neither truly alive nor truly dead, she was a vampire—though she could never bring herself to say that word aloud. Still she would trade places with the boy, with her Hsu, if she could.

Many nights, long after they had made love and murmured softly of their dreams and hopes, she had lain awake and stroked his face, his cheekbones sharp and high, his skin smooth and unlined. He was twenty, but he looked like a teenager, especially when he laughed, his black eyes alive with gaiety. He was brilliantly funny and quick-witted, able to manipulate words in clever ways to amuse her. He said his greatest happiness was making her squeal with laughter. "Your laugh is like my grandfather's crickets," he had said. "Music to me."

Tessa, frozen in time at thirty years of age, had first locked eyes with Hsu after a performance of the opera. She was used to being stared at, a British woman, green-eyed, once the lover of a diplomat who had called her his wife, though they were not really married. After Sir George Ashton III, a charmer who had scandalized his family by taking up with Tessa, died of typhoid, she had stayed in Shanghai, where she felt comfortable in her home and gardens, water lilies growing in the small, cool-water pool in the courtyard.

But meeting Hsu had changed her. He had threatened the very serenity she worked so hard to find at the altar of Buddha.

The intensity of the love affair frightened her. She thought she couldn't feel so strongly again. Her passion made her ache when Hsu was away from her, and shudder with desire each time he returned to her bed. Sir George had been a pleasant distraction, a merry bit of English wit. But Hsu had surprised her. Every breath she took was just in anticipation of seeing him again, of touching him. Their lovemaking went on for hours, and afterward they curled around each other breathing as one.

That had all changed. Tessa had her secrets. But so did Hsu. Over time, his secret destroyed them. The opium had started to take over his life, until he spent evenings languid and glassy-eyed, seemingly content to let Tessa stroke his face, but unable to do more, or uninterested in anything other than the featherlike touch of her fingertips along his flat stomach.

That night, at the sight of his body, cold, stiff, hands frozen in a position of torment on the cushion of the opium den, Tessa had felt a rage build in her belly. And after arranging for Hsu's body to be brought to his family, after mourning and chanting, she felt the rage grow.

Two weeks later, Tessa hired a guide, and, along with Shen, journeyed by night to the opium fields. Fire was an enemy, one of the few ways to kill a vampire, but Tessa didn't care. She would play with it. Fight with it. If she died, that would be better than living with this suffocating grief.

The opium fields she targeted belonged to a warlord, one of the last few warlords, a dying breed, in the country. The fields, in full bloom, were guarded by men along the perimeter. With a tendril of Hsu's hair in a gold locket around her swanlike neck, visions of her beautiful lover filling her mind, Tessa fought the guards one by one, picking them off with a furious crescendo of violent kicks and punches. Her strength was that of three men. One of the guards called her a devil and drew a dagger from his belt.

"You will pray for the devil by the time I am through with you," she spat at him, drawing her leg up and delivering a rib-shattering kick to his chest. He was doubled over and trying to catch his breath, gasping and sputtering blood, when another guard approached, hurling curses at her. He struck her face, hard, catching her by surprise and throwing her backward onto the ground, the poppies breaking her fall, a cushion of evil.

She rose up, gifted with the ability to, not fly, but raise herself, levitate. Then she had struck at him with her open hand, surprised at how the emotions of rage, guilt and grief combined to make her even stronger. She heard a *crack* as his cheekbone smashed beneath her fingers. He clutched at his face and receded into the darkness with a guttural scream.

Soon, six men surrounded her, threatening rape and a slow death by torture. She fought them off with all of her strength. She was unafraid. As a Buddhist, she knew how to contain her emotions in chanting. Now, she trained her mind; she thought of Hsu laughing as they ate rice and spoke of opera and the arts and Confucius until almost dawn, when she needed to withdraw to her secret chambers. His eyes, glassy and vacant when he smoked his opium, had once crinkled with joy when he was around her, his dimples deepening. These thoughts strengthened her resolve.

Her kicks landed with an accuracy like the slice of a blade, and in the end, the guards were defeated. She ran with a torch, letting the fire lick at the opium blooming red in fields of poppies as far as the eye could see.

As the fire rose higher, the acrid smoke choking her, Shen, her servant and friend, pulled on her arm, urging her back to the river where a boat lay at anchor waiting to take them south.

"Come. You have won. You have avenged the boy."

Tessa's regal profile was outlined in an orange glow from the fire, her dark hair pulled back from her face. Her cheeks were smudged with dirt and dried blood from the hand-to-hand battle she had fought. She shook her head sadly, a permanent grief settling deeper still in her chest.

"I haven't won, Shen. They'll plant more poppies. Opium, Shen, will be the downfall of mankind. They just can't see that yet."

"Come, Madame Tessa. Come." Shen looked nervously at the unconscious bodies of the guards, dirty, large men. One of them groaned. Two were dead.

Finally, much to Shen's relief, she nodded. They set off down a rough-cut path, picking their way through the blackness. When they reached the bottom of the hill, Tessa turned to look at the flames kissing the sky.

"I haven't won yet, Shen. But I will…. One day I will."

She kissed the locket around her neck and turned from the sight of the flames.

A boy. It had all started with a beautiful boy.

Chapter 1

Manhattan, present day

Tessa Van Doren looked out the window of her loft onto the madness on the street below her. Eleven-thirty p.m., and the city's beautiful people were packed six deep down the block and around the corner, behind velvet ropes, all vying to get into her club. She sipped at her forty-year-old cognac and spotted Flynn and his partner in their car across the street. Her hands shook ever so slightly, and she took a deep breath and then another sip of cognac. Flynn had lousy manners, always looked like he needed a haircut and a shave, and dressed in Salvation Army castoffs, but he thrilled her in a way that made a century of loneliness fall away.

She could have her pick of anyone. Men, dressed in expensive Italian suits, would try to pass Jorge, her head bouncer and guardian of the most desired velvet rope in all of Manhattan, a cool one hundred in neatly folded twenties, palm to palm. But Jorge, as far as she could tell, never took the money, was never swayed. He selected the crowd based on his own indefinable criteria. Somehow, by the end of the night, those inside the Night Flight Club would include the right mix of supermodels and celebrities, beautiful women and powerful men, journalists and sports stars, rappers and rock-and-rollers. And occasionally, the NYPD's Flynn and Williams. Flynn always drew stares, as if people wondered what the bouncer, Jorge, was thinking letting this joker past the velvet ropes—though Williams blended in perfectly. Detective Williams's skin was smooth and coffee-colored, and he wore his hair cut so close to his scalp that he looked almost royal, all cheekbones and strong jaw, with dark eyes and lashes that women would kill for.

Tessa walked over to the oriental desk she had brought with her years before from China and dialed the downstairs phone. "When detectives Flynn and Williams arrive, tell Lily to show Mr. Flynn into my office. Let Williams mingle."

Every night at midnight, Tessa would descend in her private glass elevator and make her way through her club to the back room, to the select few who made it into her inner sanctum, the VIP room, with its opulent deep-purple velvet couches and soft lighting. There she would hold court until nearly dawn with the big names and high rollers.

Tessa went back to the window and looked down on the near-mayhem below, then walked through her loft to her bedroom. The living room was full of antiques she'd collected over the years. She enjoyed the hunt, and could recount with startling accuracy the origins of each piece and how she had acquired it. On the walls hung paintings by Goya and Chagall, and one by Picasso—not her favorite, though—from his Cubist period. She loved her Rousseau most, the solitary moon peeking over the jungle vegetation. And of course, her tapestries from Shanghai, though she still felt a pang sometimes when she looked at them. Other oriental treasures sat on the mahogany custom-built shelves—jade figurines and porcelain vases, illuminated by recessed lighting. They reminded her of the happiest and saddest time of her life, her unnaturally long life. Later, when Tessa exited the loft, the best alarm system money could buy would protect her paintings and treasures, as well as her vintage clothing and jewelry collection—and her secrets.

She entered her bedroom, which was like walking into a vault of luxury. The bed was covered in pure silk sheets she had brought from Hong Kong. The canopy was a rich brocade. The carpets covering the dark hardwood floors, knotted with handmade craftsmanship, were from Iran, Pakistan, China and Turkey. Her furniture was heavy mahogany wood, late nineteenth century. Yet she mixed ruby-red glass-and-silver candleholders and candles and a collection of Steuben glass, as well as a whimsical collection of elephant statues and figurines, all with trunks raised, a sign of good fortune. The result wasn't stuffy or overdone, but simply spoke of great elegance and wealth. Far from being ostentatious, the loft was decorated with a taste and class honed over time. In actuality, the entire room *was* a vault, into which she could recede before dawn cast its first light over the island of Manhattan, and a Wellington lock and special alarm protected her from intruders. It was as if her bedroom was a giant panic room.

She walked to her cavernous dressing room, the size of a small New York City apartment. Mechanized racks rotated her clothes so she could see her incredible collection of vintage clothing: Dior, Chanel, Edith Head, Oleg Cassini, as well as new but elegant fashions from her favorites, including Dolce & Gabbana, one of the few new design teams of which she approved. Tonight she chose an Oleg Cassini gown, velvet, midnight-blue and strapless. Downstairs, amid the noise and drinking and the heavy techno-beat of the music spun by her DJ, who went by the simple moniker of "Cool," she knew most of the women would be dressed in miniskirts and knee-high boots—the season's latest. But Tessa never wavered from her vintage clothing. She always looked, Jorge told her, like she had just stepped into the room from another time, another place. Even if she hadn't owned Night Flight, she would, she knew, make the crowd part with her entrance.

Tessa zipped up her gown, expertly put on her makeup and then sipped her cognac again, thinking of Flynn and berating herself for this stupid infatuation. She wore her black hair up in a French twist, and diamond earrings dangled from her lobes. She chose a diamond brooch for the center of her cleavage and pinned it to her dress. Next she donned a diamond watch, a single sapphire ring that had once adorned a queen's hand, and, as always, she wore a gold bracelet with a small key attached.

Tessa approved herself in the triple mirror in her dressing room. She knew certain myths about mirrors and vampires—the work of the overactive imagination of Bram Stoker. She was vain enough to not leave her private quarters unless she was perfect. She knew, correctly, that she was always flawless, yet she never tired of that twirl in the triple mirror. Perhaps it was the reassurance that despite all she had lost, she still was eternally young.

Finally, she went to a small alcove off of her bedroom and knelt at the gold statue of Buddha. The idea of reincarnation appealed to her, as opposed to a Christian heaven or hell, Satan or Christ. She decided that she simply wouldn't die between reincarnations but would grow and learn with each human lifetime she lived, until she reached Nirvana. It was a bastardized version of Buddhism, she realized. Buddhists were not supposed to take lives, however evil the soul within the body was. But she chanted briefly and spoke a silent prayer nonetheless, the chant always taking her back to a time when she truly had been at peace. Then she left the loft, setting the alarm and taking the elevator down to the club.

Parked in their unmarked car, Alex Williams looked with disdain at his partner's attire.

"*Please* tell me you're not walking in there wearing that sorry-ass tie," Alex snapped at Tony Flynn as they sat across the street from the Night Flight Club, Manhattan's hottest night spot of the moment. "You'll make me look bad just by being *seen* with you, man."

"What's wrong with my tie?"

"For one thing, it's ugly. What is that? Puke-green? For another, it's right out of the eighties. Do you think you're a member of Duran Duran? Just how long do you keep these things hangin' in your closet? And three, it's a living history of your day. Is that a mustard stain?"

Flynn looked down and rolled his eyes. "Yeah…. From breakfast."

"I have to tell you…that's just *wrong*."

"I'd rather have a Sabrett's hot dog for breakfast than one of those friggin' soy shakes you drink."

Alex patted his washboard abs. "Pays off in my beautiful physique, man…. But you…hot dogs? And I think that white smudge is shaving cream."

Flynn stared at a smear of white on the pointed tip of the tie. It *was* shaving cream. He sighed. He hated shaving. He was blessed and cursed with thick black curly hair and a swarthy complexion and dark beard that three hours after shaving looked like five o'clock shadow, as if he hadn't shaved at all.

"And," Alex continued, "the pièce de résistance, ladies and gentlemen? Blue pen marks and a spot of Wite-Out. My friend, you write on *paper,* not your tie."

"Fuck you, Williams," Flynn muttered as they opened their car doors. They stood on the sidewalk a minute. "And what do I care what my tie looks like?"

Alex, always impeccably dressed in suits tailor-made for his former quarterback's body, shook his head. "The caliber of ladies at Night Flight, Flynn. The caliber of ladies. They're gonna take one look at you and run screaming. And that reflects on *me.*" He feigned hurt.

"I'm not here to cop a bunch of women's phone numbers, I'm here to check out the disappearance of one low-life drug dealer whose last known hangout was the Night Flight Club."

Alex sighed as the two men stepped from the curb and started walking toward the club with the confident yet slight swaggers that a combined total of twenty-eight years on the NYPD force buys two of New York's finest. Alex continued egging on his partner. "You can lie to your ex-wife. You can lie to your sainted mother if you want to, but don't lie to me. Your partner. The guy who took a bullet for you…right here." He pointed to his shoulder.

Flynn rolled his eyes. "Enough with the bullet already. It *grazed* you."

"Yeah, well, it entitles me to harass you for the rest of our lives. And I know one thing as sure as I know you had a microwaved hot dog for breakfast. I know you want *one* phone number…the home number of

Tessa. And she digs you, too, ugly ties and all. Makes me wonder about her."

"Yeah, well, I wonder all right. She's running a dirty club."

"Maybe. Maybe not. Look, it's a free country. She can't control every person who enters the club. Maybe she's legit."

"Sure, Williams. And the Carlucci family just *happens* to like the place a whole lot. They're not Boy Scouts. And she ain't no Girl Scout."

"If she was, I bet you'd buy a lot of Thin Mints."

Flynn slugged his partner in the arm. "Shut up already."

"You punched my bullet wound."

"I fuckin' give up." Flynn threw his hands in the air and tried not to let Williams see him smile.

As they neared the club entrance, the sidewalk was packed with women in low-rise skirts and Prada boots and men smelling of heavy cologne. The two partners pushed and squeezed their way through the crowd to the bouncer and flashed their badges, unaware they were being watched.

The minute Tessa walked into the club, she was greeted from every direction. "Tessa! Tessa! Over here." Someone snapped her picture, though she turned her head just in time, hating to be photographed, knowing photographs were dangerous. It was too hard to cover your tracks, to make a new life somewhere else if need be. She made a mental note to remind Jorge to emphasize that no photos were to be taken in the club and to confiscate the camera.

Tessa worked her way through the crowd, smiling and occasionally stopping to talk to someone she knew. Then she entered the back room. It was packed tonight. As she scanned the faces she spotted six A-list actors and actresses.

"Tessa," Michael Carlucci called. He was surrounded by three models, but he whispered something to them, and they vacated the overstuffed velvet couch. Tessa liked Michael because he had an American Express black card and liked to use it at Night Flight to buy Dom Pérignon. Last month alone, he charged thirty-two bottles. Tessa didn't care that he was acting boss of one of New York's crime families. His black card was good every time.

"Michael." She smiled and sat down next to him.

He leaned over so she could hear him over the music. "You look perfect as always, Tessa."

She gave him a sly look. "I'm always perfect...at everything."

"You make me crazy." He slid an arm around her. "I'd like to fuck you right now on the dance floor. How long's it been since you had a good fuck? Because all the ladies say I'm the best, baby."

"Tempting as that discreet offer is, I'll pass. Who are you romancing tonight? Wasn't that a Victoria's Secret model?"

"She can't hold a candle to you, and you know it. You're a hell of a piece of ass."

"She's probably half my age. I'd bet she's not

even of age. My bouncers must be falling down on their duties."

He shrugged his broad shoulders. "I like 'em young and anxious to please."

"Well then, why do you bother calling me over?" Tessa pouted, sliding in still closer to him. She wore a custom perfume she had had made in Hong Kong by a perfumer who was a master at creating the scent she alone wore—an intoxicating mixture of jasmine and lilies of the valley.

"You smell so fucking good, I could eat you alive."

"I'd like to see you try, you bad boy."

With that, she moved smoothly away from him.

"You drive me wild, Tess. So when are you going to go into business with me? We could have a night-club in Vegas just like this one. Vegas is where it's at now."

"I like being a lone operator, but if I ever change my mind, you'll be the first to know."

She stood and walked through the VIP room. She was hungry, and much as she tried to keep the serenity she found at the altar of Buddha, every nerve was on fire. Did anyone seem an appropriate victim? Was anyone causing trouble at the bar? She surveyed each club-goer with eyes that never failed to see through to their shortcomings, a sense of smell that could tell who was high on drugs, who was lying, who was nervous, who was weak, who was evil. After so long, evil, she knew, had a scent all its own. Just like drugs did. She relied on that scent. Maybe that was what drew her to Flynn. The detective worked on instinct, not unlike her own.

Jorge suddenly poked his head through the velvet curtains and motioned to her with his eyes. Tessa walked over to him. "What's up, darling?"

"He's in your office, like you said."

"Tell him I'll be there in a few minutes. Bring him a drink. He likes single-malt scotch. Neat."

"Fine taste for a...cop." He clenched his jaw. Jorge and cops didn't mix.

"Well, we like to keep our Mr. Flynn happy, Jorge." *And waiting,* she thought to herself. She liked dragging out the anticipation of seeing him just a little longer. That was half her problem. Life held so few thrills anymore that this chemistry with Flynn was almost addictive. She needed it to break the boredom.

She checked her delicate wristwatch at twelve-thirty and made her way out of the VIP room, back through the crowd to her office. Once she shut the door behind her, it was totally soundproof.

He was standing with his back to her.

"Detective Flynn." She smiled.

Flynn turned around. He'd been drinking his scotch and wondering why her office was so devoid of personal mementos. Of course the furniture was antique. Real old. He wasn't an expert on fancy furniture or period pieces, but he guessed the couch, desk, bookshelves and carpets cost as much as he would make in a lifetime. The thought depressed him. However, no photos of the rich and famous dotted her walls as they did those of most celeb-hangout owners. She seemed unimpressed by money, by movie stars. He was equally unimpressed, and this made him like her—despite telling himself she was out of his league—and probably in bed with the mob.

"Ms. Van Doren." He had taken off his tie and shoved it in his pocket. Maybe Williams was right about that tie. Still his pants were wrinkled and so was his shirt.

"What brings a detective of your stature to my humble little nightclub?"

"Humble nightclub? This is Studio 54 all over again. My guess is there's almost as much coke in the bathrooms. Or is it Ecstasy these days?"

"I throw people out for doing drugs. Ask anyone."

"I'm sure you do. That's probably what the owner of Studio 54 said, though. You know, this place is so popular, I think people would kill to get past your velvet rope outside."

"That's their foolish prerogative."

"You don't much care about the people in this club, do you."

Tessa shrugged her creamy porcelain-like shoulders, shown off nicely in her gown.

"What? You think they're *beneath* you? Not in your league?" Flynn always found himself baiting her. He didn't know why. It was like when he was in junior high and he thought he was in love with Maryanne Mooney; he used to tease her relentlessly about her freckles until he made her cry.

She stiffened. "No. They're not beneath me. But this is a business. I'm not caught up in the thrill of having my name on Page Six in the *Post* each week."

"I thought people like you lived for that shit." His voice dropped an octave with anger.

"Other people, maybe. Not me, Detective."

"No. You want to know what I think? I think because you're a classy lady with diamonds and a fancy club, you think you're better than the rest of us, including this working-stiff detective. Which is why you never give me a straight answer."

"I always answer your questions honestly," she said with mock innocence.

"Then how about telling me if you remember seeing Claude Montegna in your club the night he was found murdered. You were going to check your credit card receipts."

Tessa moved closer, until she was just a few inches from him, her scent not overpowering him but still making his stomach churn. He had a knot forming in the back of his neck. It always took all his energy to avoid being sucked in by her. He had to keep it in the forefront of his mind that he was investigating her. This wasn't a social call.

"It appears Mr. Montegna used cash," Tessa purred. "That's still legal last time I checked."

"You know, I could get a search warrant for those receipts. Don't fucking push me, Tessa."

"Oh, now it's *Tessa?*" She smiled smugly, obviously loving the way she got under his skin.

"I meant Ms. Van Doren."

"I like it when you call me Tessa. Or you can call me Tess. That's what my closest friends call me."

"Look...it doesn't matter what I call you. I'll call you busted if you don't watch out. The last thing any legitimate—and I use that term loosely—club owner wants is her books being pored over."

She touched his hand as he held his scotch glass. "You seem very hostile, Detective Flynn. A little edgy. How come?"

"I've got two unsolved cases."

"I have nothing to hide. I told you once before that Montegna was here. Jorge remembers him. But neither of us knows what time he left or with whom he left. I'm a club owner, not a baby-sitter. Maybe you should have gotten him one of those attractive little electronic ankle bracelets last time he got out of prison. You lost your man, Detective. I didn't."

"Well, he's the second high-end drug dealer killed in the last three months who'd been a regular here. And both of them had the blood drained out of them, their throats garroted. Ugly crimes." He put his now-empty scotch glass down on the desk. "How do you know you're not next?"

Tessa leaned still closer to him and whispered, her breath hot on his ear and causing him to become even more aroused, "Because I have you watching over me. You're my guardian angel."

She pulled back from his ear and smiled. He stared into her eyes. They were green and slanted slightly at the outer corners, giving her the faintly exotic look of a wild feline. He was convinced she was playing him for a fool—a poor fool with lousy suits and a detective's salary who couldn't afford to come to her club. But then when she smiled, it seemed so real.

"Let's have another drink." She took his glass and walked over to a wall faced with custom mahogany cabinets. She opened a double set of doors, revealing a bar, then poured herself a cognac and Flynn another scotch.

"May you find your killer." She raised her glass.

"I will, eventually."

"Perhaps you're closer than you even know." She winked at him.

They sipped their drinks. She didn't say anything, and neither did he. That was another thing that drove him crazy. The entire time he was married to Diana, they never had a single moment of "companionable silence." They just didn't fit together, and it was clear they'd made a huge mistake before the ink was dry on their marriage license. But Tessa…each time he came here, they ended up in her office, and each time they had a drink, or two or three. And each time, they fell into a silence that was…comfortable. As if they could talk to each other without saying anything out loud. He didn't even tell Williams about these silences 'cause his partner would give him shit about it forever.

After a while, Flynn asked, "How come you don't have any pictures on your walls?"

"I don't need pictures to tell me the Night Flight Club is successful. And I don't need to be poised on George Clooney's arm, or, heaven forbid, wrinkled old Mick Jagger's, to know who I am. I don't define myself that way."

"No family pictures? No boyfriend?" He regretted bringing it up the minute the words left his mouth. He expected her to mock him, but she didn't.

"No." She smiled but looked mournful. She stared at him, as if weighing whether or not to say something.

"What?"

Tessa shrugged those perfect shoulders again. Then she crossed behind her desk. "I *do* have one photo." She took a key from the bracelet around her wrist and unlocked her top desk drawer. She removed and then held over to him a small four-by-five photo. It was a candid shot of him and Williams at the bar in black and white, a bit blurred.

"My surveillance camera took it."

Flynn was puzzled. "Why?"

"If you have to ask, then I'm afraid you're not as smart a detective as your press clippings seem to imply…. Well, if that's all in the matter of Mr. Montegna, I need to get back to work."

Flynn was still looking at the photo. He looked terrible in it, haggard, as if he hadn't shaved, of course. "Here's your picture…Tess." He handed her the photo.

She showed him to the door of her office. "Always a pleasure, Mr. Flynn. Don't be a stranger."

She leaned over to him and kissed him, not on the cheek but on the neck. It was more intimate. And it took all his discipline to keep from kissing her back.

As Tony Flynn returned to the noise of the club,

he instantly missed being in Tessa's company. He missed the silence between them. He searched the club until he found Williams at a back table seated next to a beautiful redhead. A natural redhead by the looks of her, with slightly freckly alabaster skin and rosebud lips.

"Time to go, Alex. She ain't giving anything up."

Alex whispered something to his new companion, and she scribbled a phone number on a napkin.

Outside the club, Flynn was unusually quiet.

"What's up, man? She's got you bewitched, doesn't she. I never thought I'd live to see the day when Tony Flynn would be gaga over a woman. This from the guy who thinks a great date is dinner at the pizzeria with a pitcher of beer."

"I think she knows more about Montegna. I just have a feeling. I can't shake it."

"So we keep digging." They got back to the car, and Williams asked, "Wanna go get a drink at that place on 86th?"

"Nah." Flynn shook his head.

"Did you know you've got red lipstick on your neck?"

Flynn wiped at the spot with his thumb. "It was nothing."

"Whatever you say, partner."

"I said it was nothing."

"Sure. Okay. Nothing."

"I mean it!"

"Yup. Sure you do."

"You're an asshole."

"Now, there you're wrong..."

"You should have gone to law school, Williams."

As Flynn drove the two of them away, all he could think about was the silence. How good it had felt to share the silence. And that damn perfume of hers.

At three o'clock that morning, a man squirmed in a chair in the basement of the club. He was tied up in a room covered in tile, similar to a mortuary.

"So...do you like hitting women?" Tessa asked, her eyes full of ice-cold rage.

He shook his head, sweating, nervous, trying to shake off the drugs he'd taken.

"I don't like when men hit women. Not in my club. And I *especially* don't like men who think they can get away with trying to rape someone in my alleyway."

The man's oily skin grew slicker. Tessa drew closer to him. She was so close she could hear his heart beating. "And you know what else? I know you've been trying to deal coke in my club. I can also tell this isn't your first time to throw a woman against a wall and rape her. You're a *very* bad man. I like the taste of very bad men."

She smiled as she drew back and then sank her teeth into his neck, her canines growing longer as she fed. He struggled against her, moving his neck back and forth, fighting the terror consuming him now. She was like a dog with a limp mouse in its jaws. Though the man shook from side to side as much as his ropes allowed, she never relaxed her jaw. Her heartbeat and his became one in a dizzying struggle.

It was like a bird's wings beating against the inside of her rib cage—a hawk's wings, by the strength of the pulse inside her. She felt his blood being drawn into her. Eventually, his heartbeat stopped and hers grew stronger. The wings against her rib cage stopped. The air grew still once more.

When she finished feeding, she had, as always, that moment of remorse. She thought of Hsu and the long journey that had brought her here, to this club, to this moment, always on some quest she couldn't quite define, to rid the world of a scourge. She would pray to Buddha later. This time, the remorse for the drug dealer before her also mingled with something else she hadn't felt in a long time.

She'd dispose of this victim. Then she'd sleep all day. She never dreamed. She likened her sleep to someone losing consciousness. But sometimes, after she'd seen Flynn, she'd wake up the following night aware of him, with the feeling of longing that she had now, as if somehow he'd invaded that lost consciousness. It was the closest she ever came to dreaming.

And it was only and always about Flynn.

Chapter 2

The phone rang at seven o'clock the next night. Tess heard it from the recesses of a deathlike sleep.

She had once tried to describe her sleep to Hsu. But it was impossible. Though she did not sleep in a coffin, preferring to create a vault of her bedroom, her sleep was coffinlike, suffocating, dark, deep. Almost comatose. Rousing herself from it was difficult. After a feeding, she always slept well, though, the incessant craving that was like a frantic buzzing in her heart and head quieted.

She stirred now and answered the phone.

"Hello?" Her voice was raspy.

"It's Hack."

"If it isn't my favorite computer vigilante. How are you?"

"See today's *Daily News?*"

"No. I just woke up." By now she had gotten used to reading the "morning paper" after supper.

"You're the only person I know who's more of a night owl than even I am. Listen…it's another small item about a drug overdose. And word is, the cops don't know quite what to make of it."

Tessa sat up in bed, her eyes perfectly attuned to the darkness. She reached, rather than fumbled, for her bedside lamp, though she didn't need it, her eyesight was so keen. Next to the lamp was a glass of water. She drank gratefully, her throat always dry after such a deep sleep.

"What do you mean, they don't know what to make of it?" She ran her left hand through her hair and then rubbed her eyes.

"It's something new, the drug…like a hybrid. Something they haven't seen before. At least, that's what I'm picking up in e-mails I hacked into. I can try to find out more for you."

Hack was a compulsive junk-food lover, and an equally compulsive computer hacker.

"What are you eating?" Tessa asked.

"Hmm-mph" came the muffled reply.

"I'm almost afraid to ask, you know."

"Box of HoHo's."

"A *box.* Not just one or two. I don't understand how you can eat that crap." Of course, she fed on blood, so the irony wasn't lost on her.

"I'd have a seizure if I ate something green. Listen…I gotta go, Tessa. Did you get it for me?"

"It's winging its way to your apartment as we speak." Hack refused payment for all he did for Tessa. But, over the course of many nights on the telephone and computer, she had discovered that besides HoHo's and fried Twinkies and pork rinds, he loved a hard-to-find soda. Tessa soon started sending him cases of Manhattan Special soda from a distributor in Brooklyn. Like most night-owl techies, he thrived on caffeine, and the rich black coffee soda was a particular weakness of his.

Tessa had originally hoped to entice "Technofreak"—his online handle—with champagne and models at the Night Flight Club, but Hack wasn't interested in clubbing—just revenge, like she was. Either way, she wanted to keep him happy because when she wanted information, he was able to get it. She never asked how, but he was brilliant at what he did…if a little quirky. She had never been to his apartment, but she assumed it was wall-to-wall gadgets and equipment. And security systems. Not unlike the abode of a vampire, she mused.

"You're killer, Tess."

"Thank you…I think. *Ciao,* Hack."

"Fight the good fight."

"Always."

Tessa had met Hack in an alternative drugs newsgroup on the Internet. She was Nightlady. Over time, she and Technofreak discovered neither was interested in learning how to make homemade methamphetamine—recipes that called for mixtures of prescription pills and over-the-counter caffeine pills.

Unlike the other members of the newsgroup, they were both against drug use. One night, well over two years before, around three o'clock in the morning, they had met in a private chat room Technofreak set up. Over the next two hours, she learned his story.

Technofreak: U say U want to know my story.
Nightlady: I do. Sincerely.
Technofreak: I've never told anyone.
Nightlady: I'm good with secrets.
Technofreak: I can tell…. I don't know. I've got a feeling U R cool, ya know?
Nightlady: U 2.
Technofreak: OK. So here goes… I'm 24. And I haven't left my house in three years.
Nightlady: How come?
Technofreak: I can't.
Nightlady: Why?
Technofreak: I wish I knew. Agoraphobic. Like, I step outside my apartment and I just freak. Get it? Techno-freak. When I go outside, I feel like I'm having a fucking heart attack.
Nightlady: I know a little bit about feeling trapped.
Technofreak: Yeah?
Nightlady: Long story. Go on…
Technofreak: So I had a brother. A twin brother. Identical. Only way to tell us apart was he had a small scar over his left eye where our dog Huck scratched him once when we were kids.
Nightlady: Cool. I don't have any siblings. U close?

Technofreak: Super close. Were close, that is. We grew up with a crazy-as-shit stepfather. It was me and my bro against this dude. This asshole beat my mother. He beat my brother Roger. He beat me. Left big-ass bruises. Starved us. It was really nuts. Always too clever to get caught by Social Services. I have cigarette burns, scars, on the inside of my thighs. Hidden. He thought he was so fucking clever.

Nightlady: Depraved piece of shit. It's no wonder U don't want to leave your house. U went through hell. I'm so sorry. Though I know that sounds so weak.

Technofreak: It doesn't. I know U mean it. Thanks. Yeah. Shit. This is hard. OK, so we both turn 16. Me and Roger. We're athletic (I am one handsome dude, Nightlady) and we beat up the bastard. Bad. We go in one night when he's passed out half- drunk. I had a bat and my brother had a golf club, and we just go to town. We beat him up and break one of his legs at the kneecap, and kick him out and tell him if he friggin' shows up on our doorstep again, we'll kill him. Meant it too. I would have done it and not looked back.

Nightlady: Good for U. You were brave to do that.

Technofreak: We just had reached our limit, and we had grown. We weren't going to be pushed around anymore.

Nightlady: What about your mom?

Technofreak: She was relieved. So, we think we're

free. Man, months go by. Months. We start to laugh. Relax. Mom is smiling. She just is this new person. It was like the best fuckin' four months of my life. And then the motherfucker just shows up at the restaurant—this little diner—where Mom works and blows her away in the parking lot as she's locking up for the night.

Nightlady: Shit. I am so sorry. I am so sorry. Fuck. I don't even know what to say.

Technofreak: I know. So after he shoots Mom, he shoots himself. Right in the head. So he doesn't even go to jail. Doesn't suffer. Doesn't pay for his crime.

Nightlady: U ever study Buddhism?

Technofreak: A little.

Nightlady: He is paying for that crime wherever he is.

Technofreak: I hear you, but still. Anyway, my brother and me, we graduate high school. We both get football scholarships (did I tell U what a hunk I am?) to a school in Connecticut. We try to hold ourselves together. But more and more, I'm afraid to go out in open spaces. And more and more, he's using drugs.

Nightlady: U both had been through so much.

Technofeak: I know. And he's using meth like there's no tomorrow. He gets cut from the team, drops out of school. He has a habit like $300 a friggin' day. He's robbin' me. Stealing from old roommates. Selling everything he owns. Selling *himself. Man, it was bad. Eventually, Nightlady, he overdoses.*

Nightlady: What is a person's limit on loss? I am so sorry, Technofreak. So that's why U R so against drugs.

Technofreak: I try to hack into and destroy sites that promote drugs. Sites that tell kids in high school how to make meth. Sites that R just bad news. I couldn't save my mother. I couldn't save my brother. But I fight the good fight. From the four walls of my apartment. So, what's your story?

Nightlady: It's complicated. A lot of secrets. I once loved a man so much that seeing him made me feel like I was spinning around, dizzy. It was so intense, and as much as I would tremble when I would see him, I also knew a peace with him I never had with anyone else. And he got addicted to drugs. At first, he just smoked to relax. Then— Well, it's all the same story isn't it? It all spirals down to the same place one way or another. He died. Overdosed. And since then, I have the money and the means, the will and the ability to destroy every dealer I come across. I take no prisoners. I don't care if I die, or others die. Like you say, I fight the good fight.

Technofreak: You're a vigilante?

Nightlady: Kind of. So what do U think of that? Of me? Do U judge me?

Technofreak: No. Let me help U. I can hack into anything. Any computer. Any system. NYPD. Fed-

eral government. I can fight the good fight from
here. And you can-go out there and bring them
down.

Tessa nicknamed him Hack, and learned more
about his special skills. Soon, he was seeking out files
from the NYPD, from the medical examiner's office
and from a reporter at the *Daily News* who seemed to
have an edge when writing stories on drug wars and
crimes—he always had the scoop first. But that wasn't
all. As the first case of Manhattan Special arrived on
Hack's doorstep (if indeed he lived where he said he
did) Hack revealed to her that he also combed the alternative drugs sites, and visited dozens and dozens
of newsgroups and sites frequented by addicts and
users. In this way, he was able to check out rumors
and find out the latest street names for the club drugs
that had become so fashionable—special K, Ecstasy,
MDMA—as well as learn about places where buying
drugs was like going to an open market.

Tessa thought back on all the information he had
given her over the last couple of years. He was in-
valuable to her, a part of her, though they had never met.
He never asked, when he read, as he surely did, about
a drug dealer's death, or a shell of a ghetto building that
housed an Ecstasy operation going up in flames. He
didn't ask if she was a killer or an angel. A sinner or a
saint. Somehow, he simply accepted her, and accepted
that together they were a team, united in grief.

Tessa stretched across her bed. The room was
windowless; a series of intricate locks decorated the

door, making it akin to a "safe room" in the mansions of the rich. Like the entire apartment, the room was wired for security. Once the door was locked, the room was soundproof, silent, and, for Tessa's purposes, safe. From daylight. From intruders.

She had memories of the sun. They were fuzzy, out-of-focus memories from her childhood. Vague flashes of sun dazzled in her daydream but conveyed no warmth. She often found herself watching the Travel Channel for its shots of the beaches of Bali or the sunny shores of Hawaii. She felt a longing for the sun on her face. Something about the fact that she couldn't, ever, see the sun, made her crave it. It was an ache, like the mourning she felt for Hsu, and it had taken many years to grow used to it. She once heard someone say, about grief, that you never get over missing a person, you just move to different kinds of missing. That was how she felt about Hsu…and the sun. First it was a sharp pain that took her breath away, and now it was only a mild throbbing, like a dull headache.

Instead, Tessa tried to revel in the night. The night allowed her to carry out her mission. The night hid her in the shadows. It had been so long since she'd seen the sun, but the memory, like memories of Hsu, of her home in Shanghai and the gardens was still with her, however faded.

The phone rang again.

"Hello?"

"Are you feeling remorseful, my Buddhist friend?"

"Shut up, Lily."

Lily and Tessa were, in a sense, sisters, both "sired" by the same vampire, Marco. Both under similar circumstances, in London, though Tessa was the daughter of a landholder, and Lily a servant. They had escaped Marco as his appetites grew stronger and the sense of evil about him increased. But, though friends, their similarities ended there.

Tessa was determined not to lose what threads of humanity she had, however tenuous. She would never become like Marco. She embraced Buddhism, in her own fashion, a spiritual mixed bag, and meditated and chanted nightly to keep her appetites from consuming her. Lily, on the other hand, found Tessa's sympathy for humanity, her quest to eradicate drugs, amusing. Lily also wasn't like Marco. She didn't radiate darkness. She enjoyed Tessa's company, as well as singing at the Night Flight Club on Tuesdays and some weekends. She would feed on whatever victim suited her, but out of deference to Tessa, she kept to Tessa's odd code: dealers, pushers, pimps, murderers, child abusers. Lily's reasons weren't as pure, but she was along for the ride.

"You're always such a bitch when you just wake up. All I'm asking is, are we going hunting tonight?"

"Yes."

"Fine. Meet you on the roof of your place at midnight?"

"To fight the good fight."

"To feed, Tessa. To feed. But if you want a fight, you know I like kicking ass as much as the next vamp."

"Meet you at midnight. It's a full moon."

Tessa rose, checked both her watch and three clocks in her room, both battery-powered and electric, to confirm it was truly dark out, and unlocked the bedroom door, turning off the alarm. She stepped out into the hallway, which still afforded her shielding from the sun, and then the living room—with its custom blackout blinds. The place was in total darkness. She turned on a Tiffany lamp and then, walking through to the kitchen, the halogens that illuminated the kitchen island.

Her eyesight was keen, as were some extra senses that let her maneuver in sheer blackness, but she found lighting her loft was comforting in some way, a connection to her old life. The life before she could see in darkness. Before she lived in darkness.

She sat down at the breakfast bar and turned on her laptop, then scrolled through her e-mail for anything from Hack. Over time, she had come to really care for him. She had even offered to pay a top Manhattan shrink to do home visits, to the tune of five hundred dollars an hour, in the hope of curing Hack of his agoraphobia. But after a time, she had just accepted Hack, as he did her.

He, of course, did an Internet search on her, she learned later. He could find nothing on Tessa Van Doren. Sure, there were gossip column snippets where she was always termed "the elusive Ms. Van Doren," "the stunning nightclub owner" or "the beautiful lady of New York's nightlife." But after that, nothing. No college records. No driver's license— she never did learn to drive. No record of anything.

She wondered what he thought; once he even called her "Lady Dracula" because she never ventured out in daylight. But he said nothing, just as she no longer asked Hack when he had last eaten real food or tried to step foot in his hallway.

Hack had forwarded her a couple of news articles on a new "club drug" that seemed to be making the rounds. Deemed more intense than Ecstasy, it allowed party-goers to dance all night—and make love all night. They might also die, because the new drug was so untested, so pure, that guessing how much to take in one hit was like Russian roulette.

Tessa stretched her arms skyward, then picked up the remote and tuned in to the news on her plasma flat-screen TV. Then she rose, showered and dressed in her hunting clothes. She kept those clothes in an armoire under lock and key. Black leather pants and vest, black leather gloves, black boots with steel toes. A dagger strapped to her hip. She braided her long black hair. The braid fell halfway down her back. She added black makeup around her eyes so that she bore no resemblance to Tessa Van Doren, the elegant mistress of the velvet rope. She was someone else. She was a huntress.

Chapter 3

At midnight, the view from the rooftop of Tessa's building afforded her a look at the hordes of party-goers vying to get into her club. They were all well-dressed, and long, black stretch limos lined the street. For club kids, getting beyond the velvet rope was like reaching Nirvana. Wind whipped at Tessa's face, but she stared out into the night, waiting to feel the arrival of Lily.

Tessa's senses operated on a heightened level. That was another reason her master bedroom was silent, vaultlike. She could hear minor annoyances like the drip from a faucet or the far-off beeping horn of a yellow cab. So, in a city that never slept and was never quiet, she sought silence, a retreat from the way in which every noise reverberated—including her own pulse, which grew louder when she needed to feed.

She felt Lily before she ever saw her. Both of them had the ability to leap from rooftop to rooftop, looking, to those below, like flashes of black on the darkness of the sky. They moved so fast that anyone who saw them and looked again would see nothing, and would assume a trick of the eye, a flutter of pigeons taking flight.

"Lily." Tessa smiled as her friend landed silently beside her.

"Tessa, you look ready for the hunt. Shall we fly?"

"In a minute." Tessa stared up at the night sky. "I was enjoying the stars. The stars and the moon. That's all we have."

"You're always so dramatic."

They were a study in contrasts. Tessa, dark and green-eyed, with pale skin and aristocratic features; Lily, a platinum blonde with spiked hair and a diamond nose-piercing. She wore purplish lipstick, and her cornflower-blue eyes gazed out from beneath heavy mascara and black eyeliner. She wore a black scarf over her head to hide the platinum color, attempting to blend in with the night, though little spikes still poked out from beneath, fighting the confines of the scarf. On Lily's right breast, just showing in the cleavage of her black jumpsuit, she had a tattoo of a Chinese symbol. She had asked Tessa to come with her and draw the symbol for the tattoo artist, a burly former Hell's Angel called Boulder with a parlor down by New York University. The symbol Lily chose was for *revenge*. In Lily's case, she had no desire to pay back drug dealers for the havoc they wreaked on humankind. Instead, Lily wanted to kill Marco, and she knew, as Tessa did, that eventually he would find them. But this time they would be ready for him. This time it was him...or the two of them.

They stared up at the night sky, its stars obscured by cloud cover and the reflected lights of Manhattan. Tessa invoked Buddha and asked for forgiveness. Then they leaped over the alleyway to the next roof, seemingly frozen in the air, and landed almost in slow motion.

"Race you." Lily smiled over at her friend, not even breathless. She bore no resemblance to the fair-haired, rosy-cheeked, naive servant girl she had once been. The modern Lily loved to shock. She liked to race. She liked speed and danger and power. She liked to walk into a room in over-the-knee boots and a miniskirt and to straddle a man—any man—who was appealing to her. Lily liked to tempt and tease. And now she wanted to race across the rooftops of Manhattan.

"You know I love a challenge," Tessa said. The two friends eyed each other. Then Tessa winked.

Without another word, they flew. They ran across rooftops in fast strides, a blur of black, then took huge leaps to the next building, racing on, faster and faster. Occasionally, Lily let out a squeal of delight. She loved rushes of adrenaline. She had even been sky-diving, at night. Lily had once even convinced Tessa to break into the confines of the Bronx Zoo at two o'clock in the morning one November, where they had stealthily crept from the giraffes to the wolves, to the edges of the pride of lions. They had sat there, in the grasses, and listened to the lonely roars of the lions, knowing the lions would prefer the grassy plains of Africa, just as they would prefer the daylight and delights of their own home country.

Lily, especially, loved to leap between buildings, delighting in the one gift being a vampire afforded her. In her immortality, her fears of lifetimes ago, fears of height and darkness, and even of sex, no longer mattered. She was invincible. She was powerful.

Tessa, though, always beat her friend. For a time, decades before, the two women had been separated. In their time apart, Lily had succumbed to her appetites, and she had lived the hedonistic life—or walking death—of a vampire. But in that time apart, Tessa, instead, had honed her fighting skills. She fenced. She practiced ancient martial arts and swordplay. She acquired samurai swords and ancient weapons and learned how to use them. Those years of training had paid off with a precision in her fighting skills and an effortless grace in her flights.

When Tessa was first sired, she had no skills as a fighter, even less skill as a huntress. But she would be ready to face down Marco this time. He would never again imprison her—in body, mind or spirit. She swore this on Hsu's soul.

Tessa and Lily continued their race until they reached the very edges of a scarred area of Alphabet

City, those New York City streets with letters in their addresses. Long a place inhabited by fringe elements of society, it had a rough reputation, though certain buildings and streets had been rehabilitated during Mayor Giuliani's term, when cleaning up New York had been his vow and community policing had brought results. But Tessa and Lily also knew apartments that housed crack dens.

Standing on a rooftop, they looked down, watched cars hurtle down the street—New York City drivers were fearless. Outside the building across the street, two homeless men were passed out, leaning against each other. A cluster of men nearby seemed to be keeping watch on the front door of that building. Hack had told Tessa he'd tracked the address from the file of a crack addict arrested eight weeks ago.

A fairly steady stream of traffic entered the building, its windows fronting the street blacked out, boarded up, or simply pitch-black on black in the darkness.

"You ever think…" Lily asked, "that if we weren't so intent on doing what we do, fighting this kind of crazy shit, that we might be just like them? Just drugging to get away from what it is we are?"

Tessa shrugged. "You know my story. If I didn't do what I do, I think I would climb on the roof of my building one day and wait for the sun to kiss my cheek…and then kill me."

"That's a scary thought." Lily shuddered.

"No scarier than letting your soul get swallowed

alive by the smoke curling up from a crack pipe. When it was opium, they called it 'chasing the dragon.' That's all it is."

"You ready?"

Tessa nodded. "Dealer's name is Baby Rock."

"Poetic."

"I know. A regular William Wordsworth."

"Let's do it, Tess."

Tessa nodded, and they leaped from their vantage point to the brick building across the street, undetected, as part of the wind that seemed to pick up, howling through the canyons between apartment houses.

Using the fire escape, they entered through a hall window on the third floor of the building. Hack's information was that Baby Rock kept a place on the third floor; actually, Hack said Baby Rock kept *all* of the third floor.

Tessa and Lily crept down the hallway in synchronized silence. Tessa knew they were as invisible as shadows to the crack addicts, some slumped against walls that were painted a dull, almost military gray. Tessa and Lily paused outside the door of what had once been 3B, but which now was simply the entry to the maws of hell for anyone caught in the throes of addiction. Baby Rock had quite a business, Hack said. Crack wasn't all of it. He had a veritable stable of whores who worked the streets in exchange for drugs. Lily had seen their type before, often leaving their children in the care of relatives or the overburdened foster care system, or even on nearby sidewalks, sleepy and hungry. These women were hollow-eyed, as much zombies as Marco's slaves. She pitied them—but pitied their children more, often pressing money into the hands of sleeping youngsters, hoping beyond hope that they could escape this life lived in darkness and emptiness. She knew what darkness was like. She knew what it was like to lose your soul to it through no choice of your own.

Tessa and Lily silently read each other's signals, then Lily kicked in the door in one swift motion— Bam!—while Tessa immediately flew at one of the drug-addled bodyguards of Baby Rock, crushing his right kneecap with a sickening crunch of bone with her boot as she landed a strong roundhouse kick. He screamed in agony and fell to the ground, spitting fury.

Out of the corner of her eye, Tessa sensed and saw, in the same moment, two men drawing semiautomatics up near their chests. Bullets flew as crack-dazed addicts shrieked and fell to the ground, taking cover beneath tables and behind ripped easy chairs and stained couches. Panic and confusion reigned in the room as gunfire blazed, but Tessa and Lily moved with practiced, methodical, cold fury.

Lily spun with such speed, she became just a blurred whirlwind, ripping the gun from one man's hands as she broke his ribs with an accurately landed elbow. She sank her teeth into the soft flesh of his neck. Tessa knew that Lily always felt empowered with the first kill, knowing that the fear generated by this act alone would stun, then scatter most of the rest of their prey—in this case the foot soldiers of Baby Rock.

Tessa watched as the second gunman aimed for her and let loose a blast of ammunition that echoed in her ears. Her vision was so accurate she could see bullets in the air. She hit the floor and rolled to avoid being shot, even as she felt her canines growing from the very roots of her bones, felt the pain of that transformation. She rolled and then rose to standing, seizing the shocked man. She snapped back his neck by pulling on his hair, and bit his throat. His last words were a prayer for salvation. Even as she tasted him, she knew he had killed many times in the past. Maybe it was the ability of killer to sense killer. Salvation would elude him—at least this time around.

"Karma's a bitch," she whispered as she dropped his limp body to the floor and walked toward another gunman who had emerged from what appeared to be a back bedroom.

Lily joined her. Screams still emanated from the addicts around them. The gunman from the bedroom opened fire, but Lily and Tessa ducked to either side of the blast of bullets, then flew toward him, their pupils dilated to large black saucers and their fangs now clearly not human.

"Holy fuck! What the hell *are* you bitches?"

Tessa reached him first. Glancing in the back bedroom, she could see a young girl, not more than thirteen, naked, splayed across the bed, her body bruised and unnaturally bent.

"Never call me a bitch." Tessa sneered. She grabbed the gun from him as if she was ripping a toy from a baby's hands. The gunman, lanky, with pockmarked skin and dreadlocks, dropped to the floor and covered himself with his arms. Tessa could smell that he was high. For a moment, she took pity on him, but smelling death, she realized the girl on the bed was beyond abused. She had been murdered.

She grabbed him by the arm and pulled him up to her height. "Look me in the eyes, you fuck."

He trembled and hid his eyes with his hands, so she pried them away from his eyes and commanded him again: "I said look at me."

He reluctantly returned her gaze. "P-please…I— I didn't know she was only twelve."

Tessa didn't even want this man's blood within her. She wrapped her hand around his throat and lifted him off the ground. She didn't feel anger—at least, not the rage she used to feel when she was young, passionate, and with all the foibles of humanity. She snapped his neck, and then went into the bedroom. The little girl had an almost beatific look on her face, with long black hair tied into ponytails with dirty pink ribbons. Her breasts were just tiny mounds, her skin smooth and the color of café au lait. She had a small smile on her lips, but her big, brown eyes were frozen and fixed.

Tessa closed the eyelids of the girl. Then she covered the body with a sheet from the floor. The dingy sheet was stained, but it offered a modicum of modesty. No mother or father, however messed up, deserved to see his or her child this way. Tessa whispered to the dead girl, "You've probably had some terrible suffering in this life, baby. Next one will be easier. I promise."

She turned from the sight. All that was left was finding Baby Rock. She sensed movement at the far end of the apartment. The addicts were all still hiding, clustered in groups of two and three, moaning from fear, but she felt vibrations from the other side of a large door. It was his safe room. Tessa was sure of it.

Tessa moved toward the door, her beyond-human hearing picking up on panicked whispers on the other side. Lily was next to her, her strength even greater from feeding. They didn't even need to speak to one another, communicating on some other level, not, Tessa mused, unlike cops who'd worked with a partner a long time. Tessa nodded to Lily, who took three paces back, then ran and kicked down the door with a crash that reverberated through the apartment. Tessa entered quickly, crouching, expecting bursts from semiautomatic weapons at any moment. She was not disappointed.

Two men at either corner of the room, wearing gang colors and obvious prison tattoos on their massive biceps, fired at Lily and Tessa, shooting up the walls in the process. Cement pieces and plaster flew along with bullets, and dust from the destruction of the walls billowed around Tessa. She advanced on one man, Lily on the other.

Tessa leaped toward the ceiling, coming down with a side kick that landed at Baby Rock's bodyguard's throat. His gun dropped to the floor as he fell to his knees, no air coming from his crushed windpipe. He drew another gun as his final act, but Tessa kicked that one from his hand, and he was dead moments later. Lily was at the neck of the other man, feeding. And that left Baby Rock, who cowered in a corner, holding on to a gun in each hand, eyes wide with disbelief and the expression of someone on crack.

"What's the matter?" Tessa approached him. "Too fucked up to fight?"

He mumbled something and fired one gun, wildly missing her. She kicked that hand, forcing the gun from it, and with a loud clatter it spun across the linoleum floor. In a split second she had his other hand in hers, gun pointed safely at the ceiling. She released the clip, and it, too, fell to the floor.

"Don't kill me!" Baby Rock pleaded, a shiny gold tooth glinting in his mouth. He wore the latest "gangsta" fashions from Sean John and enough chains around his neck to give Mr. T a run for his money. "I'll give you all the crack you want. Ask anybody…Baby Rock has the best supply in the city."

"That's what we hear. But we didn't come here for your crack."

"Money. You want money? Yeah, yeah." He grew excited. "Sure…I got a bag full of it over there." He nodded toward a closet.

"We don't want money, either." Tessa shook her head. "Do you believe in reincarnation?"

"Reincarnation? Yeah…sure, whatever, lady. Just don't kill me."

She pulled him to her and sank her teeth into him. As his body went limp, she released him and whispered, "You'll pay in the next life for the suffering you've inflicted…"

Stepping over his body, Tessa went to the closet where he had said he kept his money. She had a "Robin Hood" fund of her own. She never used the money on herself, but would dole it out to the homeless, to the children of addicts, to church poor boxes. She and Lily went through the apartment, urging the addicts to emerge from their hiding places and get outside on the street to safety. Shaking, shuffling, they slowly got up. They were like ghost people, soulless. As they made their way out of the apartment and then the building, Tessa and Lily went to the bodies of the men they had fed on, and, taking their daggers, slit the area where their fangs had left telltale vampire bites. Tessa knew that the crack addicts would either keep mum or would rant about supernatural phenomenon the cops would think were hallucinations. As sirens echoed in from the windows, NYPD cars making their way onto the street in response to the gunfire, Lily and Tessa moved out of the apartment and up the stairwell to the rooftop. They were five buildings away before the first officers reached the front door of the building.

* * *

Technofreak: *Got the files of the Daily News guy who covered the Baby Rock home invasion.*

Nightlady: Not sure I'd call it a home. More like a prison for the addicts.

Technofreak: *Stearn's files say throats were slit. Place was a bloody mess. Not to mention almost 700 rounds of ammunition were fired.*

Nightlady: Interesting.

Technofreak: *The reporter, though, found a couple of crackheads who swear they saw vampires. Vampires who never were hit by a single bullet.*

Nightlady: So they were superhero vampires? See what drugs do to the mind? "This is your brain. This is your brain on drugs." Remember that commercial?

Technofreak: *Yeah. Sizzled fried eggs for brains. I remember. But one crackhead even thinks he saw a vampire feeding on the neck of one of the guys.*

Nightlady: Maybe whoever it was was simply slitting the throat.

Technofreak: *Maybe.*

Nightlady: Anything else?

Technofreak: *No. Except to say, whatever your secrets, Nightlady, we're cool. Me and U. Fighting the good fight.*

Nightlady: The good fight. I hope it's the good fight.

Technofreak: *Baby Rock had ten prostitutes working for him. Two were 12 years old. One was 14.*

That's in Stearn's files. They're going to be helped now. It is the good fight. Never forget it. Never doubt.

Nightlady: Thanks, Hack. I needed that.

Technofreak: U got it.

Nightlady: And Hack?

Technofreak: Yeah?

Nightlady: Didn't U say there was a charity for victims of domestic violence that U gave donations to?

Technofreak: Yeah.

Nightlady: I'm sending you a check for $5000. Give it to them, will U?

Technofreak: U R cool. Sure thing.

Nightlady: Good night, partner.

Technofreak: Good night, good lady.

Chapter 4

The next night, Tessa awoke and went to her altar to chant. She lit jasmine-scented incense and placed her palms together, bowing as a sign of respect. Many people, Lily included, mistakenly believed Buddhists worshipped Buddha, but Buddha was simply an example of one who lived an exemplary life. Buddhists aspired to be like him, but did not *worship* him. The Buddha on her altar was a pale green jade with gold inlay, and she had found it in Shanghai, in an old man's store. She had bartered, trading some gold and an ivory-handled dagger for it, and carried home her treasure to the altar in her bedroom in Shanghai. She'd moved it with her to every city and home she had lived in since.

After Tessa completed her chant, she rose and opened the locket she wore around her neck, the one containing the lock of Hsu's hair. Tessa sighed. Buddhists followed five laws or precepts. They avoided taking another life, avoided taking things not freely given, refrained from false speech, avoided sexual misconduct, and avoided intoxication, which could impair someone's judgment enough to make them ignore the other four precepts. Tessa's very existence defied the first precept. And though she told herself that fighting the scourge, fighting the intoxication of millions of hollow-eyed addicts, was a mission that ultimately helped humankind, not hurt it, she wrestled with her conscience and beliefs each night. She owned a nightclub—that alone was difficult to reconcile with her beliefs. But it provided her a nocturnal cover—and drew to it the evil she made it her existence to hunt.

She walked into her cavernous living room, fighting ennui. She had lived in New York City for ten years now, owned the club for four, and had not taken a lover in all that time. She had vowed many years ago not to bury a lover again. She was through with mourning. She supposed some would think the gift of immortality was priceless, their fear of death deluding them into believing it would be wonderful to live forever. In fact, when she looked back on the years of her very long life, all she could recount was a string of losses, each heartache like the pearls on a necklace, strung one after the other, poignantly beautiful.

Detective Tony Flynn was the first man in many

years who made her even think of giving up her self-enforced celibacy. Perhaps it was one lonely soul glimpsing another. They seemed to understand each other. But she hardly needed to take a lover who wore a badge. Her life was complicated enough.

Her cell phone rang, playing an electronic bar or two of Beethoven's Ninth, jarring her from her melancholy thoughts.

"Hello?"

"Hack here." He sounded short of breath.

"Hello, my dear, sweet, hyped-up Hack. How many Manhattan Specials have you had tonight?"

"I'm on number six."

"Six bottles of pure caffeine and sugar. Don't you know that stuff will kill you?"

"Not as fast as this new drug hitting the streets."

"The one you called me about the other night?"

"Yeah. Remember how I said they didn't know what to make of it—it's that new?"

"There's never an end to those who want to invent the perfect drug, is there?"

"Well, this one is far from perfect."

"They all are."

"This one's got a kicker. It's tough to gauge how much should be in each hit. It makes users feel so good that, like OxyContin, they figure if a little feels good, more will feel better."

"Terrific. Just what we need on the streets."

"And there's a pureness to it. It's a love drug, like Ecstasy—but you know how they can make Ecstasy with household bleach and lye and all kinds of crap?"

"Yeah."

"This is some kind of synthetic something—doesn't appear to have that stuff in it. In fact, it's like it's manufactured under pharmaceutical guidance."

"What do you mean?"

"Well, you know how big drug companies have to follow the FDA and everything?"

"Yeah."

"Sure…well, with this drug, it's like some anal-retentive chemist is overseeing production. Then, there appears to be a touch of opium to it. So not only do you want to fuck all night, you feel real happy doing it."

"Do they take it at raves?"

"Nah. It's more of a designer club drug. Seems to be concentrated in Manhattan proper. Not even out in the five boroughs yet."

"That's just a matter of time. Then the burbs. And usually when suburban white kids start taking it, then…*then* the politicians and law enforcement will take it seriously."

"I don't know…seems like a lot of internal e-mails at the NYPD on this one. Know what they call it?"

"Hmm?"

"Shanghai Red."

Tessa shivered, as if a cold breeze had swept over her. "What did you say, Hack?"

"Shanghai Red."

She was silent.

"What Tess?"

"It's nothing. Just a weird coincidence."

"What is?"

"Nothing. Will you keep me posted if you can…. Follow this one like a bloodhound, okay?"

"Sure thing, Nightlady."

"Why do they call it that?"

"What?"

"Shanghai Red."

"I don't know. I thought maybe it had its origins in Chinatown."

Relief flooded Tessa's body. "Of course. You are quite clever, Hack. Chinatown. That makes perfect sense."

"I'll keep nosing around."

"Good. Talk soon."

"Fight the good fight."

"Always, Hack. Always."

Tessa hung up the phone. Just the mention of Shanghai made her homesick—and worried. She had been born in England, the willful daughter of a no-bleman. It wasn't until after Marco, after she had wit-nessed atrocities she could barely think of, let alone give voice to, that she had escaped to China. It had become her second home, a place she adored that of-fered her peace. But then changes there had forced her to take flight and she had returned to Europe, and then continued on to America.

Shanghai represented gardens to her. Fragrant flowers, bamboo trees with delicate thin leaves. And her koi pond safe behind a graceful high fence to pro-tect her privacy. She used to go out at night to feed the koi and watch their gaping mouths kiss the surface of the water as they waited for their mistress to drop their food into the pond. They'd even let her pet them.

And then there was Shen.

She sighed. Shen, her loyal servant, had become a true friend. His devotion to her had touched her deeply, and she had made sure that after his death from a bout of tuberculosis one winter, his son was able to escape the Communist Revolution and come to England to study. She was the young man's unseen benefactor, always there with both money and influence, making sure his path was free of obstacles. His Chinese medicine clinic, in the heart of London, was world renowned. She wondered if the kindly doctor, who had died ten years before, after leaving his clinic to *his* child, a daughter named Anna, ever knew where his scholarship and the secret funds to purchase the building in Notting Hill had come from.

Shanghai Red. It made sense that Chinatown, long a seat of corruption and gangs, though recently much cleaned up, might be the source of the latest drug that people felt they needed to make them forget life, forget their problems. Shanghai Red. The color of blood.

Chapter 5

Tessa's DJ was a white kid from the Bronx who had blond dreadlocks down to his ass. He had been a Calvin Klein underwear model for about a year, and his face was like a painting of Michelangelo's, with classic features and perfect lips and large, wide-set, blue eyes. When he smiled—which was any time he was playing music—he looked like a little boy, with two dimples and a sparkle to his eyes. Each night he dressed in tight black jeans, a black T-shirt, and black leather boots from Italy, and he took his music very, *very* seriously. "Cool" remixed the hottest techno and club music, and he had a following. His music *was* the drug that drew people to the Night Flight, and though Tessa didn't kid herself that the club kids and celebs wouldn't try to snort lines in the bathroom, fuck in the stalls, and in general try to outsmart Jorge and her security team, she ran a clean club and was sure Cool was part of the secret to its success.

The night after the raid at Baby Rock's, he had bounded into her office and opened one of her mahogany cabinets that hid her stereo equipment and a flat-screen plasma television like the one in her apartment. He pressed a button and opened the CD drive, then put his homemade CD in it, shut the drive and pressed play. "Listen to this. You're gonna love it, Tess." He grinned.

The bass line was intense. She felt it reverberate through her, almost hypnotic. She shut her eyes and listened, getting lost in the sensuality of the music. When the new remix, a Madonna classic with a Moby sound, was done, she kept her eyes shut for a full minute more.

When she finally opened her eyes, Cool was leaning against her desk, his arms crossed and face expectant.

"Well?"

"What can I say? Beyond brilliant. Once again, you prove you are the hottest DJ in town."

"Felt like sex listening to it, didn't it?"

"You could say that." Tessa pursed her lips. Cool thought everything about music was like sex. He seemed to live, breathe, eat and dance to sexual music twenty-four/seven. And he had enough groupies that if he actually wanted to *have* sex, there wasn't a shortage of willing partners. Right now he was involved with an A-list sitcom star, which meant even more stargazers trying to get past the velvet rope. The TV star brought her L.A. friends out whenever she could, meaning real star sightings were now as commonplace at the Night Flight as cosmopolitans and apple martinis.

He was clearly pleased with the mix. "People are gonna be fucked up tonight. In the groove. Cool."

"You're the king of cool, so that makes sense." She smiled at him, bemused. All of her employees were loyal. She interviewed extensively, paid them well—she had all the money she needed in this life…or the next. But some of them were intimidated by her. Lily said it was because she was so mysterious, and somewhat taciturn with them. That, and the fact that she dressed like a 1940s movie star, which, Lily said, "can be a tad off-putting to someone with four nose-piercings." But Cool was never intimidated, as far as she could tell. He came into her office whenever he could catch her, always with a "new sound" that he insisted she listen to.

"If I'm the king of cool, you're the queen, Tess."

"Stop flattering me. Your girlfriend will think you're trying to get me in the sack."

"Come on, Tess. We're old friends."

She smiled at him. "Of course we are. And one of these days, I'm going to retire and leave the club to you and Jorge."

"You always say that…but you're shittin' me, and I know it. You can't fool a guy from the Bronx."

"You wait and see."

In truth, the papers were already drawn up. If she died, or if she simply gave her lawyer the word, or if she "disappeared" for more than three months, the club would transfer ownership to the two employees she trusted the most—and that the club meant the most to—and who would also never betray the loyalty of the people who worked there.

"Okay, Tess. In the meantime, I better go do some sound checks and get ready to rock the house."

Cool turned, his dreadlocks swaying slightly across his back as he walked away. She admired his passion.

About ten minutes later as she was going over the liquor orders, she heard a knock on her office door.

"Come in."

Jorge entered. He was a hulking figure with piercing black eyes and a tattoo on his enormous right biceps that read "Bella"—his daughter's name. He was married to a woman less than half his size, a quiet but strong-willed schoolteacher named Delorean who had tutored in the New York State prison system as a volunteer and fell in love with the convicted felon. Believing his protestations of innocence, she contacted an old college professor who had written a textbook on DNA testing. After much persuasion, letter-writing and promises of Delorean's undying gratitude, she had convinced her old professor to have Jorge's DNA tested against a single strand of hair from inside the panties of the rape victim. It wasn't a match. In fact, when the case was reopened, nothing about any of the DNA evidence matched Jorge. Soon, the actual rapist was behind bars, and Jorge was exonerated. He and Delorean married four months later, and after a long job search with many doors slammed in his face, he began working for Tessa.

"Tess, I need off next Wednesday."

"Okay." She smiled and then looked back at the Excel graph she had up on her computer screen.

"Aren't you going to ask why?"

"No."

"Why not?"

"Because if you need off, you have a reason."

"I do." He stared at her, willing her to ask him, eyes sparkling.

Tess put down her pen. "Okay, Jorge. I'll bite. Why do you need off?"

"We got the baby."

"Oh blessed Buddha!" Tessa leaped up from her desk and crossed the room to hug him. Jorge and Delorean had been trying to adopt a baby for two years, and recently they had been very close to getting an infant boy born to an unwed teen mother. The baby was blind, but otherwise healthy and in need of a special home. Delorean and Jorge had no problems getting pregnant—Bella was their biological baby—but Delorean had been adopted as a child, and they believed too many special needs children needed a family.

"I know." His eyes were shiny. "We're going to name him Micah. It's a biblical name."

"You two are going to give him a wonderful home. I bet Bella can't wait to be a big sister."

"I know. She's over the moon. But if you hadn't found us that lawyer, we'd still be mired in red tape. You have to let me pay you what he charged you."

"No. And there's a ten-percent raise as of next Friday. You have another mouth to feed."

"What are you, Tess? An angel?"

Tessa mused at the irony. "No. I'm no angel. But Delorean is. And so are you. Do me a favor and send in Colleen?"

"Okay." He couldn't speak any more and rubbed at his eyes. "I have a son now. Bella has a brother. Thanks, Tessa."

"It's nothing. Really. Bless you all."

He left and shut the door, and she mused at how such a big, hardened man had been softened by the love of a good woman.

Colleen came a few minutes later and poked her head in. She was one of Tessa's best bartenders. She also auditioned constantly for Broadway parts. She was talented, too, and Tessa expected to lose the five-foot-eleven-inch strawberry-blonde to a role any day now.

"You asked for me?" Colleen looked worried.

"Yes. I'd like you to plan a baby shower for Jorge and Delorean."

"You heard the good news?"

"Yes. I'm ecstatic." Tessa walked over to a Paul Klee painting on the wall and removed it from its picture hook, revealing a wall safe. She spun the dial back and forth a few times, opened it and withdrew ten crisp hundred-dollar bills. "This will cover decorations, a cake, and call Anya over at Zenith to cater pastries. We can do appetizers from the kitchen. And then take whatever's leftover and get...what do they need?"

"Everything. Little Bella's four now. They still have their old crib, but no boy clothes, and their old stroller is just a wreck."

"Get a stroller from me. If you need more money, let me know."

"When do you want to hold the shower?"

"Thursday, before we open."

"Want to make it a surprise?"

"No. We'll never pull it off. He's too smart. Just tell him we're doing it, and if he doesn't show up at seven o'clock, he's fired."

Colleen looked like she would bubble over with happiness. She grinned and stared at Tessa, shaking her head.

"What?" Tessa asked.

"Nothing. It's just whatever anybody says... you're a softie."

"Well...don't tell anyone."

"Your secret's safe with me."

Colleen shut the door, and Tessa thought about the trials and challenges her employees faced. They didn't appreciate the humanity of the day-to-day struggle of life. She would have given anything to be, once again, a twenty-something woman with human frailties and human needs. To wonder about what the future held...

Tessa continued with her paperwork, getting lost in numbers and her financials. The club was doing remarkably well. When she left it to Cool and Jorge, they would become rich men.

Around eleven o'clock, she decided to see how Cool was getting the house rocking. Wearing a black Edith Head pantsuit she walked out into the club, where the feeling was electric. The dance floor was packed and the energy was palpable.

She watched the dancers grind into each other. Looking around her she saw all the younger women had stomach-baring tops and naval piercings. Everyone seemed lost in Cool's music. Couples kissed, and the bar was unbelievably crowded. Cocktail waitresses, their round trays aloft, maneuvered expertly through the crowds.

She had virtually no turnover. For one thing, she made allowances for their "real" lives. If they needed a day off to attend to personal business, they didn't have to lie and call in sick. For another, on a good night the cocktail waitresses would clear three hundred fifty a shift, the bartenders double that.

As she made her way back to the VIP lounge, she thought she glimpsed something out of the corner of her eye. Turning to the dance floor, she looked intently, uneasy with how her very being registered danger. But she saw nothing.

She took two more steps. Again, she felt it. She whipped around, focusing her senses on both what was seen—and what was unseen. She had learned over the years that she could detect things the rest of the world couldn't, like a metal detector could find lost rings and pieces of jewelry and beer cans beneath the surface of sand on the beach.

She stood near the dance floor, allowing her instincts, animallike and eerily accurate, to take over.

And then she saw him.

There, dancing on the perimeter, was a vampire she had known decades before, in 1946 to be exact. She was sure it was him. Their eyes locked, and she was even more convinced. It was Jules. Minus the haircut of that era, of course, and now dressed like a typical New York club-goer with a black T-shirt over perfect, sinewy chest and arms, and black dress pants. His black hair was long, almost to his shoulders, and he wore a single diamond earring in his left ear. He was dancing with a girl who looked drunk out of her mind. Tessa was anxious. He could take that girl and feed on her in a bathroom stall and she'd never even know what bit her.

He smiled the false, menacing smile she always knew him to have. His crooked mouth seemed dangerous, even when he wasn't smiling or contorting it into an evil leer. Tessa moved toward him, trying to squeeze past dancers gyrating on the floor to Cool's remixes. As she neared Jules, he pushed his dance partner and stepped back off the dance floor, hurriedly making his way to where the unisex bathrooms were. Tessa followed him, trying to stay focused, ordering herself to calm down and keep her wits about her.

Jules was the worst kind of vampire. He was a follower of Marco and his hedonistic band of disciples. They believed virginal blood brought them greater power. She shuddered to think of how many lost young runaways had succumbed to them. She had to get to Jules.

The hallway by the bathroom led to a locked storage room, an office and an extensive CD and record room, sealed with an alarm, that Cool used to catalog his exhaustive collection. Beyond that was an exit that led to both a back door in case of fire, and a staircase. The staircase ascended all the way to the roof.

Tessa was just at the entrance to the hallway when she saw Jules reach the door at the end, his face illuminated by the red neon Exit sign. He turned and licked his lips, taunting her, then pushed on the door and disappeared.

She raced down the hall. Just before she reached the door, Jorge called to her. "Tess!"

She turned. "Don't follow me, Jorge."

"If you're not back in twenty minutes, I'm coming after you." He fidgeted with his watch and set its alarm. She sighed and pushed through the exit door. She knew Jorge had gotten used to his employer's mysterious ways. He respected her wishes, but would come find her when that alarm went off, damn him. She had twenty minutes.

In the stairwell, Tessa climbed cautiously. At the third-floor landing, again she felt Jules's presence. Looking up, she saw he was attached to the ceiling like a spider clinging to a wall.

"Tessa," he hissed, a slight lisp to his *S* sound. "It's

been a long time since I've had the pleasure of your company."

"Hasn't it, though? I thought it was you. I thought I smelled shit, Jules."

"Always the bitch, ever the fucking bitch. Tonight, you will be a dead bitch."

"Still hoping Marco will relent and let you suck his cock? How many decades are you willing to wait for him, Jules?"

"Fuck you!" He flew down from the ceiling and attacked her with a powerful kick to her jaw.

Tessa reeled for a minute, but she knew she needed to remain aware, alert and ready to fight.

Before she could even kick him back or fly at him with a flurry of punches, he was on the move again, racing up the stairs. She chased after him, hearing him breathing as he kept three or four steps ahead of her, out of reach. Then she heard the door leading to the roof slam. Tessa pushed through the door, too, cautious that it might be a trap, but feeling she had no choice.

Jules stood, poised on the ledge at the far end of the rooftop, his figure outlined against the backdrop of the lights of Manhattan.

"What are you doing here?" she demanded, looking around and seeing no one else on the roof—just the two of them.

He flung his hand back with a flourish. "What am I doing where? On the roof? I like a little night air. It's good for my constitution."

"No. I mean my club. New York. Last I heard you were in Germany."

"So dull once the Communists got their hands on half of it. Hitler…now that was a man with vision. I could really follow a man like that."

Tessa shook her head. "Is Marco here?"

"I don't know. I haven't seen him in years. No, I'm here to track down an old friend."

"This old friend wants you gone." Tessa moved toward him, adopting a stance she had learned while studying with her martial arts master in China.

"You look a little…aggressive. You always wanted a fight. Couldn't just go along, could you? Couldn't be happy with immortality. We defy the gods, Tessa. We are equal with them. But you had to adopt your code, from your little slant-eyed friends."

"Still spewing hatred and racism, are we? My 'code' is as ancient as Buddha."

"Too bad it means nothing against my strength."

Jules leaped from the ledge and flew at her, trying to strike her with his hands, but she was quicker, blocking him and sending him off balance.

"Oh…I see your fighting skills are still sharp. This is going to be a pleasure," he hissed, recovering.

Tessa knew she could never take one of Marco's spawn lightly. They had great strength, derived not only from Marco's strength, but from how much they fed and from the rituals of evil they performed.

She struck quickly, using her fists, landing a strong punch on Jules's sternum. He gasped, and then his face turned dark. She had stirred his wrath even more.

The two of them faced off, delivering flurries of

furious kicks and blows, then striking defensive postures. Finally, Tessa was able to corner him near the building's air-conditioning shaft.

"Tell me who sent you and why you're here, and I'll let you go."

"You have it all wrong. Before I kill you, I'll fuck you. Tied to the roof, staring at the moon and waiting for the sun to rise. Burnt to a crisp like a side of bacon come morning."

Tessa struck with a powerful sidekick. It landed with brutal force on his ribs, and she heard the bones snap like twigs. But Jules, despite a momentary winded reaction, drew a dagger from a sheath hidden beneath his shirt and waved it in her direction.

While she focused on avoiding his blade, Jules landed a kick on her collarbone. Pain coursed through her, but she responded with a roundhouse kick near his kidneys. He struck back, kicking at her again and again, his knife still drawn, leering at her.

They fought, Tessa feeling muscles aching and bruises forming. She would hurt tomorrow—provided Jules didn't win and leave her to be burned by sunrise—one of the four ways to kill a vampire.

She flew backward, needing to catch her breath, but Jules was soon near her. She could smell his very sweat.

A drizzle had started, and as Tessa drew back to strike at him again, she lost her footing on the slick tar of the roof. She found herself flat on her back, and rolled quickly twice, avoiding the downward trajectory of Jules's dagger. He slashed at her arm, catching it and making a sharp slice from elbow to near her wrist.

Groaning with pain, she clutched at her arm. She struggled to her feet, ready to fight Jules to the death now. But he suddenly rose, levitating before her.

"Consider this a warning."

"A warning about what?"

"It will soon be apparent. Oh, you'll die, finally, and no one will weep for your passing. But you're going to suffer first."

"Speak for yourself." Tessa sailed through the air with a flying sidekick. But by the time she reached where he had been floating, he had transformed and was away, a dark-winged raven four feet across, darting through the night sky and the rain.

Breath ragged, Tessa look down at her arm, dripping blood on the rooftop. She winced with pain. The rain was icy cold, and she was completely drenched.

Suddenly, the door to the rooftop opened, and a beam of light from the stairwell illuminated the figure of Jorge.

"Tessa?" he called out.

"Over here." She wrapped her uninjured hand across the slice on her arm. It was healing already, but still it hurt, and her teeth chattered from pain and the chill.

Jorge dashed over to her, saw the dripping blood and looked at her with eyes radiating concern.

"What happened, Boss Lady?"

"You know better than to ask. An old enemy from a lifetime ago, I'm afraid. Hard to explain."

"Where is the bastard?"

"He leaped to the next rooftop."

Jorge looked at the roof of the next building. He squinted in the rain, seeming to judge the distance. Tessa sensed he didn't believe her, but he knew better than to ask. She never asked him about his past, his time in juvenile hall, the tragedies that led him to associate with the people that got him thrown in prison. He afforded her the same courtesy.

He took off his outer shirt, leaving himself in his white undershirt. Wrapping her arm in the shirt, he escorted her, limping and tired, down to her loft apartment.

"I know you don't want me to call the police."

"I'll be fine."

"What about calling Detective Flynn? He seems to like you, even if he snoops around a bit."

"No, that's okay."

At the door to her apartment, she withdrew her keys and unlocked three separate locks to gain entry, then shut off the alarm. Tessa stood on tiptoe to kiss Jorge's cheek.

"I know you like to fuss over me like a mother hen, but I'll be fine."

He gave her a dubious look. "Whatever you say."

Tessa entered the apartment and locked the door behind her. Looking down at her arm, she saw the edges of the knife wound healing. She walked into her bathroom and applied a bandage. The blood flow had, at this point, stopped, though the cut still throbbed.

Tessa retreated into her bedroom. She felt like her

brain was buzzing. What did the appearance of Jules mean? What did he want?

Thinking of Jorge's suggestion, she pictured Detective Tony Flynn. Maybe it was time to see what, exactly, he knew about the creatures of the night who made Manhattan their playground.

Chapter 6

Early the next evening, Tessa had dialed the cell phone number on Flynn's business card.

"Flynn."

"Detective Flynn, I've missed you snooping around my club. It's Tessa Van Doren."

"Hello, Ms. Van Doren." He had sounded pleased but a little wary.

"In the past, you've offered to talk with me should I have any information that might be useful. Is that offer still valid?"

"Yes."

"Well, I was hoping that maybe we could talk when you get off duty."

"I'm off in about an hour."

"Great. Can you come by the Night Flight? Ask for Jorge, and he'll show you to my loft."

Just before nine o'clock, Detective Tony Flynn knocked on the door to Tessa's loft, having gained entrance to her private elevator and hallway courtesy of Jorge. Tessa answered the door wearing a little black Zac Posen dress.

"Detective Flynn…" Tessa smiled as she made a sweeping gesture of welcome with her arm. "I'd like to welcome my favorite detective to my humble abode." His clothing was as rumpled as usual, though his shirt looked freshly ironed and he smelled of a pleasant, musky cologne.

As he entered her loft, Flynn let out a long, low whistle. "Humble? Uh-huh. For Donald Trump— maybe. And even then I'd say it's a question mark."

"Well, I'm sure Mr. Trump's got me beat."

Flynn looked at a Marc Chagall painting on the wall. "I'm an idiot when it comes to art, but this I recognize from somewhere…a museum or something. And I'm guessing it's not a reproduction."

"No, it's not. It speaks to me. When I had the opportunity to buy it, I felt I couldn't pass it up."

"Yeah, well, a nice Porsche speaks to me, but that doesn't mean I have one parked downstairs. And this?" He gestured toward a small statue of Buddha on a high teak table, incense burning next to it and filling the air with the scent of sandalwood.

Tessa smiled. "It's how I maintain my serenity in a city that's a far cry from serene."

"I was raised Catholic."

"And now?"

"Well, it's kind of like this...once a Catholic, always a Catholic. I don't go to church every Sunday. I don't even make it on Easter, to be honest. But I tell you, after 9/11, my ass was in a pew at St. Patrick's Cathedral. I lit candles for three guys I knew real well who died. And I had my late grandfather's rosary beads in my hand."

Tessa saw him shift his weight from one leg to the other, looking down, and she sensed he regretted sharing something so personal, so she changed the subject. "Can I offer you a drink?"

"I'll take a scotch."

Tessa moved over to a mahogany hutch, hand-carved, from the 1800s. Polished to a sheen, it housed crystal decanters of liquor and Waterford glasses. Tessa had filled a sterling ice bucket just before Flynn arrived.

She pushed up the sleeve of her cocktail dress and poured Glenfiddich into a glass. She handed it to Flynn, "Your scotch, Detective."

"What are you going to have?"

"A brandy." She poured herself half a snifterful and raised her drink in a toast. "Cheers, Detective."

"Cheers, Ms. Van Doren."

"To serenity."

"To always getting the bad guy."

They clinked glasses and sipped their drinks. They enjoyed a moment of quiet together, then Tessa asked, "When are you going to call me Tess?"

"When are you going to call me something other than Detective?"

"What should I call you? Tony? Anthony?"

"Yeah. You just told me to call you Tess."

"I know…but you don't seem like a Tony to me."

"What do I seem like?"

"I don't know. Does your partner call you Tony?"

"No. He calls me Asshole."

Tessa laughed. "I doubt that. I can tell you two like each other very much."

He looked right at her, his eyes conveying amusement. "If there's something you shouldn't say to two macho New York detectives, it's that it's obvious they 'like' each other."

"Well, you do. Machismo aside, and all that. So what does he *really* call you?"

"Flynn."

"That suits you. May I call you Flynn, then?"

"Sure. So if you don't mind me asking, Ms. Van Doren…Tess…why did you call me?"

Tessa walked toward the living room area and motioned for him to sit on her couch. She sat next to him. She internally berated herself, thinking she should sit in the damask-covered club chair opposite the couch, away from him, but she felt compelled to be nearer him.

"You're always inquiring about drug dealers in my club."

"Yeah. We have a couple of open murder cases that seem to be related to the drug trade."

"And today I read in the paper about a dealer named Baby Rock…."

"Killed in some sort of ritualistic way… You know something about it?"

"No. Not really."

"If you've been wearing a badge as long as I have, you learn that a 'not really' is actually a 'Yes, Flynn, I do know something.'"

"What if I told you that years ago I encountered a man who was so evil that even being near him meant you risked your soul…. What would you say?" She stared at him.

"I would say I believe you. I would say that I've met more men like that than I care to count in my years on the force."

"I knew I wasn't wrong about you."

"True story, Tess—I was a rookie, maybe six months out of the Academy. Me and my partner—different partner, not Williams…old guy, long since retired—we answer this call for a domestic disturbance. We end up having to break into this apartment and—" Flynn took a breath.

Tessa could see him take a fraction of a second to collect himself before he continued.

"—and we find this guy. This young, fucking sick bastard who had killed his girlfriend in cold blood. Held her under the water as she took her bath in their fleabag apartment, and he drowned her. And then he beat her baby—his baby, I'm talking nine months old. Then he sat there and fired up some crack and smoked it. Feet up on the coffee table. When we broke down the door, he looked at me and my partner like we were pieces of shit for interrupting his

Wheel of Fortune. Asked if we wouldn't mind waiting until fuckin' Vanna White was finished before we took him downtown."

Tessa looked down into her brandy. Her voice trembled as she asked—as she felt compelled to—"What happened to the baby?"

"She died. Internal bleeding. Baby Shauna."

"Oh my God…" Tessa passed a hand over her brow, then took a long, deep sip of brandy.

"We pooled money in the squad to bury her. With an angel headstone… I'm sorry. You know, is it any wonder I haven't been on a date in a year? You spend enough time swimming in a cesspool, it starts to just ooze out of you. I'm not good company."

"Well, if you're not, then neither am I."

"That I can't imagine. You sweep into that club around midnight, and the place just halts for a second. Like everybody in there takes a breath at the same time at the sight of you."

"That's quite lovely of you to say. Really."

"It's the truth. So what do you, lady of the elegant night, know about evil?"

"Suffice it to say," Tessa whispered, "that years ago I was swayed by a man to leave my family, my home, my whole world. And he turned out to be a liar. Beyond that, he was evil. And last night I saw someone who once worked for this man. He was in my club. If I hadn't seen him with my own two eyes, hadn't exchanged words with him, I would have sworn I'd seen a ghost. But he was here. And though he claimed the man I am referring to is long gone, that he hasn't seen him in years, something in me believes that's a lie. And if he *is* alive, then I am convinced he has something to do with the drug trade in New York City. And I am equally convinced he is bringing his trash to my door to taunt me."

"Do you have a name for this guy?"

"Marco."

"Have a picture? A last name? Where he last lived?"

Tessa shook her head. "I have a last name—though he may have changed it, may have an alias. But when I knew him, he was Marco Constantine. But that's all I have. I was hoping you might find even that name useful as you go about your investigations."

"Sure. It may be helpful. And what makes you think he's around? Other than this guy you saw last night."

"Shanghai Red."

Flynn looked intently at her. "And what do you know about Shanghai Red?"

"Only that it's killing people. And that Shanghai was my home once—" She faltered. "When I was a girl, of course. And I think if Marco is alive, he would name a drug that to antagonize me."

"Well, if that's the case, then this is one cold customer. Because that drug is baffling even the best lab we use. It's mostly synthetic, but with a dash of heroin. And it's just unpredictable."

"Like a dragon."

"A dragon?"

"Yes. Like a Chinese dragon of myth. Unpredictable."

"Yeah. Hey, listen, you got a picture of the guy last night? On any of your surveillance cameras?"

"I'll have Jorge run through the tapes. We might. It's dark and crowded on the floor, shadowy, but he stuck out." She noticed Flynn was nearly out of scotch. She took his glass from him and went and poured him another. While she was up, she refilled her brandy.

When she handed him his scotch, he asked her, "How come, after all this time, me and Williams checking out your club for two years now, you decided to come to me with this information?"

"Because, for the first time, I'm scared."

"Do you want me to get a restraining order on this guy?"

"Trust me, Flynn, and I mean this. There isn't a badge, gun, judge, jail, courtroom or piece of paper that can keep this man from killing me if that's what he wants to do."

"You say that pretty calmly."

"Because I am calm. It's the truth. Maybe it's the Buddhist way. All I can do is be ready for him."

"You going to tell me more about this guy, Marco?"

"I can't. Except this…he doesn't sell drugs to make money. He does it, simply, to own the souls of those who get addicted. He gets off on the vapid stares of zombies, people beholden to him and the drugs…people he owns. It's why I despise him. Well, one of many reasons I despise him. I wasn't lying to you all along when I said I ran a clean club. No drugs.

I rely on my DJ, Cool, to be the love drug that keeps the crowds coming back."

"I'd say some of them come back to get in the gossip rags, like those two whores...the daughters of that real estate magnate."

Tessa laughed. "The two strawberry-blondes? Pathetic, aren't they? They throw up in the bathroom so they can drink more. You can hear them out in the hall even over the music."

"Charming. You have more class in your little finger than they do in their whole emaciated bodies...and I bet a lot of men come back here to catch a glimpse of you."

"No. I think you're the only one who does that."

"See, that's when I think you're just stringing me along, pretty lady."

Tessa could see him swallow, then clench his jaw, wrestling with his feelings. She moved closer to where his arm was draped along the back of the couch. She fit into its crook.

"Some things I've said make no sense. Some things I feel toward you make no sense. But you just have to trust me."

"Trust ain't my strong suit. Not after all these years on the job."

She leaned her head back to look at him in the soft light of the Tiffany lamp on the side table. She traced her finger up the side of his neck, to his jaw, and then up along his cheek. She felt the tingle of his stubble against her soft skin. She leaned in still closer. How long had it been since she had kissed someone with passion, not sucking blood and life away?

Flynn looked at her face. Then he leaned in and kissed her. First he was tentative, but then he maneuvered himself, taking one hand and then the other and placing them on either side of her face, pulling her to him. She kissed him hungrily, wanting so much to move toward the light and life, to move toward a human being. To *be* a human being. She didn't know how much time passed, each of them kissing and moving their lips up and down each other's necks, then her lips finding his ear, his temple, kissing each part of his face, his eyelids, his forehead. She wanted to memorize the taste of him, the smell of his cologne, the way he ran his tongue across her bottom lip, tantalizing her before kissing her full on the mouth.

Eventually it was she who pulled back. For all her talk of trust, she wasn't ready to allow him to know her secrets. How could she tell him? How could she make love, in the dark, behind triple locks, in a bedroom that was a vault, devoid of sunlight?

"I know," he murmured. "I should go."

"It's not that…I just…someday I will tell you more, Flynn, but tonight, this was enough. It was perfect."

"Yes, it was. You know I didn't come here expecting this, right?"

"I know. You may be a tough cop, but you're also a very honest and decent man."

"Thanks. Sometimes I forget that." He disentangled himself from her and stood. She rose from the couch and escorted him to the door.

"If you find out more about Shanghai Red, will you please tell me?" she asked.

"I'll tell you what I can."

"In the meantime, I'll get you a picture, if I can."

"Be careful."

"I live my life with caution."

"Me too."

"I know. I think that's why we understand each other." She stood on tiptoe and kissed him again. "Good night, Detective Flynn."

"Good night, Ms. Van Doren."

She opened the door, and he stepped through and headed down the hall. She shut and locked the door, setting the alarm code and working through the locks.

With her keen sense of smell, she smelled his lingering musky fragrance. She hungered now for something else. Blood, yes, but also to make love. She wanted Flynn as she hadn't wanted a man since Hsu. But she knew if Jules was in the city, all who were part of her inner circle were at risk. And something told her that Detective Flynn was the most at risk of all.

Chapter 7

Detective Tony Flynn rode the subway to Queens and walked three blocks from the station to the tiny fourth-floor walk-up of Gus O'Hara. He rapped on the door.

"Tony, my boy!" boomed a voice from the other side. The door opened, revealing a stocky old man, about seventy years old, with rosy red cheeks and a shock of pure silvery white hair. With his girth, big grin and pink cheeks, had he grown a beard, the resemblance to Coca-Cola's vision of Santa Claus would have been uncanny.

"Brought you two bear claws," Flynn said, thrusting a plain brown bakery bag containing two sickeningly sweet pastries at Gus.

"Perfect with our morning coffee. Come on in, kiddo. Come on in!"

Flynn entered the apartment, the smell of freshly brewed coffee making his mouth water. He hadn't gotten any sleep. Thoughts of Tessa and an agonizing ache to make love to her had kept him up all night. He hadn't even bothered to shave.

Flynn walked into the living-dining area and sat down at the small wooden table where they had their coffee and pastries, a weekend ritual. Gus had been Flynn's mentor for his first couple of years out of the Academy. Everything Tony Flynn knew about being a good cop, an honest cop, he had learned from Gus. Much of what he knew about life in general, he had learned from Gus. Flynn's own father had died of complications following smoke inhalation and burns—he'd been a firefighter—he had suffered in an awful blaze that had claimed the lives of three other firemen. Flynn's mother raised Flynn, just eight at the time, alone. It was Gus who changed him from an angry young man of twenty into a real cop. It was Gus who gently told him his ex-wife Diana was a mismatch from the start—that she would never be happy living on a cop's salary. That she was not a giving person—not in the way Flynn was. And it was Gus who picked up the pieces after she left him.

Gus's small one-bedroom apartment was a shrine to military history. World War I and II memorabilia filled the place. He was an amateur, but he had amassed a rather amazing collection of photos, medals, books, yellowed newspaper clippings, shrapnel, uniforms. It was the hobby that kept him from going mad in retirement without his beloved late wife, Irene, to keep him company.

"You look tired, Tony," Gus said as he came in from the kitchen with a pot of coffee and the bear claws on two plates. The cream and sugar and mugs and spoons had already been set on the table waiting for Flynn's arrival.

"I couldn't sleep."

"Why not? A case?"

"You could say that."

"Anything a useless old man could help with?"

Gus was lost without his badge. Flynn knew their friendship, their father-son kinship and connection, was one major reason Gus was still as energetic as he was. Flynn honored that by coming to him with difficult cases—even if he didn't really need Gus's "take" on them—and asking his opinion.

"Uh…it's actually a woman thing."

"A woman?" Gus raised one eyebrow. "I haven't heard the *W* word since Diana, and you know how I felt then. She was hard on you, son. Now, my Irene…feisty. But she understood me. She understood me in ways my own partners didn't. So, who is this woman?"

"She owns a nightclub. And I think I was all wrong about her."

"What do you mean?" Gus poured coffee and passed Flynn a bear claw, which Flynn promptly dunked into his mug of steaming black java.

"Well, at first I thought she ran a crooked club. A

couple of high-end dealers hung out there and then they ended up dead. Weird shit. Killings…with their blood drained from their bodies."

"Was that the Bogdanovich case I read about?"

"Yeah. He was one of them. Russian mob. At least, that's what we thought. Maybe them moving in on the Italians. We thought perhaps a territory dispute. Who the fuck knows with these lowlifes? We thought the blood draining was a sign. A warning. But when I asked this woman what she knew, she always said 'nothing.'"

"Is the place mobbed up?"

"Well, that's the thing. I thought so at first, but now I'm not so sure. See, everything about this woman makes me question myself. First, I was sure she was as crooked as the proverbial three-dollar bill. Then, last night we talked, and man…she *hates* drugs. Hates them as much as I hate them. She tries to run a clean club—not easy in this city."

Flynn was also adamantly against drug use. His father died a hero, and after his death, looking for a role model for her son, his mother had sought out his father's brother, Sean. But Flynn's uncle had turned out to be a two-bit hood, a low-level, dime-bag pot dealer. So Flynn's mother had isolated her son from the Flynn family, raising him as best she could on a widow's pension and social security, and what she earned as a teacher's aide in the school system. Drugs were the enemy in the Flynn home. And though she had lost her husband in the line of duty, doing what was right was the goal she taught her son to aspire to.

"Sounds like this nightclub owner's a fine woman, then," Gus mused.

"There it gets tricky. She's too fine."

"Too fine?" Gus dunked his bear claw and waited for Flynn to go on.

"See, we have this kind of antagonistic thing going on. Gus, plain and simple, she's loaded. *L-O-A-D-E-D.*"

"Like Diana?"

"No." Flynn's face darkened. "Diana was from old money. Her parents were mainline Philadelphia, for God's sake. I was never going to make her parents happy, let alone her."

"And this woman?"

"She's different, is all I can say. She doesn't seem to care about money, even though she obviously has a lot of it. She has this club—as hot as the old Studio 54. I mean, Gus, it is like in Page Six of the *Post* every Friday and Saturday. Knee-deep in heiresses, movie stars, rappers, New York Yankees—you name it."

"Ah, the beautiful people."

"But you want to know something a little strange? The thing is, when you go in her office, she doesn't have nothin' on the walls."

"That's kind of atypical for a club owner. No black-and-white five-by-tens of her and the latest movie stars? Rock stars?"

"No. Nada. Nothin'. No pictures. She is totally unimpressed by the A-list her place draws."

"So maybe she is just good at what she does—running a nightclub. And maybe she doesn't care about all the trappings of wealth. You ever think that's possible?"

"Yeah. But I know she's got secrets."

"Secrets. Please. You got secrets. I got secrets. Remember the Moreno case?"

Flynn nodded. Moreno was a child molester. Flynn and Gus had gone to Moreno's house to search for an abducted eight-year-old girl. They found a veritable child porn empire. And they found little missing Annie Bey's underpants. And Charles Moreno, elementary school psychologist, wasn't about to give anything up. Only after Gus and Flynn inflicted some serious pain did he confess the little girl was buried alive in a bunker twenty feet in back of his house—within view of the bedroom where he slept with his pregnant wife. Had Gus and Flynn not broken Moreno's jaw and the bones in his left foot, and fired a gun two inches above his head to terrify him, the little girl would be dead. Of course, they had pinned the injuries on "resisting arrest." Moreno was serving twenty years to life. And neither Flynn nor Gus had lost a moment's sleep. But yes, they had their secrets....

"I don't know, Gus. She's mysterious. And beautiful. And for the life of me I can't figure out what she could possibly want with the likes of me."

"Did you ever stop to think that a principled man might be attractive to some women? My Irene...now she loved me precisely because I was going to make sure the bad guys went away."

"I don't know. This woman unnerves me. She's

got art in that loft of hers that costs more than I make in a decade. I saw this painting. I was positive I had seen it before. I went home last night and found it in a fuckin' art history book from a course I had to take in college. It was a Marc Chagall. He drew these kinds of weird people with the eyes flat on the side of their faces. Not my taste, but Jesus…it's museum-quality shit she has."

"And what? A classy woman can't love you?"

"Well, look what happened with Diana."

"Diana, despite her money, wasn't classy. She was bossy and controlling. And she loved you in direct proportion to how fast she thought you would rise to police commissioner. To how quickly she could convince you to go to law school, become a DA, join a fancy law firm and make headlines. This woman you describe, I don't get that sense. Not from what you've told me this morning."

"I don't know…I just feel like a loser around her."

"What does Williams say?"

"He thinks she's amazing. But of course he loves going to her club and scoring phone numbers. I mean there are supermodels there, Gus. And you know Williams. The ladies love him."

"What's the name of her club?"

"Night Flight."

"Night Flight…Night Flight. Where have I heard that name before?"

"The newspaper, probably."

"No. That's not it."

"What, then?"

"Nothing. Want some more coffee?"

"Sure."

Gus poured Flynn another cup, but the retired detective still looked puzzled.

"What is it, Gus?"

"I don't know. I'm just getting old."

"Bullshit." Flynn knew Gus did the *New York Times* crossword puzzle every day, read five books a week and did everything in his power to stay at the top of his mental game. He and Irene had not been able to have children, so Flynn was named in his will as sole beneficiary. Flynn also had all the papers necessary to make medical decisions on Gus's behalf, and what Gus feared most was someday being senile and sent to a home where he would just waste away and die, no longer alert and bright and sharp-minded. Flynn knew nothing escaped Gus, no detail.

"It's nothing."

"It is something. Tell me."

Gus shook his head. He sipped his coffee, then suddenly downed the rest of his cup. Furrowing his brow, he rose from his chair and went over to a four-drawer file cabinet in the corner of the room.

"I seem to remember…"

"What?" Flynn asked. Gus's hunches were legendary at the precinct.

"I'm not sure. But I seem to remember a nightclub in Germany. World War II. Called the Night Flight Club. A very hot place. Played American jazz, had a chanteuse. And the owner of it was a very beautiful woman. Dark-haired. Green-eyed. One newspaper called them 'emerald eyes.' She was mysterious, elusive. But described as stunning by anyone who met her."

"Night Flight, huh?" Flynn's heartbeat quickened. "Kind of an odd coincidence. Tessa is very beautiful herself. Black hair. Green eyes."

Gus opened a file cabinet. "I have everything cross-referenced." He fumbled through some files. "It's not under Night Flight. Or nightclub. But I just *know* it's here somewhere. I seem to remember, also, a picture. Let me see what I find. Of course, it can't be the same person, same club, but it just makes me curious."

"Me too."

Gus shoved closed the heavy file cabinet drawer bulging with research and clippings. Returning to his seat, he said, "Don't judge her for being rich, or owning a nightclub. Judge her by what you see, what you *feel*. Trust your instincts, Tony. You do as a cop."

"Yeah, but my instincts as a man left me divorced."

"And you can't judge yourself forever because of it. So Diana blinded you to her true self. Doesn't mean every woman will."

The two men sat and had another whole pot of coffee. Then they watched the Giants game on television, and finally, yawning, despite the caffeine, Flynn felt ready to go home. Riding on the subway, gently rocking with the train, he thought of Tessa. He thought of kissing her. And he thought of Gus's words. *Trust your instincts.* His instincts told him that he could trust her—and that whatever her secrets were, they were more intense than any he previously could have encountered, let alone managed on his own. And his instincts also told him that he didn't care. He'd take her. Secrets and all.

Chapter 8

That night, Tessa dressed in a classic black crepe Bill Blass pantsuit and rode down around eleven-thirty in the elevator to check in with Cool, who was trying out a new sound system on the upper level of the club. It sounded great, so she proceeded to her office. She was in a horribly bitchy mood, and she knew it.

In the first place, she hadn't slept well at all. She needed to feed, and soon. Her pallor was such that she'd been forced to use pancake makeup, and though she applied it better than a Hollywood makeup artist, she hated feeling like a slave to her condition.

Condition. She shook her head. How many euphemisms had she used over the years to kid herself? She just couldn't bear to think of herself as she was—as she really was. *Undead.* Neither alive nor truly dead. Just in a state between two worlds. She was reviled. Movie after movie portrayed vampires as blood-sucking evil creatures. And spiritually, she knew immortality achieved through blood was wrong, an affront to all religions.

Adding to her bad mood was waking up this evening with a feeling that her longing for Flynn was a weakness. She had lived as a celibate, but now she hungered for the taste of Flynn, for his mouth on hers. Kissing him hadn't cured her of her infatuation—it had made it far worse.

She was poring over her accounts on her computer when there was a knock on her office door.

"Who is it?" she asked sharply, an edge to her voice.

"Cool."

"Come in." She tried to soften her voice, but she knew it still sounded irritated. Like she had PMS. She and Lily joked they had "Pre-Monster Syndrome"— since neither menstruated anymore. Though she had considered her periods an inconvenience when she had them—most especially at the end of the nineteenth century—she knew now a monthly cycle meant the opposite of her. It meant life.

"Tess?"

"Hmm?" Her face was impassive.

"Lily is a no-show."

"What do you mean a no-show?"

"I mean a no-show. As in not here, and she's supposed to go on in a half hour."

"Did you call her place?"

Cool nodded.

"Her cell phone?" she snapped.

He nodded again.

Tessa took a deep breath. "Cool…I'm sorry. I'm just in a really bad mood. Insomnia. Of course you'd call her place and her cell before you'd come in here. That's just really unusual."

"I'm going to go on the assumption maybe she's sick or something, so no live show tonight. Unless I can get Miss Divine," he added, referring to a drag queen who sometimes did a fun, over-the top disco set.

"Miss Divine needs three hours of makeup and prep. Just go without the live show."

"Okay. But I figured you'd want to try to track down Lily. She's never not shown. Not as long as I've worked here."

"Thanks. And sorry for being so bitchy."

"We're cool." He winked at her and left.

Tessa dialed Lily's apartment in Chelsea, a place on the top floor with access to the roof. The phone rang and rang. No machine came on, something else that was absolutely unlike Lily, who adored being part of the twenty-first century and had every technological gadget she could get her hands on. Hell, she coordinated her outfits on her Palm Pilot, used her iMac to download songs to her iPod. She was wired to distraction, and there was no way she'd leave her apartment without the machine on or without forwarding the calls to her cell phone—which was a tiny fold-up Nokia in bright red with rhinestones.

Every nerve inside Tessa was now alive and working overtime. She massaged her temples, then she buzzed Jorge. He wore an earpiece not unlike that of a Secret Service agent.

"Yeah?"

"Listen, Jorge, you need to cover everything tonight. Lily isn't picking up her phone, she didn't show up to sing—and you *know* how much she loves being the center of attention. Something's wrong. I can feel it. I'm going by her place to check it out."

"Maybe I should go with you."

Tessa was sure Jorge was replaying the sight of her on the roof, her arm bloodied by her battle with Jules, but she tried to put his mind at ease. "No, really. I'll bet she's got something as simple as the flu, and just turned her ringer off. I'm concerned, but not in panic mode yet. I'll call you if I need you. Meanwhile, I'll have my cell on. If she should show up, call me."

"Sure thing."

Tessa hung up the phone and mused over how twenty years ago, she wasn't even online. Cell phones, gadgets, her friendship with Hack didn't exist. The world was changing at a faster pace than at any other time she could remember, except perhaps during WWII—though then the frenzy had been a furious worldwide spiral downward. Now it was about keeping in touch and wired to the rest of the world all day, every day.

Riding back up to her loft, she tried not to feel a sense of dread, but she was worried. She unlocked the door and quickly dressed in what she thought of as her kick-ass attire. If Jules was waiting for her, he'd find that she was more than willing to finish what *he* had started.

Turning to leave her bedroom, she saw that her answering machine was blinking. Thinking Lily had called, Tessa pressed play. She heard Flynn's voice.

"Tessa... It's Tony Flynn. I want to thank you for the drink last night. I enjoyed...shit...I enjoyed your company. And in the meantime, I'm trying to see what I might be able to find out about Shanghai Red... And I was wondering if I might buy you dinner. You have my card. Call me. All right, then...good night."

Tessa's finger poised over the button. She decided not to press erase. She liked the sound of his voice, so instead pressed save.

A second message began to play.

"Tess...Tess, pick up. Please. Please...it's—"

Lily's voice. Sounding scared. And then cut off. Tessa wondered if her machine had malfunctioned, even as she knew it hadn't. Something—or more likely someone—had prevented Lily from continuing.

Tessa pulled on her leather jacket and donned a pair of dark glasses. Whoever it was, Tessa was ready to do battle.

Chapter 9

Lily's apartment was as much a reflection of her being as Tessa's loft was a reflection of herself. Whereas Tessa's home was a collection of art, beauty and Buddhism, Lily's apartment was about music and bohemia. Giant posters of Charlie Parker and Miles Davis, as well as movie stills from old silent films Lily had watched—when they were released—and loved, mingled with hanging tapestries from Morocco and Spain. Whereas Tessa's clothes hung in a dressing room fit for a queen, Lily's clothes were strewn haphazardly or draped over one of several dressmakers' mannequins. Lily often sewed her own clothes, never losing the skill she had learned as a seamstress and servant over a century ago. She haunted a thrift shop over on St. Mark's that stayed open until eleven o'clock at night during the week and later on the weekends, and brought home vintage clothes that she then altered into nouveau funk.

"Lily?" Tessa called out cautiously. She entered the apartment through the bedroom window, muscles taut, ready for whatever faced her. "Lily?"

Tessa crept from room to room. Lily was very untidy, so Tessa was hard-pressed to determine whether or not a struggle had occurred in the apartment. She entered the kitchen, and there she saw a knife thrown on the floor—a meat cleaver. Tessa looked at the butcher block where Lily stored her kitchen knives. It was the cleaver from the block. Tessa picked up the knife. Why had Lily drawn it, if not because she felt danger? Tessa spotted blood on its edge—

And then, from behind, he hit her.

"Fuck!" She whirled around, momentarily reeling, and faced off against a vampire easily six feet tall.

"So easy when you take the bait, Tess," he hissed at her.

"Who are you?" She demanded, drawing back and preparing to fight. Her head pounded. In truth, she was in a weakened state—she really needed to feed. She imagined it was like when Delorean, Jorge's wife, complained of the migraines she sometimes suffered.

"Please…before I kill you, we should be on a first-name basis. Call me James."

She struck him quickly with a strong kick to his side. He barely registered the blow, just blinked once slowly, and then shot his hand out, grabbing her by the throat and lifting her two feet off the ground. Tessa struggled to breathe, gasping and trying to pry his fingers from her neck. She began seeing actual stars. Damn this one. If her head hadn't hurt before, it would surely hurt now.

Tightening her grip on the cleaver in her right hand, she sliced his arm, deep, not stopping when she felt the knife meet the resistance of bone.

James screamed out in anger and pain, a primal howl, releasing his fingers from her throat. Blood spattered across the walls and cabinets of Lily's kitchen. With him momentarily distracted, Tessa kicked with all her might, then slashed at him again, catching his shoulder with the full force of the cleaver and burying the blade in his collarbone, where it stuck. He clutched his shoulder, the blood spilling through his fingers, and opened his mouth wide in pain, showing lengthening canines.

"You'll fucking pay for this," he snarled at her, but Tessa was already on the move.

Certain Lily was not in the apartment, and certain that the strength of this vampire was greater than her own because she was weakened, she retreated, almost in full flight, out into the living room and, in a flash, out to the fire escape and up to the roof.

She could hear him clamber through the window after her, his motions making a flapping noise like the beating wings of a mighty bird, an eagle. A vulture.

But she had a head start. With a leap, Tessa was on the next roof, and then another one. She wanted as much distance between herself and the very angry, very injured James as possible. She needed time to think.

A drug nicknamed Shanghai Red had arrived in Manhattan.

Lily was gone.

Two vampires had come to find her.

Feeling herself further tangled in a spider's web she didn't yet understand, she knew there was but one place to go for answers.

Underground.

Chapter 10

The night air rushed past Tessa as she hurried as fast as she could down to Grand Central Station. Lying over subway grates, Manhattan's homeless struggled to keep warm. Cops clustered in groups of two, some with German shepherds, part of the increased security after 9/11.

All in all, she found the extremities of Grand Central misery-inducing. The atrium was beautiful, almost like a cathedral, but deeper into the catacombs of tunnels, the air smelled of urine and the unkempt and dirty, as well as exhaust fumes and steamy grime. She rushed past leering men, a prostitute or two, and listened to the droning voice of someone announcing train arrivals over the P.A. system. Tessa walked quickly, making her way on to a track in the farthest reaches of the station. But her destination was still farther, to a place few even knew existed.

Slipping onto the tracks, she looked at her watch. No one was around, and she walked up the tracks to a series of tunnels. The slightest vibrations of the tracks told her which path to take, and she moved along past rats and trash until she came to an area of catacombs leading to still more tunnels and switchbacks. From there, she slipped into one particular tunnel, grateful for the eyes of the undead, able to pierce through darkness.

After walking for ten minutes, she heard hissing and whispering, and she knew she was near the encampment of King. A small fire burned in a trash can, and she could see the outlined figures of three men. One of them whirled around as she approached.

"What the f—" he muttered, his hair was matted and greasy, his face filthy, almost black with grime, making him almost unrecognizable as human.

"I'm here to see King," she said, widening her stance, ready to pounce, to fight, or to defend.

"Who's you?" the man challenged her. She smelled alcohol on his breath.

"Tessa. He knows who I am."

"Wait here." She saw his eyes narrow untrustingly in the faint glow of the fire. Then he moved further back into the manmade caves of the tunnel. Every nerve of Tessa's was alive as she waited. She knew, watching her, unseen, were all of King's "children," the lost souls he protected who worshipped him as an underground deity. They'd kill for him. She'd even heard rumors of cannibalism.

Finally, after waiting uneasily, she was summoned.

"King will see you now." The wild-eyed man came close to her and sniffed at her. "You smell like the undead."

"So do you," she sneered. She couldn't let him see her unnerved. Not for a minute could she show weakness. Not down here. Not now.

She followed the man back into the tunnels. She passed makeshift campsites strewn with old newspapers and litter, not much more than refrigerator boxes and clotheslines with dirty blankets thrown over them. Mattresses and chairs, the stuffing falling out of them, were strewn about, and people clustered in small, familial groups. Shockingly, she even heard the wails of children. She saw an old shopping cart being used as a crib, a small, dirt-covered baby inside it. This was King's city.

Finally, she stood in front of King. His throne was constructed of cinder blocks, and then covered in tinfoil. Oddly enough, despite being thrown together from trash and construction debris, it glinted in the firelight. And there sat King, his long grey hair nearly to his waist, his face covered in grime, yet his eyes a youthful blue. Tessa never could figure out his age.

"King." She bowed, placing her two palms together as she did so, a gesture of peace.

"Tessa..." He nodded.

"I don't have time for niceties, King. I come in peace. You know that. You know me."

"Ah, yes. The Buddhist. Avoid intoxication. Refrain from false speech. Avoid sexual misconduct. You do all the things a good Buddhist does. Except that one little precept: Avoid taking lives. You undead filth."

She clenched her jaw. She didn't have time to defend her principles, her existence, not to King. Not right now. "You know my story, King. You've always known. It's probably in that book of yours."

He nodded. King was a vampire hunter. He was as crazy as anyone in Bellevue—from where he had escaped once. But he was also sane enough to wage a true war on the undead. He once had a wife, once had a daughter, but he had lost them to two vampires. At least that was the story he told his followers.

King used to be Brian Harper. He was driving somewhere out in the deserts of Las Cruces, New Mexico, living the hippie life, dropping acid, listening to the music of peaceful protest. He created Native American musical instruments, and he sold them at craft fairs throughout the West, traveling with his wife, Estella, and little girl, Chiara, in a run-down Chevrolet van.

They called the van Ethel, and "she" was stocked with all a man, woman and little girl could need—a small refrigerator to keep milk and cold drinks in, a bed, their clothes, food, even a little porta-potty. Brian did most of the driving, and Estella and Chiara's job was to sing and keep him awake.

One night, Brian and his family had the misfortune to break down in the middle of the desert near sundown.

"What's wrong with Ethel?" Chiara asked.

"Poor Ethel is a little sick, is all. I'll get out and see if I can't fix her."

Brian worked with a flashlight and a few tools, and tried to see what the problem was. In the end, he concluded there was a very good reason he failed automechanics in high school. He had no idea what was wrong with his van.

Climbing back in the driver's seat, he said, "Ethel has a virus. We're gonna have to spend the night out here, Chiara. And wait for someone to come along in the morning."

"Is this an adventure?" Chiara asked, her blue eyes so like his own.

"Sure is, honeybun."

As night fell, they heard a keening, a wailing.

"What's that?" Estella asked.

He rubbed her shoulder. "It's nothing honey. Probably some desert coyote. You know…it's getting chilly. Let's roll up the windows just in case, climb in back and just get a good night's sleep. Some truckers are bound to pass us in the morning."

He turned to roll up his window, and Estella reached over to roll up hers. Chiara was in between them. Then, from seemingly nowhere, two vampires descended, reaching in through the open window on Estella's side of the van and plucking his wife and child like a pair of rag dolls out through the window. Inexplicably, they left King to scream out in the night.

He jumped out of the van and called for his wife and child until he was hoarse, then voiceless. At first, he could hear Chiara's screams. Then nothing.

Taking a flashlight, he began to walk to where he had last heard a scream. Eventually, he seemed to know they were dead. He collapsed in the sand, where he lay, barely coherent, until morning.

When the sun came up, he shuddered awake, wondering if it had all been a nightmare. But then he stood and saw, not too far off, two bodies lying sprawled on the desert floor. He ran to them. His wife and child stared up at the sun, unseeing, vampire bites on their necks, much of their blood drained. They weren't "turned"—in the way vampires can create new vampires—they were drained to skin on skeleton. Dead.

He already had no voice, having screamed himself mute. He cried silently, clutching them to his chest, rocking, crying.

He trudged back to the van and returned to their bodies with a makeshift shovel—the lid of their cooler. He dug shallow graves and buried them in the desert. Brian had once, when he was a teen, been arrested for assault. He'd served time for breaking and entering when he was nineteen. No policeman would believe his story of depraved vampires. He told no one—and went mad. He had no idea how many months he lost to drugs and alcohol. Finally, he woke up in a state psychiatric hospital—sobered up. And in part madness, part despair, he decided to become a vampire hunter.

Perhaps the two vampires had spared him out of a sense of cruelty. They would leave him to grieve. That had been their mistake. Because King, after burying his wife and child, the horror of having heard their last cries echoing through his head, after his months of insanity, had decided he wouldn't rest until every vampire on earth was dead. He set about discovering all there was to know about vampires. He traveled the country taking odd jobs and took all the money he had and even went hunting in Europe, reading in musty manuscripts about different legacies of different vampires from the Dark Ages to the present time. He chased down half truths and small leads, and he learned to kill them, and he kept all his kills and clues and legends in a book he called The Bible.

Now, he ruled over a small band of society's outcasts. And he and Tessa had an uneasy truce worked out years before, after her arrival in Manhattan. She had proved to him that she was on a mission herself, to rid the world of a different scourge.

"My friend Lily is missing."

He nodded, not reacting.

"And there's a sudden spike in the vampire population in the city of Manhattan, all of whom seem to want me dead."

"And how do you think *I* can help you?" He spread his palms out, mocking her with a look of wide-eyed curiosity.

"My guess is, King, you already knew about the sudden escalation in the vampire population. Nothing escapes your eyes." She looked around, knowing from the darkness she was being watched by the eyes of King's people. His unseen spies. They were the homeless that people stepped over and didn't really see.

"Don't try to flatter me," he spat.

"I'm not. That's the truth…and my guess is you may even know where Lily is. I'm going to get her back, and I don't care who I have to kill to do it. We can either work on the same side, as we have in the past, or we can declare an end to our truce. But I *am* going to find her."

Tessa stared at King and willed him to help her. She wanted to rub at her temples, which throbbed, but she didn't want him to see how badly she needed to feed.

"They're European."

"Who?"

"The band of vampires who arrived here. Lineage goes back to Italy. Back to him."

"Are you sure?"

"Your sire. Yours and Lily's. It's all related somehow. By taking Lily, I presume they're trying to lure you out into the light of day—or at least into the battleground of darkness."

"Do you have any idea where Lily is?"

He shook his head.

"You know she started out as a servant. She had no desire for immortality."

He nodded. "I'll keep my ears to the ground."

"Thank you, King."

"And in return…"

"I know." Tessa bowed to him. In exchange for his help was the agreement that any news on Marco would be relayed to him. King had only killed one of the two vampires who destroyed his wife and child. He had tracked down a vampire by the name of Damien, whose origins spanned back to Romania. The second one, her own sire, had remained elusive for the thirty years King had been hunting. And King wouldn't stop until he succeeded in killing Marco. Though rumors persisted that Marco had died in a fire, Tessa never knew what to believe. She needed the truce with King, and so she had promised to share with him any news about Marco's rumored whereabouts.

Tessa turned on her heel and made her way back through the catacombs and caves. The acrid smell of unwashed human flesh and urine assaulted her nostrils. Finally, she emerged from the bowels of Grand Central Station and into the night air of Manhattan. She needed to feed, and made her way down to an open air drug market on the Hudson River. She and Lily often came here, usually stumbling on dealers with AK-47s and posses of killers. She would find prey here.

"Lily," she whispered, as she stood on the shore, the wind whipping her hair around her face. "Hang on." Then she turned in the direction of the glow of crack pipes.

Chapter 11

Tony Flynn slept fitfully.

And he woke up with a raging hard-on. Christ, he thought, what am I? Fourteen?

But there it was, the hard-on, taunting him. Because no matter how much he tried to deny it to Alex Williams, Flynn knew Tessa Van Doren occupied his dreams almost as much as she occupied his waking thoughts.

He stretched and shook his head in disbelief. Yup. Like he was fucking fourteen.

Finally, the hard-on subsided, and he rolled over and climbed out of bed and hit the shower. A cold one. After showering, he shaved. Then he ran a comb through his hair—though he knew it was as unruly as his dick. Finally, he went out into his kitchen and started the coffeemaker.

His ex-wife had let him keep the coffeemaker.

He could never get over how calculated their separation was. Whereas he would curl himself into a ball at night, agonizing over what went wrong, Diana had moved out and into the Park Avenue pad of the dermatologist she was servicing on the side. Then she'd returned to their shabby apartment with a goddamn *clipboard* on which she had itemized every one of their possessions. And she'd proceeded to keep everything of value. In the end, all Tony Flynn had asked for was the coffeemaker.

He took his coffee black, and breakfast was often a microwaved hot dog or leftover pizza. This morning, it was the vestiges of moo goo gai pan. He shook his head. How could Tessa Van Doren's world intermingle with his? He dug into the moo goo gai pan in the white takeout box with a fork that had a bent tine, washing his breakfast down with coffee in a mug with a chip in it. He imagined Tessa taking her coffee out of fine bone china and a sterling coffeepot.

Midbite, his cell phone rang. He pressed Talk. "Flynn."

"Tony, my boy, it's Gus."

"Hey Gus…what's up?"

"I think you should come by after work if you can. I have something to show you."

"Yeah?" Flynn raised an eyebrow.

"I don't want to say anything more. Consider it a surprise."

"Okay, Gus. I'll be by around seven. You gonna be there?"

"Eh, Tony…where am I gonna go? Think I got an invitation to dinner with the mayor? I'll make us some kielbasa with a nice rye from the bakery up the street. How does that sound?"

Tony looked down at his ice-cold moo goo gai pan. "Better than you know, Gus. Better than you know."

At ten minutes after seven, Tony Flynn got off the train in Queens with a crowd of commuters and walked three blocks to Gus's place. He could smell the kielbasa out in the hallway, and his mouth watered.

"Tony!" Gus opened the door and enveloped him in a bear hug.

"Hey, Gus." Flynn smiled and patted his friend's back. He walked into the apartment, where the small table was set for two. It was dinner—so that meant Gus put out a tablecloth. The television was tuned to a sports channel with the volume all the way down.

"Sit down."

Flynn did, and immediately saw a brown envelope on his plate.

"What's this?"

"Open it." Gus looked very excited.

Flynn cautiously opened the envelope and slid out a black-and-white picture. In it, five S.S. officers smiled at a camera in a nightclub, their ominous uniforms crisp-looking, their grins somewhat dangerous-looking. And there, in the corner of the picture, was a beautiful woman with dark hair, her face in profile and one hand raised to her face, as if to block the camera shot. Even blurry, she looked like Tessa's twin, and his stomach tightened.

"Holy shit."

"Yes. The Night Flight Club in Germany. It's a copy of the original picture. And that one—" Gus pointed at the man second from the left "—is Goebbels. That's why I couldn't find it in my files. I had it in *his* file."

"And her?" Flynn pointed to the woman.

"She was the proprietress. A contessa. Mysterious. No one was sure of her exact background. European. But not German. Not Aryan, certainly, by the looks of her. But she ran a hot spot where the S.S. liked to play, and so she was tolerated."

"A contessa, you say?" Flynn whispered.

"Yes. And that's not all. There was supposedly an explosion. An assassination attempt. Place blown up when it was filled with German officers."

"Including Goebbels."

Gus nodded. "He escaped, but whoever planted the bomb got more than a few S.S. Now you understand some of this isn't substantiated. Rumors. Rumors passed down amongst World War II buffs."

Flynn ran his finger over the picture. "What happened to her? After the war?"

Gus shrugged. "No one knows. It's as if she vanished into thin air. She could have died in the explosion. It wasn't like there was DNA testing back then. Even if she didn't die, it was common to lose track of people after the war—the world was insane then.

So not knowing what happened to her isn't surprising in and of itself."

"She looks like someone I know."

"This woman? Does she look like the one who runs the club?"

Flynn nodded. "They could be twins."

"Maybe this was her grandmother or something."

"Maybe." Flynn shook his head back and forth while Gus stood and brought in a platter of kielbasa.

"Well, it's not like it could be her."

"Huh?" Flynn was distracted.

"I said, it's not like it could *be* her."

"I know. But the resemblance is so close, it's eerie."

"They say we all have a doppelganger."

"You think?"

"I don't know. Sometimes I wonder."

Flynn slathered a piece of rye bread with mustard. "Can I make a copy of this picture?"

"That is a copy. I took it down to the photo shop two blocks over. They scanned it or something on their computer and made me a print. It's yours."

"Thanks, Gus." Flynn put the photo down by his plate. The two men ate, talking about old cases and memories. But Flynn's eyes kept zeroing in on the face of the woman in the picture. The woman who had run Germany's Night Flight Club. It wasn't just the uncanny likeness to Tessa.

She was wearing a vintage dress *exactly* like the one he'd seen Tessa wear the first time he met her. Once again, the mystery of Tessa Van Doren had Flynn completely intrigued.

Chapter 12

The first thing Tessa did when she awakened the next night was try to call Lily. No answer. The answering machine didn't even pick up. Tessa let the phone ring thirty times, willing Lily to be there. But of course Tessa knew she wasn't.

Tessa hung up the phone when the ringing sound just made her more upset, jangling her nerves. She climbed out of her bed and went to kneel in front of Buddha. She prayed for her friend's safe return, but she knew that the longer she was missing, the less likely her disappearance was to have a happy ending. She had known Lily almost as long as she had lived. The idea that someone was perhaps holding her old friend against her will—or worse—consumed Tessa's heart. She finished praying and then rose and went out to her living room and then to the tall window that overlooked the city.

She thought back…back to where it all began. More than a hundred years ago.

"Madame." The tall, dark-haired gentleman standing in front of her raised her hand to his mouth. When he kissed her hand, he allowed his lips to linger just a moment too long, then turned her hand palm up and kissed her hand again, this time more intimately.

Tessa glanced around at the crowded party, wondering if anyone saw the man's impertinent move. But no one glanced in their direction. Even if someone had, the look in his eyes said that he didn't care. She had never met anyone so bold before.

"Sir." She nodded her head coolly, holding his gaze, noticing his eyes were black.

"Madame…you look flushed."

"It's a bit stuffy in here."

"Would you care to take some fresh air on the balcony, or would you prefer I fetch you a glass of punch?"

"Punch will be fine."

"Walk with me, then."

He linked his arm through hers, and she felt the muscles of his biceps through his shirt. He confidently led her past the dancers and into the parlor, which was empty of revelers.

"Sit down," he commanded. "I'll be back."

He returned with a cup of punch. "You must drink. You look pale."

Tessa sipped the sweet lemony drink. "Thank you," she said haughtily. She couldn't help but feel he was undressing her with his eyes.

"You are the widow, are you not? Mrs. Van Doren, am I not correct?"

Tessa nodded. "Yes, I lost my husband—" she inhaled "—thirteen months ago." She had not spoken of her husband in months, since the melancholy overtook her, and she wasn't sure why she felt compelled to tell this stranger the story, but she found the words tumbling from her lips. "A young girl, the child from the next estate over, had fallen through the ice on a small pond near our home. John saved her life, but at the price of his own. He caught a terrible cold…terrible. We could hear a rattling in his chest. Then he started running a high temperature, high fevers night after night. Delirium. He was lost within five days. My name was the last word he uttered."

The man in front of her pursed his lips. "Such a shame. I am so sorry to hear this."

"My John was never in the finest health…. Always rather sensitive. I suppose that was the poet in him."

"Were you in love with him?"

Tessa felt a blushing of her cheeks—something that happened when she was embarrassed or angry, or, as tonight, both. "That seems a very rude question, Sir Constantine." She knew this stranger's name. He had arrived on the London social scene in late summer. The entire party had whispered of him. He was mysterious and supposedly very, very wealthy. More than a few women were pushing their unmarried young daughters at him. He was never impolite to them, but when she observed him from afar, she sensed his bemusement.

"Rude? You call me rude? I think not. It's a simple question. Did you love your husband? Or are you one of the many unfortunate women who find themselves sold off like chattel by their families?"

"That's none of your business!" Tessa placed her punch glass on a small table and rose.

"Please..." Sir Marco Constantine placed his two hands gently on her shoulders. "Sit down," he soothed. "I mean no harm. Let me just say that I am—how shall I put this?—enlightened."

Tessa's heart beat wildly. Something about him made her want to dash out the door of the parlor and out of this house entirely. It was as if she heard a whisper, John's voice, which she sometimes heard in the night. Now that voice was saying, *"Run, Tessa."* And yet, something in Sir Constantine's carriage, an arrogance, a strength, made her stay. "Enlightened in what way?"

"In the way I feel women should be treated. In the way I saw you on the outskirts of the dance floor last week at the Duke and Duchess's party, your eyes so clearly expressing boredom. Why is that? Perhaps as a woman you long to escape the proper ways of society. Perhaps you long for freedom in much the way my horse despises having the bit in his mouth."

"You liken me to an old nag, then?" She lifted her head. He had power and strength, but so did she. Her beauty was legendary in London.

"No. I liken you to a wild horse that yearns in its very soul to be free."

"Please. I have freedom. I am hardly a slave…or a servant."

"But surely your father married you off to your husband to increase familial alliances."

"My father, sir, allowed me to marry for love. My husband was a poet and a gentleman farmer. We—I—reside at Willow Pond."

"Yes. I had heard as much. Was he not your best friend since childhood?"

"Yes. And what of it?"

He leaned in very close to her, his breath hot on her neck. "I would have thought a beauty like you needed real passion. Have you ever had real passion, Mrs. Van Doren?"

Tessa had never been spoken to in such a way. She tried to push past the dark-haired stranger, suddenly finding the upturn of his mouth cruel and cold.

"Don't leave on my account," he said, his eyes dancing with laughter. "Sit. I will leave." And with that, the gentleman retreated from the parlor and rejoined the party.

Tessa's hands shook, and she frantically wiped at the spot on her hand where his lips had caressed her palm. She discreetly found her aunt Lydia and told her she felt light-headed and would be returning home. Then she called for her carriage and had her driver return her to Willow Pond, where she quickly retired.

But lying alone in her four-poster bed, beneath the quilt her grandmother had made her as a wedding present, sleep eluded her. She felt physically ill, and every time she shut her eyes, she saw Marco Constantine. Her head throbbed. She had never had such a visceral, physical reaction to anyone. She even had one fitful dream in which they were making love. Tessa awoke, breathless and in tears. John *had* been her best friend. And yes, she had been curious about deep passion, but she had known her husband since she was a little girl and hadn't ever imagined being with anyone other than him. Their lovemaking had always been tender, and though she sometimes longed for something more, her home at Willow Pond and being able to be close to her parents, both gone now, had seemed like an acceptable compromise. Why this dream? Why when that very man had so infuriated and humiliated her?

Passion. She knew her appearance, like that of a high-strung thoroughbred, invited speculation. She, the aristocratic beauty, with the quiet and studious John Van Doren, had seemed a mismatch. He had hair the color of wheat, and pale blue eyes, and he was soft-spoken. But, in truth, though very different, they walked in the fields in perfect companionship.

So why did Marco Constantine invite such dreams? Tessa dissolved into nervous tears, feeling unfaithful for the very thoughts that kept her awake. In the darkness of her bedroom, she wept for John, for herself, and for this strange longing inside of her.

She assumed that by dashing away from the party, she had discouraged Sir Marco Constantine from trying to pursue her. After all, he was always pursued

by the loveliest of London society's high-born ladies.
But she was not free of Marco Constantine. In fact,
he spent the next month or so ingratiating himself to
her aunt Lydia and uncle Henry, her sole surviving
relatives, and he had an uncanny way of appearing
at every social event she attended. Whenever she saw
him, she felt her breath leave her, and although she
would try to avoid him, she felt a pleasure when he
sought her out, which he always did over the other
young ladies. Soon, all of London knew it was the
widow Van Doren he seemed to desire. Tessa had
never felt such daggers of jealousy in the stares of
other women whenever she made an entrance during
a party.

One night after a party, very late, he offered to see
her home in his own carriage when her horse suddenly
went lame, his back hind leg unable to support its
weight.

"All right then." She smiled to hide her nervous-
ness and climbed into his carriage. On the ride back
to Willow Pond, he pulled her to him and kissed her
as John never had. It was as if he devoured her, pas-
sionately pressing his chest against hers. She was
dizzy, frightened, and thrilled all at once. The kiss
held a promise of what their lovemaking would be
like. And she knew it would bear no resemblance to
the sweet nights spent with John.

Marco walked her to her door, and saw her safely
into the confines of Willow Pond. She could barely
walk after the kisses they shared. And foolishly, when
he returned two nights later and proposed, she accepted.

Their wedding night was indeed all their kisses had promised. Tessa felt her passion in waves that left her literally weak and aching for more. His mouth found both her nipples and then traced a path down her belly. He was not afraid to touch every part of her, to tease her to heights she had never experienced before. No, her John had never loved her this way. Marco took her over and over and over again, not tiring. But shortly before dawn, he retreated, telling her he had business to attend to at his own country home and promising to return to Willow Pond that night.

"I love you, Tessa," he said, kissing her.

"I love you, too."

"You are my one true love."

All day she slept, and he kept his word, returning after sundown, when they resumed their lovemaking. He liked to lie on top of the blankets, watching her shiver, her nipples hard, her flesh pale in the orange glow of the fireplace in her bedroom. Just when she thought she could bear the cold no longer, her nipples almost painful, her fingers icy, he would cover her body with his own, warming her, feeling her goose bumps turn to heat as he entered her. She liked hearing his breath in her ear, hearing his passion for her.

"You were the one I was searching for," he whispered.

"You always say that, my love."

"It's because it's the truth I speak. You are my one true mate. We each have one. You are mine. I knew it. I knew behind those dark green eyes was a tigress. Don't you feel it, Tessa. Don't you?"

She stared at Marco. He was a stranger to her in many ways. The wedding had been a small candle-lit affair, at the chapel on Uncle Henry's property, and only her aunt and uncle and Marco's servant girl, Lily, and his houseman, Charles, had attended. And yet, she chided herself, could he really be a stranger when they made love in this way?

As weeks passed, Tessa found herself addicted to his touch. She would sleep all day, waiting with agonizing anticipation for the moment she would see him, naked, standing before her, his body as perfect as the statue of David she had seen in Florence with John on their honeymoon. They rarely left the house.

And yet, something nagged at her. Whereas with John she had romped through the fields of Willow Pond until both their cheeks were a rosy red, she never saw her new love in daylight. He explained it away as his business keeping him far afield during the day, but she didn't believe him. Occasionally, too, she was frightened by him. He had secrets, she was sure of it, but fear kept her from prying. She loved him, and part of her didn't want to know the truth. Fear and the passion bound her to him. He never tired of her, nor she of him. Still, when she looked in the mirror, she was sometimes surprised by her appearance. Circles had settled beneath her eyes. She couldn't sleep most days now as her fears took root, and she felt restless and strange. But she couldn't let go of her obsession for him.

Finally, one night, near dawn, he made her a strange offer.

"Do you trust me, Tessa?"

"Of course I do, my beloved." She traced the muscle of his biceps with her fingertip. Then she stroked down his belly to his thigh and up to the small black line of hair from his navel down to where he was hard, as always, for her.

"Do you believe that we are each meant for one person, forever? Even beyond this world?"

"Now I do," she whispered.

He rolled on top of her and kissed her. "You are mine. And I need you to trust me. We are to be together forever. And not even God can pull us apart."

"Why would God do such a thing?"

"Because He sits on His throne and He gives, and then He takes away. He took your John. I know you cared for him. Shh, my love." He put his fingertips to her mouth as she started to speak. "I am not jealous. I know he was your best friend, just as I also know that what we have comes along maybe once in a century. Once in two centuries. It is a love for the ages. It *defies* the gods. Do you want to be with me forever?"

She nodded.

"Then believe," he whispered.

And then he bit her.

Tessa screamed. She felt a sickening rush, as if she were hurtling down a pitch-black tunnel. She fought against him with all her might, beating at his arms and back, feeling her heart beating harder and harder. And then…nothingness.

She wasn't sure how long she was in a world of

shadows and darkness. She only knew that when she next awoke, every nerve was alive, and Marco was there, ready to make love to her, ready to bring her further into that dark world. She clung to him, frightened, certain it was all some sort of bad dream. He then explained, talking softly as one might to a child, what she was now. What *they* were. Then he made love to her again.

If she had thought before that their lovemaking was intense, nothing prepared her for the explosion within her body now. Every cell inside her was on fire, and she knew anything in her previous life paled compared to this. The bond between them was so strong, and now she was tied to him in darkness forever. Yet she was repelled by what she was, still not quite believing the nightmare she found herself in.

She was wracked by guilt and disgust. She still heard John's whispers. Sometimes, hiding from the sunlight, she would come upon one of his books in the library, and she would touch the pages and will John to come back to her, to rescue her from what she had become.

The whispers of John became stronger and more urgent. The first time she killed a man in London, a drunken man in a dark alley, with Marco encouraging her, she felt shame…and then heard her beloved John's voice. He was luring her to the light, just as surely as she knew by her new form, her new life in darkness with Marco, she was to be separated from John forever. Even if she died—as she would if the sunlight touched her, Marco said—she would not go to heaven with John. She would be a lost soul. Forever.

She missed Willow Pond, ached for it with something akin to homesickness. She and Marco spent more and more time in London proper, in the city, the better to blend with the shadows. Some nights, she would find herself crying, longing for Willow Pond, craving the feel of the sun on her face, John's hand in her own, picking daisies, climbing in the old willows, laughing.

She wasn't sure of the precise moment when she decided to leave Marco. She knew she was addicted—not just to feeding on blood, but to *him.* And she felt pity for Lily, the servant girl so faithful to her master. Turned, just as she was.

When Marco had to go to Paris on business, to settle the estate of his great-uncle who had left him a large inheritance, by the third night without him, she felt panicked. But it was in the dark of that night that she heard John's sweet voice. He told her to leave. To return to Willow Pond, and from there to leave England.

She told Lily what she was doing. "And if you are smart, dear girl, you will leave also. Make a life for yourself, such as we can have life." She shook the girl by the shoulders as she packed hurriedly.

"Take me with you, then," Lily begged her. "Don't leave me with him. Have pity on me and take me with you."

"Fine. We will stick together, then."

She and Lily fled the following nightfall and headed on horseback to Willow Pond. From there, she wrote a letter to her aunt Lydia and uncle Henry telling them she was going overseas on holiday, and not to worry for her. Then she took her jewelry and anything of value she could pack in her trunks and left Willow Pond with only the vaguest of plans. She and Lily traveled by night to Italy, to an isolated villa in the countryside that she rented. There, they lived behind shuttered windows, and anxiously paced the floor, unsure of where to go next.

Surviving was difficult. They couldn't go to the market in daylight. They couldn't travel in daylight. Tessa hired a gardener who also ran errands for them during the day. Feeding was difficult, too. They needed the isolation of the country place to protect them from Marco—and yet that meant they had to ride long and hard when they had to feed, always making sure they returned to the house by dawn.

The house was beautiful, with olive trees that swayed in the breeze and an arbor under which they took their supper….

There, at the house one night, Marco found them.

He kicked in a window and tore the shutter clean off its hinges.

"My wife," he sneered, sweeping in through the window, glass shattering on the tiled floor.

Tessa and Lily both screamed, Lily cowering behind her.

"My darling," Tessa said, her voice quivering with fear.

"You left without a goodbye, my love. Without a *proper* goodbye." He was across the floor of the villa in an instant, his boots clicking on the tile. He grabbed Tessa and his lips were upon her neck.

Later Tessa didn't even recall picking up the candelabra. She remembered striking him with it, though. Marco fell to the floor, blood trickling from his temple. Tessa stood over him and struck him again, the heavy silver candlestick landing with a sickening *thud*. Lily shrieked.

"No, my child. Don't: We can't panic."

Hurriedly, they raced for their bags, and then, still feeling fear, Tessa set the villa on fire. Then they took off on horseback.

Miles down the road, their horses tired, they stopped at a stream near a fork in the road. Tessa told Lily, "I am headed for the sea. I will take a boat. You, head to Paris. Get lost amongst the masses. You will be anonymous there. Godspeed." She pressed a sack of gold coins into the girl's hand, the name God feeling foreign on her tongue.

From there Tessa traveled, eventually, to Morocco, where she met the diplomat George Ashton, and then it was onward to Shanghai.

Chapter 13

Hack called at eleven-thirty that evening. "I got your e-mail. I'm really sorry, Tessa."

"I know, Hack. I'm worried sick."

"You gonna tell me what you think this is all about? Or is this another one of your deep, dark secrets?"

"Hack, I trust you. But I also know it's better for you, the less you know. I think someone from the past, someone with a grudge toward Lily and me, has returned. I think he may be using her as bait."

"And do you think it has to do with Shanghai Red?"

"Yes."

He was silent.

"What is it, Hack? You can tell me."

"Well, I've gone over it a hundred times."

Tessa's body stiffened. "What? Tell me."

"All right. I was playing around on the computer. I took all of the Shanghai Red death locations…every place where someone had OD'd on Shanghai Red…and I configured them on a map of the city. Then I added locations where police reports indicated Shanghai Red was being sold."

"And?"

"And, it's a bull's-eye."

"What do you mean?"

"I mean, they form concentric circles on the island of Manhattan."

"Circles."

"Yup. And not just ordinary circles. I mean perfect circles. You couldn't draw them more perfect in geometry class."

"That makes no sense."

"But you didn't ask the sixty-four-thousand dollar question."

"Which is?"

"Where's the bull's-eye?"

"I don't understand."

"Come on. Archery, babe. The bull's-eye. The circle in the center. Well, let me tell you, Tessa…it's the Night Flight Club. Bull's-eye."

Tessa clutched the phone in one hand and reached out with the other to steady herself against her dining room table.

"You still there, Tessa?" Hack whispered.

"Mmm-hmm. But I don't know what it means."

"It means you are the bull's-eye and someone's

planning on using you as target practice. Someone's out to send you a message. I'd watch it if I were you. I'd double watch it. Something about this is really messed up. I think you pissed off the wrong person."

"You could say that…. Thanks, Hack. You'll keep playing with your computer, then? Keeping your ear to the ground?"

"Yeah. If I hear anything about Lily, I'll let you know."

"Thanks, Hack."

"Fight the good fight."

"Always."

Tessa hung up the phone. Long ago, she had run from the man who sired her. But here, in Manhattan, she was determined to take a stand. This was *her* home, her streets. Her world. And Marco wasn't going to take it away from her.

"Surprise!"

When Delorean walked into the Night Flight Club on Thursday evening, she started weeping as everyone shouted "surprise" and emerged from behind the bar. Even Jorge had moist eyes as he clutched his new son. Delorean turned around and playfully slugged her husband on his rock-hard biceps. "You devil, you kept this surprise from me?"

Jorge winked at Tessa. "My boss would have fired me if I told you."

Tiny Delorean rushed over to Tessa and, standing on tiptoe, threw her arms around Tessa's neck. "This is so amazing. It looks magical. Thank you."

They had stuck a Private Party sign on the door and were opening an hour later. For now, the entire place had been decorated in blue tulle. Against the back wall was a large banquet table covered in presents. Several other tables were covered in white linens with baby-blue flowers in vases in the center. Cool even toned down his techno mixes and was playing some Latin music he knew Delorean loved.

The kitchen staff had created platters of canapés, and they'd brought in pastries and a sheet cake as elaborate as one for a formal wedding.

"Come on, everyone, eat, dance, greet the baby," Tessa urged, her arm around Delorean. She heard several bottles of champagne being uncorked with celebratory *pops*.

Little Micah slept blissfully in his father's arms. He had pale brown skin and a crop of black curly hair. Tessa peered at his angelic face, feeling that familiar tug that she experienced whenever she saw children. She disguised the longing, telling herself a baby was not only an impossibility, it would never fit in with her lifestyle. She and John had wanted a baby. But that was from another time and place; she no longer entertained such thoughts.

Tessa allowed Delorean, Jorge, baby Micah, and his older sister, Bella, to take center stage. Her employees clustered around them, oohing and ahhing over the baby, who was bundled in a Winnie-the-Pooh layette set that Cool had bought and given Jorge in anticipation of the blessed event.

Bull's-eye. Tessa looked around at the people she

cared about. From the dishwashers to the bartenders
to Jorge, she knew their names, faces, children's
names, their dreams. She helped them get green cards
and work visas, she paid college tuition, she let them
have days off for doctor appointments, their children's plays, and to sightsee with visiting relatives.
When Cool dated a waitress with a cocaine habit,
Tessa even paid for rehab. Cheryl was now clean
sober, and living in upstate New York, enjoying a
fresh start.

Tessa knew she couldn't allow Marco's relentless
pursuit of her to destroy them. She watched Jorge
feed cake to Delorean in celebration of their new
son. Looking on, she felt a pain that they might all
be in danger. Tessa now knew that whatever it took,
she would have to destroy, once and for all, the vampires who pursued her.

Later that night, after they opened the club, Tessa
called Hack. It was a little before midnight, and she
knew he'd be up, nursed along by his caffeine habit.

"I need to know something, Hack."

"Sure thing, Tess."

"Can you use those circles to predict where
Shanghai Red will strike next?"

"I've been toying with some formulas and predic-
tions all night."

"And?"

"And I'm pretty damn wired, but I think I have a
general idea where they'll strike next."

"Where?"

"Tudor City."

"Got a cross-street?"

"Yeah. Got a pen?"

Tessa took down the address. Tudor City was an enclave of Manhattan between 2nd Avenue and the East River, delineated by 42nd Street to the north. The buildings there had more character than typical skyscrapers. Stone apartment buildings were grouped together in an area that felt like a true neighborhood—though it was just a stone's throw from the hustle and bustle of Midtown.

Tessa checked her watch. The club was just filling up. She hurriedly dressed in black leather pants, black leather gloves and a black motorcycle jacket. She donned dark glasses and braided her hair. She wouldn't wait until they came to the bull's-eye. She would go to them.

As she traveled by rooftop, her teeth chattered. It wasn't the cold. It was the fear. She had spent a century putting distance between herself and that woman—her youthful self, who had been so easily swayed by passion for a man. Now, she would not only face him but the origins of the life she led now.

In Tudor City, she descended a fire escape to the streets. The November wind rushed through the alleyways with a *whoosh*. Tessa crept like a cat, every nerve alert, on fire. She waited for James, for Jules, for the half creatures under Marco's spell. Hearing footsteps, she turned around, and faced a trio of vampires— James and Jules, the two she had already encountered, plus a woman who carried an ancient-looking dagger.

"We've been waiting for you," the female vampire taunted, her voice raspy and menacing.

"Have you?"

"Yes. Our Master said you would be smart enough to find us. But stupid enough to think you could fight us."

"He underestimates me, as always."

The vampire James came toward her first. They circled each other. Then Tessa found her center, found her strength and lunged toward him with a flying sidekick that snapped his ribs. When he doubled over, she brought her boot up and connected with his nose, which instantly spewed blood.

"Bitch!" he spat, gasping.

But Tessa had no time for name-calling. She pulled the lid off a garbage can in the alleyway and flung it like a discus, hitting Jules in the throat, causing him to spit blood and clutch at his neck. But of course, they had their tricks, too. She knew fighting them would not be easy.

First, a wolf appeared at the female vampire's side. Though Tessa did not shape-shift, she knew enough about other vampires to know some of them did.

Next a fog descended. It grew so thick, she couldn't see them, but she also knew it provided them cover from prying eyes.

She heard the four paws of the wolf coming toward her. It leaped up, and its jaws snapped at her neck, spittle flying and a snarl emanating from deep in its throat. She lifted her hand in defense, and its teeth closed around it, biting her with razorlike incisors. She fought the urge to scream in pain and, taking her other hand, she formed a hard fist and punched the wolf's snout with all her strength. It recoiled with a loud growl and then a whimper, then it withdrew and lay down, its paw atop its snout.

Tessa pulled her belt through its loops and hurriedly wrapped it around her wounded hand, trying to stanch the blood flow. She crouched low, straining to hear and see where the next attack would come from, trying to catch her breath.

Hearing footsteps on the pavement, she guessed it was the woman next. She knew the woman would be her fiercest challenge. Tessa understood Marco too well—the woman would be both a vampire slave and a sexual slave to him. And she would be jealous of Tessa.

The woman burst through the thick fog, knife drawn, emitting the eerie shriek of the undead.

Tessa thrust out her fist, landing a punch squarely in the woman's stomach. It didn't stop the vampire, who sliced through the air with her dagger. Tessa could feel a soft breeze as the dagger whipped close to her face, back and forth. She raised her arm and felt the blade cut through the thick leather of her jacket. A warm ooze told her the knife had found flesh.

Tessa again crouched, this time searching and then finding the kneecap of the female vampire and landing a sharp kick that snapped the bone and brought the vampire down to the ground. Quickly standing, Tessa kicked her in the jaw. The other vampire started rolling away from Tessa, reflexively pulling her arms up to her face and wailing.

From behind, Tessa heard Jules and James. Of course she hadn't wounded them enough to stop them, only enough to stun them. The two of them moved in tandem, almost as if dancing, drawing their legs back and then kicking out, spinning, kicking, spinning, kicking. Tessa raised herself off the ground and came at them with kicks and punches, and her full repertoire of fighting skills. When she first trained in the martial arts, she did it for discipline. Here in New York, she had added Kav Magra training—a form of martial arts used by the Israeli military. It wasn't quite so elegant as her initial training, but Kav Magra was designed to render a kill.

One of two vampires, Tessa couldn't tell which, managed to land a solid kick to her face, crunching against her cheekbone and immediately causing her right eye to swell. Tessa had to fight a panic rising in her when she realized she could no longer see out of that eye. Summoning all her remaining strength, she knew she could not allow herself to pass out.

"Buddha be with me," she whispered, and from somewhere deep inside, she heard Hack's voice. *"Fight the good fight."*

Regaining her strength, she thought of Hsu, and of Hack's brother. The images, their stories, energized her, and she whirled around and around, spinning with roundhouse kicks in the direction of Jules and James. She landed more kicks than she missed, and soon they retreated.

Then, without warning, the fog lifted. Tessa surveyed the ground. The wolf was lying on its side. The woman was crumpled in a heap, clutching her face. Jules and James were limping away from her.

Tessa's eye was swollen completely shut, but she sensed Marco. At one time in her life, when both would be in a crowded room, sheer chemistry between them would magnetically pull her to his side. But now she considered that awareness of his presence a warning of deadly danger. She gazed up at the rooftops.

He was there. And in the crook of his arm, he choked a limp Lily. Tessa could see through her good eye that time had not diminished his strength. He was breathtakingly powerful and evil, all wrapped into one.

"Let her go, Marco," Tessa called up to him, the words muffled, coming from lips swollen where she'd caught a punch. She tasted blood in her mouth.

"It's a pleasure to see you, my beloved. My wife."

"Take me. Leave her."

"No. Our time to dance will come later."

"Why not now?" she shouted up to him, but her voice just reverberated into emptiness.

He was gone. Vanished in a rush of fog.

Tessa saw that her enemies were stirring. She took off on foot, racing through the night. She'd deal with it all later. For now, she had to get home and nurse her wounds.

When Tessa reached the club, she took the back entrance. She didn't want anyone to see her. Placing her hand to her face, she could feel the swelling. She knew she looked frightful.

Fitting her key in the lock, she ascended the back stairwell to her loft. And then she stopped. For there, sitting on the doorstep to her private apartment, was Detective Tony Flynn, clutching a bag of Chinese takeout.

Chapter 14

"Jesus H. Christ, what the hell happened to you?" he demanded, standing up in disbelief. "Here I brought you supper, and I should have brought a doctor instead."

Had Tessa been a woman, an ordinary woman, she knew she would have wanted nothing more than to dissolve in his arms and let him care for her, but she knew his seeing her this way would raise many questions, and she struggled to think of what answers she could give him.

"It's nothing." Tessa quickly unbraided her hair, hoping her long black locks would hide some of the bruising.

"Nothing? You get the living shit kicked out of you

and it's nothing?" Flynn was at her side in three swift strides.

She avoided looking at him, tears stinging her eyes. She was unused to sympathy. She moved toward the door, deactivating the alarm and unlocking the three locks, all the while allowing her hair to fall forward, masking some of her wounds. Blood trickled to the floor from her cut arm and hand.

"Tessa!" Flynn grabbed her shoulder, causing her to wince. "Damn…I'm sorry." He released her, but looked down at the blood on the floor. "I think we've got to get you to a hospital."

Tessa opened the door. "I'll let you in, but no hospitals." She was surprised at how her voice trembled. Seeing Marco—with Lily, no less—had unnerved her. She knew many vampires felt the call of their sire. She did, too, but her years of training taught her to ignore that pull.

Flynn followed her through the door, and she reset the alarm.

"Let me see how badly you're hurt. You're bleeding. Jesus, Mary and Joseph but you're a mess."

"Flynn, suddenly you've got religion? That's two mentions of Jesus inside of a minute. Look, I'll be all right." Tessa moved from the living room through her bedroom to the master bathroom with the giant sunken marble tub. He followed her in there.

"I thought you said you ran a clean club."

"I do," she said, taking off her leather jacket slowly, wincing for just a fraction of a second at the knife wound.

"People who run clean clubs don't end up looking like they just went twelve rounds with Mike Tyson."

"This is an old score. I can't explain it right now." She continued undressing, pulling off her leather pants, seeing the mottled flesh, knowing she would awaken tomorrow night hurting. She was now in a black tank top and black panties, and she didn't care. She wanted to get into a hot tub of water, to wash away the memories of the night. She needed a plan to get Lily back. As long as Tessa wasn't captured, Marco would keep Lily alive as bait. She was sure of it.

She stared at Flynn in the soft light of the bathroom, willing him to stop asking questions.

"Look, does whatever happened tonight have anything to do with this?" Flynn took a photograph from inside his jacket.

Tessa looked down, recognizing herself from another time, another place.

"What? An old World War II photo?" She feigned ignorance.

"This isn't you?" He pointed accusingly at the woman in the picture.

"That would be impossible, Flynn. This had to have been taken…what? Sixty-five years ago? Have you been drinking?"

"Look me in the eye, Tessa…Tess." His voice was soft but commanding.

He reached out his hands and gingerly took her face in them, tilting her chin upward so she was forced to look at him. He blinked slowly, and a flash of pity fell like a shadow across his face. Then he leaned toward her and gently kissed her bruised and swollen eye. He traced her cheek with his tongue, moving down, finding her neck and kissing her again.

She exhaled and began to unbutton his shirt. It had been too long since she had had human comfort. Soon he was shirtless, and she stood in her bra and panties. She pried herself from his embrace and started filling her tub with steaming hot water. She wanted a long soak to ease her pain, and she wanted him, wet against her.

Without speaking, they each undressed completely and climbed into the water. She turned on the whirlpool jets, enjoying their massaging effect on her muscles. Tessa nestled against Flynn's chest, lying on top of him, her nipples hard against him. Taking the bar of scented green-tea soap, she began to lather up his chest, sliding her hands up and down his body.

"Tessa," he whispered, "what happened—?"

"Shh," she urged him, covering his lips with her bruised ones.

She felt him growing hard, heard him moan. Soon, they were making love, the steam from the tub rising around them. She straddled him, facing him, chest to chest, belly against belly.

"Tessa, let me help you."

"You can help me by letting me forget…if only for the night."

"Oh God…" He pulled her tighter to him, kissing her voraciously. Though it hurt her mouth, she was lost in the moment, and when they both climaxed at once, she felt a release and a peace at the same time. A wholeness.

They climbed out of the tub and dried each other off with thick Turkish towels. Tessa led him by the hand to her bed, and they climbed in under a mountainous goose-down comforter.

"I don't want to talk." Flynn pulled her close against him. "I want to keep this perfect. But tomorrow, I'm going to want to know what happened."

"That's fair." She lay on top of him, her long hair wet and splayed out against the pillows. She rose up on her elbows and kissed him, amazed at how strong his mouth was, how powerful and sexy he was.

They held each other, kissing languorously for some time. At four-thirty Flynn moaned. "Damn, I've got to go home. I'm on duty in three hours."

"I need to get some sleep before the sun comes up," Tessa said truthfully.

Flynn slid out from under the warm blankets. He dressed quietly. Tessa pulled on a robe and walked him to the front door.

"Fuck it," he said.

"What?"

"I'm falling for you. And I don't give a damn about playing games with you. I'm tired of games. I want honesty. I care about you, and something tells me I'm not gonna like your whole story when I hear it. I have a feeling it's not even gonna make sense. So I said it. And I mean it. I'm falling for you, and I still want to know the truth."

She nodded. She kissed his mouth, then whispered in his ear, "I care about you, too."

He waited while she unlocked the door, and then strode down the hall, not looking backward.

Watching him until he descended the staircase, Tessa felt a pang. He thought he wanted the truth. But even with all he'd seen as a police detective, could he handle it?

She wanted to get this over with. Part of her yearned to just tell Flynn her story. If he rejected her forever, she would go back to her life of solitude and be done with it. She found a business card with Flynn's cell phone number and called it, but she got his voice mail.

"This is Flynn. NYPD. You know what to do."

She smiled bemusedly. He was a man of few words. Just the sound of his voice filled her with both peace and dread. He was a decent man, an honest and strong man. He had the qualities of a warrior, however, and he was nobody's fool. And as much as being with him made her feel more complete, more centered, she still wondered how he would deal with her secrets.

"Hello, Flynn. This is Tessa. I'm feeling much better today. I don't look half as bad as I expected to. I want to talk. Call me when you can."

She hung up and surveyed herself in the reflection of the windows lining her living room. She was nearly healed, the miracle of vampires. But just as she was recovered, she knew her enemies were as well. They were a gathering force, and they would come for her again and again. For what seemed like the thousandth time, she worried about Lily. Tessa knew Lily had great inner strength. Over the last hundred years or so, she had transformed from a naive young servant girl to a confident ball-buster. She seemed to know no fear. Tessa hoped Lily was using that internal strength to mentally hold on until Tessa could somehow free her.

Tessa knew Marco. She had lived with him as his wife. He had taken vows with her, though surely he didn't believe in consecrated vows. Nonetheless, back then, he would have done anything to possess her, his *one*. He wouldn't kill Lily. Not yet. Lily would stay alive as long as Tessa was not yet reunited with him. But where was he keeping her? Manhattan was a big city, and there was no telling where Lily was.

Tessa couldn't go to the police for help. She didn't exist on paper or in the system. Lily didn't have a social security card. She had found a landlord who gladly took cash. She didn't exist—at least not in this century. Anyone who knew her in her first life was long buried in an English cemetery plot. The police would be chasing a ghost.

She took solace in the fact that Marco probably didn't want to kill her—his beloved wife. As a Buddhist, she believed that souls live through multiple lives—and occasionally, in those lives, a person might find a soul with whom he or she was inexplicably connected. In Marco's case, he would search for her, his *one,* forever if he had to, not to kill her but to bind her to him again.

She went to her laptop and logged on, sending an instant message to Hack.

* * *

Nightlady: Knock-knock. U in, Hack?

Technofreak: I'm in, bad-ass lady. Where else is an agoraphobic gonna go?

Nightlady: LOL. Got anything for me tonight?

Technofreak: Maybe. Just kind of a hunch. U find Lily?

Nightlady: No. Caught a glimpse of her, but that's it. One very bad dude has her, my friend. And I need U to help me get her back.

Technofreak: But she's alive. That's good news. Now we just have to get her.

Nightlady: Precisely.

Technofreak: Well, I went to some alternative newsgroups hunting down where to buy Shanghai Red.

Nightlady: And?

Technofreak: It's fuckin' amazing. U would think this stuff is gold. People will do ANYTHING to get their hands on it.

Nightlady: Hope they're willing to die for it. I mean, this stuff is so dangerous.

Technofreak: Tell me about it. But to the junkies, it doesn't matter. The Internet is buzzing about this stuff. The perfect high. That's what they call it.

Nightlady: How can they be so stupid, Hack? I feel like I'm constantly fighting a losing battle.

Technofreak: In some ways we R. But that doesn't mean we stop fighting.

Nightlady: Thanks, Hack. I needed to hear that.

Technofreak: Well, it's easy for me to say. I comb

*the information superhighway, and you're out
there getting your ass kicked.*

Nightlady: We each need the other.

Technofreak: Like Starsky and Hutch.

Nightlady: Who R they?

*Technofreak: Old cop show. Anyway, I ended up
hacking into a site and lurking. Found two guys
talking about Shanghai Red. The one guy says he
heard it's being manufactured in the city. Soon
gonna flood the fuckin' drug market. Take over the
crack trade. Take over everything. That's how
"awesome" the high is.*

Nightlady: Damn.

*Technofreak: I ran the concentric circles again.
And I think it's possible that it's being manufactured down on the docks on the Hudson. You
know. Over by the meatpacking district. The S&M
places. I plotted the next circle, and it crosses
over an abandoned warehouse.*

Nightlady: Bingo!

Hack gave Tessa the address, and she went into
her bedroom to change. Surveying herself in the mirror, she saw that her eye had a shiner that she assumed would be healed by the next day. However,
considering how badly she had been hit, she didn't
look too bad. The deep gash from the knife and the
teeth wounds from the wolf were almost healed over.
She rubbed her hand over the place where twenty-
four hours ago flesh had been torn and bleeding. She

thought about how, for over a hundred years, she hadn't had a cold, or a fever, or any mortal frailties. The good news was that she was whole again. But Marco's rage would be building.

Tessa again donned her leather jacket—a little worse for wear from the previous night, with a slash in the arm—leather pants and a black tank top. She put on her steel-toed boots, the better to inflict damage, and she strapped a knife to each leg. Next she pulled on leather gloves. Opening a trunk, she pulled out a semiautomatic. She hated mortals' fascination with guns, but she knew she had to be prepared for anything. Dressed to fight, she first needed to make things right with Buddha.

Kneeling in front of her shrine, Tessa lit a stick of incense. Quietly, she chanted. She explained to Buddha—to the universe—what had brought her, as a warrior, to this point. She was not obeying the tenets of peace, and she prayed for forgiveness.

"I need to do this to stop my sire. Forgive me. I will do what I can to make things right. If I can solve the problem without violence, I will. Buddha be with me."

She rose and centered herself with several yoga poses. Then she went over to her antique desk and called Jorge on his phone. "Jorge, I won't be in at all tonight. I know I've been asking you to run things more, but I'm hoping this will be the last night I have to."

"You okay, Tessa?"

"No, Jorge. I'm not."

"It's Lily, isn't it? She's in trouble."

"Yes. She is. But I'm going to help her, Jorge. I

just ask you to trust me. And I know that's asking a lot of you. I just can't tell you everything right now."

"Tessa, I came to you out of the joint. I'd been out, what, a year, and no one would give me a job. Exonerated or not, I was an ex-con. You had no reason to hire me. You had no reason to believe me when I said I was completely innocent. You could have looked at my prison tattoos and sent me on my way. Not only did you trust me, or at least give me a chance when no one else would, but you've continued to trust me with a lot of responsibility here. I trust you with my life."

"Well…" Tessa said softly. "Let's hope it doesn't come to that."

She hung up the phone and left her loft, ascending to the roof. Staring out over the city, she tried to feel a connection to Flynn. Then, reaching backward through time, she tried to feel for a thread connecting her to Hsu. And then to John. The universe was all interrelated. She needed their help. She needed them to guide her.

Taking off for the Hudson River, she flew against the night sky, leaping between buildings, exhilarated by the jumps, by the freedom, by the cold air nipping at her face. New York really was the city that never slept, she thought as she looked down at the busy streets, yellow cabs a blur of color on concrete roads. The concrete jungle.

She supposed that busyness was what had drawn her to the Big Apple in the first place. She had tried living in isolation. In the country. But the problem was that at night, places in the country shut down. New York was different. When she awoke each night, she had her pick of a thousand restaurants, stores, and as much action as during the day.

New York—especially now in the twenty-first century—was the first city that allowed her a semblance of normality. In 1911 and 1940—1950 even—there were no fancy security systems or panic rooms or ways to ensure her safety and keep her out of the sun. In 1940, she could not have gone to the grocery store at three o'clock in the morning. She couldn't have paid all her bills with online banking. Before New York, and before the last twenty years or so, she had to pay assistants and servants to do all her daylight work. Yes, New York was her salvation and her haven.

Finally, Tessa had made it down to the meatpacking district. Like everywhere in New York, there were inroads of gentrification. Some B-list actress had put in a sushi bar. There was a Mexican place with a reputation for good margaritas—on the rocks, with salt—and a French bistro had cropped up. But the meat-packing district still was harsh. Several rough leather bars lined the streets, with small crowds of bare-chested men in leather chaps and dog collars milling around outside. And then there were the prostitutes. This area wasn't for the faint of heart.

The closer she got to the river, the colder it got. Wind rushed past her ears, and she turned up the collar of her leather jacket, spotting dried blood on her sleeve. Her eyes teared from the wind. The prostitutes lingered by warehouse loading docks, pulling coats around themselves to keep warm, and then flashing cars as they drove slowly by. Tessa knew the routine. Men from the suburbs pulled over in their sedans and minivans, selected a girl, and got a fast blowjob for twenty bucks in the front seat. Handjobs could go for ten bucks. She watched one girl climb into an SUV. The girl couldn't have been more than fourteen or fifteen, and the SUV had a bumper sticker on it: Proud Parent of an Honor Roll Student at St. Mary's High School. Great, Tessa thought disgustedly. He's got a girl that age and he doesn't stop to think about that runaway in his car. Mortals were victims to their appetites—for sex, drugs, alcohol and darker addictions. She had thought she'd seen it all. Fetishists and S&M parlors. Dominatrixes who ruled their submissives with an iron fist—and a leather whip. A kid on PCP who axed his entire family to pieces. Crack addicts with AIDS still turning tricks while they waited to die.

She turned from the scene, pained by the sight of the teen girl. Then she decided she couldn't just fly away. She climbed down a fire escape into an alleyway that was ankle-deep in trash, exited the alleyway and went over to the SUV. She rapped on the driver's window.

"Buddy, roll down your window."

Suddenly, the young girl's head popped up, and she could see him hurriedly zipping up his pants. He opened the window.

"You a cop?" he asked. "I can't get arrested. If my wife found out, she'd divorce me."

"How old are you, sweetie?" she asked the girl.

"Eighteen."

"Bullshit."

"Sixteen."

"More bullshit."

Finally, in a voice barely above a whisper, she said, "Fourteen."

The man in the driver's seat started to cry. "Oh shit, oh shit, oh shit," he said rocking back and forth. "Damn, I didn't know."

Tessa's senses were so attuned when she was near people, she could spot a lie from a mile off. A trained vampire, keyed in to scents, was like a lie detector. She opened the car door and dragged the man out, slamming him up against the hood of the SUV.

"I'm only going to say this once. I know you knew she was fourteen, and I'm guessing you have a little honor roll student about the same age."

She pulled his wallet out of his back pocket and flipped through to the picture encased in plastic. "Beautiful family. It's a shame you're such a *fuck* that you'd jeopardize them."

"I'll never do it again."

"You're right. I'm going to keep your wallet, which has your address on your diver's license." She read his name. "Look, Bob, if I *see* this SUV anywhere *near* the working girls again, I'm calling your wife, you filthy pig. And if I see you look at an underage girl again, I'll kill you."

"What kind of cop are you?"

"I'm your worst nightmare, pal. I'm a cop outside the law."

She withdrew all the money in his wallet. "You sure carry a lot of cash."

"It was payday."

Tessa handed the thick stack of bills to the girl, who looked afraid to move.

"You must have a good job, Bob. That's a lot of money. What do you do?"

"I—I own an accounting firm."

"Hmm. All right, honey—" she nodded at the girl "—climb on out."

The girl did as she was told.

"Bob…time for you to leave."

"I need toll money."

"Bob…Bob…Bob…I don't give a fuck if you *walk* home. You're giving all your money to— your name, sweetie?"

"Cherish."

"That's what your pimp named you. What's your real name?"

"Dana."

"Okay, Bob, you're giving all your money to Dana here. Consider it a scholarship fund. Now get lost."

Trembling, Bob got back in his SUV and sped off, leaving Tessa with the girl.

"Dana, how come you ran away from home?"

"How did you know I ran away?"

"Because, despite you being on the street here, your hair and makeup remind me of a small-town girl. You didn't come here to do this kind of work. This isn't where you belong."

The girl broke down. "My mama died. Six months

later, my father marries this awful woman. He'd be
at work until late, and she would hit me and make me
do all the housework."

"It's like Cinderella, honey."

She nodded. "I told my father she hit me, but he
said I had to try to get along with my 'new mommy.'
She made me sick! So I ran away."

"How long have you been gone?"

"Five months."

"You call home in that time?"

"No."

"You like living on the streets?"

"No. It's disgusting."

"What's your home number? And your dad's
name?"

Dana gave her the number, which was in rural
Pennsylvania, and Tessa dialed her cell phone. A
man answered it on the first ring.

"Hello?"

"Hello, Fred, this is a friend of your daughter's."

He started sobbing into the phone.

"Fred," Tessa said impatiently, "I can't help you
if you're a mess. So calm down. Tell me something—
that bitch you married that hit your daughter, you still
married to her?"

"Technically," he sniffed into the phone. "Is my
baby girl all right?"

"We'll get to that in a minute. What do you mean,
technically?"

"The divorce isn't final, but she moved out two

weeks after Dana left. I was so blind to her faults. I was lonely. Please tell me if my daughter is okay."

"She's been through a rough time. I need you to go to the Night Flight Club in Manhattan. It'll take a good three hours to get here. She will be there. And then you both need counseling. I'll call and check on her in a month or so. If things haven't changed at home, I'll come after you. Do you understand?"

"Yes. Where is this club?"

Tessa gave him the street address and cross-street, and then she called Jorge and told him to expect the girl and her father. Tessa then hailed the kid a cab and sent her on her way.

"Thank you," she whispered. "You're an angel."

"No need to thank me, honey. Just don't ever run away again. Finish school, go to college. You want out of that house and that backwoods town, do it the right way."

The girl nodded and the cab pulled away. Tessa looked at her watch. Good deed done for the night, now it was time to find Marco.

She had memorized the address Hack had given her. The warehouse in question had windows painted black, a chain link fence topped with razor wire around it, and five snarling Dobermans patrolling the parking lot. Someone didn't want anyone coming in. Or, for that matter, anyone going out.

Tessa landed on the roof. She moved along the tar-paper stealthily and found a fire escape. Moving down one flight, she found an unlocked window and quietly lifted it about four inches. Just enough to see an assembly line of drug-making.

An Asian man in a lab coat walked amongst the workers. She guessed he was the chemist. She attuned her superior hearing to him as he shouted commands in Mandarin. She recognized enough of the language. Then he spoke in English.

"Faster. Move faster, you lazy pieces of shit. Move faster or this is what will happen to you." In the next instant, he had withdrawn an automatic gun with a silencer and pointed it at the temple of one worker. There was a pop as the gun went off and a woman slumped to the floor. "Faster. Faster! But do not forget to be precise."

The workers' eyes glanced furtively at the dead body. The man in the lab coat stepped over her, stopping for a moment to kick her body as a final act of disdain. Two men made a move to clear the body from the floor.

"Leave her there. As a reminder. Faster. Let's see them move faster."

Long tables were lined up, with tubes and glass containers, scales and lots and lots of white powder. Manning the tables, assembling packages and smaller dime bags of drugs were zombies. Tessa didn't know what else to call them, but she recognized their vacant expression. She had seen that look before….

Chapter 15

Germany. 19—. It was the fourth city she had lived in over the course of the previous seven years. Every time she settled in somewhere—Venice, Paris, Athens and now Berlin—she would, after a time, sense that Marco was zeroing in on her. In Venice, she had barely escaped after spotting him in a café. In Paris, had she not booby-trapped her apartment, she was sure she'd be back in his clutches.

Sooner or later, too, in every city, she would become aware of the creatures of the night. They all had a scent, imperceptible to mortals, but a scent nonetheless, and an uncanny instinct of being able to find one another. For some, it was to form groups. In groups there was strength. Less isolation. They were tormented souls, and Tessa believed that in clusters they moved further and further away from their humanity, making it easier to accept just who and what they had become. She supposed it was not unlike mortals who commit horrible acts in gangs or in riots, losing their inhibitions and sense of morality.

Tessa supposed that was the same with the Nazis. Ideals, political positions and beliefs that would have been given no credence before, now dominated. The Nazis found strength in numbers. No one questioned their lack of humanity. In numbers, it was easier to do what they were doing. They could load Jews on cattle cars, destroy the shops owned by Jews, beat people on the street, all in homage to a nationalism that made no sense.

She leaned out the window of her apartment and looked down on a crowd of young Nazis—no older than fifteen or sixteen—who were beating an old Jewish man. The elderly gentleman wore a long, black tweed coat, and pinned to its breast was a yellow star. One boy, baby-faced and Aryan to the nth degree with pale white-blond hair and rosy cheeks, stomped down with his boot on the old man's hand as he lay on the sidewalk. She heard the man's cry of agony. Around the Nazis were ordinary citizens moving about their business, glancing furtively in the bullies' direction, but not offering so much as a word of protest.

Tessa was sickened. It wasn't just the Jews singled out, either. She had a bookkeeper whose father was in a wheelchair. The bookkeeper's father was long gone—not part of Hitler's vision for a perfect Germany. She knew of a camp of Gypsies rounded up. Of homosexuals beaten beyond recognition. This was what groups of evil could do.

But Tessa wasn't interested in being part of some group—undead or living—or listening to the rhetoric of Hitler. She operated alone. Buddhism had enlightened her, taught her to keep her soul untouched by the day-to-day struggle for survival. But she believed both vampires and ordinary Germans fed into the same soul sickness. Germany was like a country of undead.

As the pro-Hitler factions became more rabid, she sensed a growing power of darkness in the city. The vampires were also gathering like storm clouds. Tessa knew it was time to leave Germany. She thought she would strike out for America if she could arrange for safe passage. But she had a mission to carry out first.

She ran a nightclub in Berlin, a jazz club actually, that she called the Night Flight Club. And as the city spiraled toward insanity, she decided she would aim to kill some of the S.S. If she had to leave Germany and be on the run in another country as the world went crazy, at least she would accomplish some good.

That night, as she had planned, Goebbels arrived at the club, along with other high-ranking German officials. Their black boots were so shiny, you could see your reflection in them. The S.S. commandeered her three best tables. They all drooled over her, and for all their talk of Aryan perfection, any one of them would have bedded her—dark hair, green eyes, questionable heritage and all.

She descended the staircase—a sweeping magnificently wide staircase that allowed her gown's train to trail behind her—at midnight. Fifteen musicians were playing big-band standards by the dance floor, and people were jitterbugging and dancing, seemingly oblivious to how Germany—their Germany—was hurtling toward madness. But something more was wrong. The minute Tessa entered the room, she felt the hairs stand up on the nape of her neck, as if a cold breeze had whispered past her.

Of course, in a sense, everything was wrong. Yellow stars adorned the coats of the Jews, and having witnessed upheaval in Shanghai and other countries over the years, she felt like screaming at the Germans—not the S.S., but the ordinary German citizens. *Wake up,* she wanted to urge them, you are hailing a madman as your savior.

But tonight, she sensed a new danger. As if in slow motion, she surveyed the room, hearing snippets of conversation, trying not to focus on any one conversation with her hearing, but instead picking up on vibes. And something more. The smell of undead. There! She felt the gaze of, not a vampire, but a slave. And another. And another. Dressed in finery, but haunted, vacant-eyed. They were not yet fully turned, and they were controlled, wholly and with no mercy, by Marco. She sensed it. Her husband was somewhere close to her. He was relentless in his pursuit of her.

She was so ashamed. How had she allowed her passions to blind her to his evilness? With the wisdom of hindsight, how could she not have thought it odd that he was never with her in daylight? How had she missed the coldness in his eyes? She would have gone mad by now had it not been for Buddhism.

Tessa realized she needed to detonate her explosives. The zombies—or whatever they were—would perish with the S.S. It was rather fitting, she supposed. A modern evil and an ancient evil would be destroyed in flames together. She only hoped Marco was somewhere in the building, somewhere where the flames would consume him, too. Fire, like sunlight, could kill a vampire.

Tessa paused for a moment. She had once loved him—or had thought she did. There was no denying the connection. She silently prayed that if she succeeded in killing him and if vampires could go on to a next incarnation, Marco would be able to atone for his misdeeds in this existence.

She strolled through the nightclub, the music lively and exuberant. She tried to act nonchalant, but she was aware of the undead, aware of the S.S., giving the acting performance of her life. She greeted each of the vile S.S. officers as if she were enamored of their manhood and virility. They lapped it up. And she casually avoided the undead, not looking at any of them. Whatever she did, she did not want her behavior to seem suspicious. She knew they were there to capture her, but she feigned ignorance.

She took to the microphone. "Thank you all for

coming," she said in perfect German. "I trust you will enjoy the band, the food, the champagne. Tonight we live to dance."

She couldn't bring herself to say "Heil Hitler." She couldn't. She had never said it. She remembered listening to Hitler's radio addresses and hearing the masses embrace him. It had sickened her.

Standing near the bandstand, she swept her hand toward the musicians, and they struck up a Glenn Miller song. And as she stood under the lights, she saw him. There, overlooking the dance floor, on the second floor, was Marco, the man whom she had once thought to be her sexual soul mate…her husband. She faltered for just a moment, hoping her recovery was swift enough that he would not realize he'd been spotted. She walked through the high-stepping, dancing crowd on the dance floor, out of the main ballroom to a back room, where she planned to start a fire. Then she would light fires at two more key spots, with a keg of explosives scheduled to explode in fifteen minutes beneath the table of the S.S. officers, hidden beneath a floorboard.

She lit the first fire, pouring kerosene on a pile of books and taking a match to them. It was a symbolic gesture as well as a practical one—she was burning multiple copies of *Mein Kempf,* Hitler's manifesto, filled with rantings. She left the back room and was racing to the location of the second fire, when Marco suddenly blocked her path, facing off against her in the hallway, three undead, expressionless monsters behind him.

"Tessa." He exhaled heavily.

She knew that, for all his ire, the sight of her weakened him. His eyes registered that his attraction for her was still intense and palpable. She avoided staring at his eyes, which had a magnetic pull.

"Marco."

"Have you missed me, my darling?"

"No," she said steadily. "Not as long as you are who you are. I was young and naive when I met you, Marco."

"Not so naive. You didn't resist me."

"I resist you now…. And who are these things— these beings you've brought with you?"

"They worship me as their father and creator. As their god. Remember, my lovely wife, how I told you not even God on His throne could keep us apart?"

"Yes. I remember, but you must know aspiring to be like God will only bring you ruin. Aspiring to be God is evil, Marco."

"I have power like God, immortality like God. I *am* God…. Come with me."

"I can't."

He stared at her, his eyes drawing her to him. "Do you not love me, my darling Tessa?"

"Marco, my husband…don't do this." She could smell the acrid smoke seeping into the hallway. The undead began squealing.

"Calm down," he commanded them. But panic set in. The creatures, despite the finery and anatomy that made them appear human, were subhuman and unable to think or react in a human way. They were animalistic, and they ran like rats.

Marco, furious, started running toward her. Tessa was trapped. Fire was now raging behind her, the flames starting to lick the walls, and he blocked the only exit. And then, as if by an act of the very God Marco defiled, an explosion rocked the club. Tessa fell heavily against a wall, but Marco was struck by a falling beam and collapsed on the floor.

Tessa rubbed her head and shoulder, where she had slammed against the wall. She held her hand up to her nose and mouth, trying to avoid inhaling the smoke filling the air. With one last glance at Marco, she ducked into a side room, opened a window and escaped out into the streets, where people poured out of the club, teeming onto the sidewalks.

Tessa hurried across the street and into an apartment building. She ascended the stairs to the roof, next leaping to the bell tower in the center of the city square. From this safe distance, atop the tower, Tessa watched her nightclub become engulfed in flames. Smoke billowed skyward, and orange fire kissed the sky. She put her head in her hands, feeling both a sense of relief and a great sadness that the man she once loved but who was so consumed by evil and hubris, had finally perished. Or so she assumed…

Zombies. The undead. Hack had been right. Tessa peered in at the drug-making occurring under machine gun-carrying guards. The creatures' eyes were flat, expressionless. They worked down on the factory floor with mechanical precision. She knew what they were. Marco hadn't fully turned them into vampires. So they remained in a state between undead and living, a suspended state of death, yet still breathing. There was no freeing them, though. She could never turn them into mortals again. They would have to die, along with their master. But she hoped that in dying, their souls might be freed from their torment.

Chapter 16

"I don't believe it. Detective Tony Flynn, the sloppiest, crabbiest son of a bitch who ever patrolled the streets of New York, is in love." Alex Williams stated it matter-of-factly.

"Look, I didn't tell you this so you could mock me, man. I told you because I think she's in some kind of trouble, and I don't know what it is exactly. I only know it has to do with Shanghai Red."

"My friend…we've been through a lot together."

Flynn rolled his eyes. "Please don't give me that 'I took a bullet for you' shit."

"I'm not." The two men sat in a diner down near the Hudson River. Alex Williams continued. "I'm serious. When you married Diana—me, Gus, even the lieutenant, knew it was a big fuckin' mistake. But who was I to tell you no? I mean, I haven't been in a relationship, ever, that lasted more than three months."

"What about Sara?" Flynn asked, referring to a gorgeous lawyer that everyone said Williams should settle down with.

"She doesn't count. I cheated on her."

Flynn shook his head. "You're hopeless."

"I know. So are you, but in a different way. Anyway, hell, we lived through Diana, through my dad's death, through Gus losing Irene, through a bullet— all right, I had to get that in there—through perps so fuckin' sick and ugly they haunted us at night."

"And?" Flynn asked. "Why bring this all up?"

"You're my best friend, and something tells me this lady...she's what's been missing from your life. So if she's in trouble, if we've got to bend a few rules to help her, we do. She's your woman. End of story."

"Thanks, Alex. You surprise me sometimes."

"Did I tell you my bullet wound hurts in cold weather?"

"Fuck off." Flynn laughed, then shoveled the rest of his fried eggs and toast into his mouth, washing it down with black coffee. The diner was a place they frequented late at night. It was a mixture of drunken club kids sobering up with eggs and coffee, people coming off the night shift, cops and a few denizens of the leather bars.

Before heading down to the diner, Flynn had

checked his voice mail. Just hearing Tessa's voice had made him instantly hard. He thought her a perfect sexual match to himself. But part of him still found it difficult to believe a woman with class and wealth could really be interested in him. He only knew that when she straddled him, when they were making love, there had been a moment when she looked into his eyes and he felt as if she looked right into his soul, battered and weary though it was.

"So what's your plan?" Alex asked.

"I want to head over a couple of blocks. There's a veritable drug supermarket by the river. Let's just hang and see what we can find out about Shanghai Red."

"You got it, my lovesick puppy."

"Fuck you."

Two blocks over from the diner, a homeless man slumped against a trash can, seemingly oblivious to the smell of rotting garbage. Flynn's mother had raised him to have compassion for his fellow man, and he always carried plenty of dollar bills. He didn't go to church often enough, but he slipped a wad of singles into the poor box of any church he passed. Giving the homeless enough for a meal was his way of doing good works. He peeled off ten singles and pressed them into the homeless man's palm.

"Go buy yourself a hot dinner, pal."

"Did you see them?" The man was crying. "Did you *see* them?" He began to cower.

"What, my man?" Flynn asked, used to the mentally ill amongst the homeless. Flying saucers, the devil, Jesus—they saw them all. He even knew one homeless guy who thought Elvis was a toll taker on the George Washington Bridge.

"The zombies."

"Zombies?" Alex asked, rolling his eyes at Flynn.

"Zombies!" the man squealed, agitated.

"Think we should call someone to come take him to Bellevue?" Alex asked, turning up the collar of his coat. "It's an awfully cold night. Even if they just keep him for a twenty-four-hour observation, he'll get a warm bed for the night, maybe calm down. Sounds like this dude can use some Thorazine."

Flynn squatted and tried to look the man in the eye. The man tried to reel away. Flynn said, "Easy there, partner. Take it easy. Now, what did you say you saw?"

"Zombies." The man was clearly terrified. Even as he spoke, he kept looking over his shoulder, agitated. "They're making Shanghai Red. Shanghai Red. Chinese zombies."

"Jesus," Williams said.

Flynn leaned in closer to the man. He was dressed in rags, and his teeth were rotted, eyes wild. But when he looked intently at Flynn, there was a hint of sanity.

"Shanghai Red?" Flynn whispered.

"Yeah. At the warehouse. Two blocks that way." He pointed toward the river.

"Okay, buddy. You get inside the diner and have a hot meal." Flynn stood and pulled a card from his wallet. "Then I want you to head to this shelter. Ask for Sister Teresa. She'll help you."

The man took the card and nodded.

"I mean it. Sister Teresa. Tell her Detective Flynn sent you."

"Flynn...Flynn..." the man mumbled. "And... and you're going to get the zombies, right?"

Alex and Flynn both nodded, then helped the homeless man to his feet, pointing him in the direction of the diner.

Flynn looked at Alex and said, "Let's do this."

They took off on foot toward the warehouse that the homeless man had indicated. They didn't see the man in the shadows a block to the north. They didn't see him snap the neck of the homeless man. They only saw the warehouse looming next to the cold and black Hudson River.

Tessa's legs were cramping. She crouched on the fire escape, her arms hugging her sides for warmth, and tried to decide what she was going to do. Panic was one option—but one she couldn't afford.

A fire was a logical choice, but with the Dobermans roaming down below, she had to do it without drawing too much attention to herself. On top of that, she wasn't sure she could ignite a blaze big enough to destroy the building—and the creatures inside it.

She could drop in through the window and fight them. Vampire slaves were poor decision-makers. Even outnumbered, she could probably beat them—for a while. But eventually, the sheer number of them would render her powerless from exhaustion.

She could let the new batch of drugs hit the

streets…and then pick off the chemist and Marco and the leaders of this new cartel one by one. But that would flood Manhattan with the most dangerous drug since crack. Right now, Shanghai Red was still elusive. If all the drugs in that warehouse hit the marketplace she imagined junkies dying in droves. And then it would, like all drugs, make its way out to the suburban shopping malls. There would be no stopping it.

She thought perhaps she could call Flynn and bring the wrath of the NYPD down on this warehouse. But involving police in vampire business wasn't her style. That would leave too many unanswered questions for the police to delve into. One look at the zombies, and the cops would know something truly strange—even for New York City—was going on.

Suddenly, it became a moot point.

Below, a Doberman began barking sharply, almost howling. Soon, all four Dobies were agitated.

Tessa moved away from the window and saw Flynn and Williams squeezing through a hole in the chain-link fence. "Damn," she whispered. Now what? They were good cops, excellent detectives, but they would be no match for what was behind those doors.

There was no time to warn them…. Then she grew excited. Oh, the gadgetry of the twenty-first century. Tessa took out her cell phone and dialed Flynn, praying he had his phone on vibrate. He did, as she didn't hear a ringing down below.

"Flynn here" came the whispered voice on the other end.

"It's Tessa," she whispered. "You are in danger. Call for backup."

"How do you—?"

"Please, Flynn. Trust me. Make the call."

She hung up, not giving him time to ask questions. She knew Flynn, or at least she thought she did. Flynn would call for backup. But he was a warrior, so he would also get inside that warehouse. And she had to be sure the odds were more even before that happened. She raised the window farther and climbed into the building.

The warehouse was a maze of metal catwalks. Tessa crept along them, noiseless. Good thing she wasn't afraid of heights. Peering down on the chemical lab below, she saw the crumpled body of the woman the chemist had shot in the temple. These weren't people to mess around with, and she prayed Flynn and Alex Williams would be able to stay alive long enough for backup to arrive.

A commotion broke out on the floor.

"Did you just stick some of this Shanghai Red up your nose, asshole?" A guard took a billy club and raised it menacingly above the head of a fidgety young man.

"No," the young man replied in a pleading voice.

"I saw you," the guard said, bringing the club down on the young man's skull with all his might. He fell in a heap like a sack of laundry.

Keep this up and you'll have no one left to work here, Tessa mused. Then again, the more of their own they killed, the fewer there were for Flynn, Williams and her to fight against. Out of the corner of her eye, she saw Flynn and Williams creeping in from the back of the building. The guard's beating of the young man had provided just the distraction they needed.

Tessa moved along the catwalk, crouching low, blending into the ceiling with her black clothes. She willed Flynn to look up at her. Focusing her internal energy, she tried to concentrate on him, speak to him with her mind. She knew Marco sometimes did that to her. She was grateful when Flynn did look up, but his dark expression told her he was worried about her. *Well,* she thought, *he'll soon learn I can take care of myself.*

Suddenly, a blood-curdling scream filled the warehouse, shaking Tessa to the core. Peering over the catwalk, she saw that a female slave had spotted Flynn and Williams. They had no choice but to dive for cover and draw their weapons.

"NYPD… Everyone put your hands up! We've got you surrounded."

"He's bluffing," the Asian man in the lab coat said loudly. He made some hand signals to the guards, three or four of them, who withdrew guns and began fanning out across the warehouse floor.

Frightened, the drug slaves started their keening sound, moaning and wailing, and covered their faces with their hands. The Asian man was visibly irritated by their noise. He ripped a gun from the hands of one of the guards and let off a burst of firepower, mowing down five slaves.

"Stay silent or that's what'll happen to the rest of you."

But the keening continued. The slaves ran behind crates and dove under tables. Chaos had taken over the once-methodical operations below.

"Put down your weapons." Williams's voice came from the shadows.

"You come out, and perhaps we'll let you live," the man in the lab coat taunted.

Tessa saw that he was the leader. She withdrew her weapon and took careful aim at the Asian man. Squeezing the trigger, she fired and landed a shot in his chest. He toppled to the ground, but the guards reacted by crouching down and firing wildly in her direction.

The sound of shots echoed in the cavernous interior of the warehouse, and bullets ricocheted off the catwalk and the ceiling, metal hitting metal. Tessa ran as fast as she could to the far wall and moved quickly along the catwalk into the shadows.

Flynn and Williams aimed their guns at the guards and fired. One, a huge man with a crewcut, shot at the boxes where Flynn and Williams appeared to be taking cover. Bullets fired with machine-gun speed. Tessa heard Williams cry out, and she could see Flynn leaning over his best friend, who was now sprawled on the floor.

Hoping to distract the guards, she fired off another round from her gun, dropped the clip and inserted a new one. She no longer needed to be quiet—they all knew she was up on the catwalk—so now she ran, her boots clanging on the metal bridges as she made her way to a stairwell. Bullets flew by her head. She fired off rounds as she ran, and eventually leaped down onto the floor of warehouse, scattering frightened slaves. One zombie drew near her, and she kicked him in the face, knocking him to the floor. She had to show them right away that she was not to be messed with.

Flynn, from somewhere behind her, picked off two of the guards. Only two were left, plus the band of the undead.

She moved straight toward one of the guards, his face covered in tribal tattoos, his skull bald. His back was to her, and he was aiming his gun in the direction of Flynn and Williams. She kicked his Uzi, and it flew out of his hands and landed with a clatter. The other guard took aim, but she ducked, and Flynn landed a bullet in the guy's leg.

The guard cursed, but she showed him no mercy, kicking his wounded leg with her steel-toed boot, and then using a roundhouse kick to his hands, which knocked his gun away. He fell to the floor in pain.

That left only the guy with the tribal tattoos. And the massive biceps.

Tessa squared off against him, drawing up her fists. He lunged at her. Swiftly she shot a leg out and tripped him. He fell hard on the concrete floor, but grabbed her ankle, pulling her down, too.

Rolling over, he wrapped his large hands around her throat and started choking her. Trying to stay calm, all the while feeling a crushing sensation on her windpipe, Tessa pulled one of her knives from its sheath and jammed it upward, landing it in the muscle and fat of his belly.

He rolled off her, placing his hands on the blade, trying to staunch the flow of blood, which was spreading across the floor beneath him.

When Tessa looked up at the undead, they were closing in on her in a circle. She had no time to recover from the choking she'd just received. Scrambling up, she ran from the zombielike slaves and over to one of the tables filled with chemistry equipment. Something here had to be flammable.

Knocking over beakers, she watched chemicals and powder spill across the tables and onto the floor. A small Bunsen burner stood at the head of the table. She raced to it and turned it over.

As she had hoped, flames shot up, and the fire spread quickly. The drug slaves screamed in panic, covering their eyes and hands, yet no one moved. One of them flailed his arms, and his sleeve caught on fire. He squealed louder as the fire spread to his chest, and the smell of charred flesh turned the air acrid. Tessa thought she would throw up. The others started retreating into the shadows, shrieking. They were too stupid to run from the building; they were waiting to follow orders. They would all die of smoke inhalation.

She now raced over to where Flynn and Williams were hunkered down. The bullet had grazed Williams, and there was some blood loss, but he was now sitting, albeit woozily.

"Did I miss all the action?" he asked.

"Yes, Alex. Now lean against that box there," Tessa urged him.

"Tessa." Flynn hugged her. "What the hell are you doing here?"

"It's a factory for Shanghai Red. They're all drug slaves. So high on this crap they don't know which end is up."

"Yeah, but that doesn't explain everything—" His eyes jerked toward where the zombies retreated.

"Look, there's a lot of smoke. You've got to get out of here. We all do."

Sirens—and plenty of them—sounded outside. Tessa looked at Flynn. "I've got to go out the way I came in. I can't have been here."

"I wouldn't even know what to put in my report."

She smiled at him, then took off for a ladder that led to the ceiling and the rooftop. She was feeling a sense of relief as she made her way along the cat-walk, hurrying, then climbed out a window. But when she looked back she couldn't believe her eyes. One of the wounded guards suddenly stumbled forward with his machine gun and fired at Flynn, who fell to the ground. Cops blazed into the room in full SWAT gear, and Tessa put her hand over her mouth to stifle a scream as a pool of blood spread beneath Flynn's body.

Chapter 17

Back in her loft, Tessa took a shower and finally, allowed herself to shed tears. She stood under the shower nozzle until the water went from steaming to hot to lukewarm and finally to cold. At three o'clock in the morning, Tessa dressed in a pair of simple black pants and a black sweater, her hair pulled back from her face, not a trace of makeup on, and went to the hospital by cab.

The bond among NYPD cops, especially post-9/11, was legendary, and the waiting area outside the operating room was wall-to-wall officers—both in uniform and off duty.

Leery of calling attention to herself, she quietly sat down in a plastic waiting room chair, folded her hands in her lap and eavesdropped, hoping to find out how Flynn was.

Back at the warehouse, Tessa had watched for as long as she could from the roof across the street. She had seen four ambulances pull away, some with body bags, and she had feared for Flynn, not knowing whether he was dead or alive.

Now, sitting in this waiting room, she learned he was having surgery to remove four bullets. He had lost a lot of blood—almost 10 percent of his blood, to be exact—and the cops were all signing up to donate type O for transfusions.

She listened to the man the others called Cap, Captain Joe McNally, and a woman she guessed was Alex Williams's kid sister, Marie.

"Your brother is already bitching he wants out of the hospital bed. He'll be fine," Cap said. "The crazy bastard wants to be wheeled to Flynn's room and donate blood."

"And Tony?" Marie's voice was laced with tears, and she knotted a tissue in her hand.

Cap sighed and shook his head. "Christ… We just don't know. I think it's gonna be touch and go for a while. He lost a hell of a lot of blood. One of the bullets pierced his spleen. They're searching for another bullet…let's pray it missed his liver."

"And what happened? Does anyone know?"

"Well, Marie, honey, near as we can figure it, they were eating in some greasy spoon and got a tip that there was some suspicious activity at an abandoned warehouse. They went to check it out, and it wasn't abandoned at all. These two unlucky sons of bitches stumbled on a gold mine of drugs. They were manufacturing this new shit, a new club drug, right there."

"Why did they go in alone?"

"These two cowboys? You know your brother and Tony. That's the kind of cops they are. Meanwhile, we're still pulling out burned bodies. In all the gunfighting, some chemicals caught on fire."

"Does Tony have any family here?"

"No. Diana, his ex-wife, is remarried. I wouldn't even waste a phone call on her. We have to call Gus, of course, but the guy's in his seventies. We call him about this and wake him up, he'll be rushing over here in shock, liable to have a heart attack. I'm sending Malone over there tomorrow morning. Better to tell him in person. Plus, we might have more definitive news by then."

"Tony's a good man, Cap."

"The best. They don't make 'em like Tony Flynn anymore."

Tessa felt a tear land on her hand. She hadn't even realized she'd been crying. She waited with the crowd of friends, but knew she had to leave by 4:30 a.m. in order to be safe in her bed by dawn. She rose from her chair and slipped out the door, determined to come back the following night.

As soon as she awoke the next night, Tessa called the hospital. They weren't releasing any information on Detective Tony Flynn.

"Can you tell me if he's even alive? Is he in a room?"

"Ma'am, are you a family member, or another nosy reporter?"

"Never mind."

Tessa knelt at the statue of Buddha. She prayed for Flynn's recovery and for his soul. She burned some sage, which had been given to her by a Native American shaman she met once. She hoped it kept the undead away and brought Flynn healing.

She dressed in black wool pants and a black sweater, brushed her hair and pulled it into a chignon, and put on her heavy black leather coat. The radio said a cold snap was pulling the temperatures down into the twenties.

She left her loft and walked down the street. At a newspaper bodega on the corner, she saw that Flynn's and Williams's heroics had made the front page. It was the third-largest single-day drug bust in the history of law enforcement in the city. The fact that two NYPD detectives made the bust and not the DEA was something the police commissioner was trumpeting to any reporter who would listen. She laughed. Only Chicago had a history of more colorful politics than New York City.

Tessa paid for the *Daily News* and read through the article for information on Flynn, who was listed in critical condition in the intensive care unit. Williams was to be released in the next twenty-four hours.

Back at the hospital, Tessa strode purposefully. She had found that she could go almost anywhere without being questioned if she looked like she belonged there. Between her confident body language and her aristocratic looks, no one ever approached her.

Soon Tess found the waiting room for the intensive care unit. The policy stated that family members could visit for five minutes every two hours. Waiting for those rights were Alex Williams and his sister, an older gentleman, and a handful of cops in uniform.

Alex was sitting in a wheelchair in a plain blue hospital gown. He started to rise when he saw her. "Tessa…"

"Don't even think about getting up, Detective."

"Eh—" he waved his hand "—it's a flesh wound."

Suddenly, completely uncharacteristically, she grew hoarse fighting back tears. "How is he?"

Alex's eyes welled up. "Not good. Not good. Our boy lost a lot of blood. He's on a respirator. He can't talk. He's not even awake. They're keeping him in an intentional coma state right now."

"I'm so sorry." Guilt coursed through Tessa. He'd never have been looking into Shanghai Red if she hadn't approached him about it. She should have known better than to involve anyone else.

"Tessa, this is my sister, Marie. And this guy is Gus, Tony's first partner when he joined the force."

"Nice to meet both of you." Tessa smiled.

"You must be the one," Gus said, a little in awe.

"I beg your pardon?"

"Tony told me about this beautiful woman…a very classy woman. And she resembled a picture I had of a woman from World War II—I'm a big history buff. You're her. I can tell... He was—*is*—very fond of you."

"Yeah," said Alex. "I'm not used to seeing my partner all tied up in knots over a woman."

Marie laughed. "Tough Tony Flynn...no. I always thought he was part of the he-man woman-haters club."

Alex chuckled, then winced. "Sorry—still hurts a little. But yeah, Tony was a founding member of the he-man club."

"He just has to pull through," Tessa said.

Gus clasped her hand in his. "He will."

A nurse came into the waiting room. "Detective Flynn can have two visitors for five minutes."

Gus squeezed her hand and looked at Alex. "I think the best medicine for Tony would be to have Tessa go in."

Alex nodded. "You go on."

"Are you sure? You're his partner."

"Yeah, but he's crazy about you. Go on, Tessa."

Tessa rose tentatively and steeled herself for what was behind the double doors leading to intensive care. She followed the nurse, who spoke soothingly to her.

"He's going to look a little frightening. There are tubes everywhere, but I've been working here a long time and have seen plenty of miracles. You talk to him. Don't think he can't hear you."

The nurse led her into an alcove where machines beeped, and green and red lights blinked from computers. Tony Flynn was breathing with a respirator, which whooshed as it inflated his lungs. Tubes ran down his nose, and IV poles dwarfed his broken body.

Tears flowed from Tessa's eyes. She nodded her thanks as the nurse left her alone.

Tessa moved toward Tony. His black hair was matted with dried blood, and his face was ghostly pale and unshaven. His hands were curled, lifeless, on the bed. Tessa knelt by his bedside and took his right hand in hers, kissing his fingertips.

"Flynn..." she whispered, "I can't believe this happened to you. I would give anything, I promise you, anything to trade places with you."

It was unnerving just hearing machines instead of his voice. "I have so much to tell you, so much to explain to you. But I can't do it while you're lying here like this. Please know, my darling, that I love you. I love you in a way I haven't experienced before."

She laid her cheek down on his hand, tears falling onto the sheets. "I won't be able to bear it if you don't pull through, Flynn. You have to come back to the land of the living for me. For us."

Almost imperceptibly, his forefinger moved. He touched her cheek.

"You can hear me?" She raised her head and looked at his face, which seemed as blank as before. "I know you can hear me. I love you."

She listened to the machines and willed him to pull through until she saw the nurse coming to signal her that time was up. Tessa stood and leaned in close to his face. "Don't give up. Come back to me."

Then she left the beeping machines, the computers, the IV poles and her lover, and walked out into the waiting room.

Tessa's life was consumed by two things: finding Lily and visiting Flynn's bedside. She spent a good part of every night at the hospital. Alex was released, and he would come each night and sit with her. Gus took the daytime shift. They were determined never to let a visiting time pass without one of them going in to see Flynn.

By the third night after the shooting, Tessa and Alex were getting worried. The doctors were trying to bring him out of his coma. They'd been told that the longer he stayed in his comatose state, the less likely he would come back without some kind of permanent damage.

"He's like friggin' Sleeping Beauty. Let's hope he wakes up. He finally has something to really live for. You know, he fessed up to me," Alex said.

The two of them were alone in the waiting room, a small TV on the wall playing a rerun of some bad sitcom.

"What?"

"He's in love with you. My boy, Tony Flynn, is crazy about you. Of course, I knew that a long time ago, from the first time he stepped in your club two years ago. He may have acted all tough, but I could see he was a goner."

"That's sweet, Alex but he's got the heart of a warrior. I have to hope that helps him right now."

"It will. That and hearing your voice. When I go in there, I call him a pussy and tell him to fight." Alex choked up. "I tell him I don't want another partner. So he's got to pull through."

"He's strong. But you know, there's something about him. From the gossip I've overheard it sounds like his ex-wife really took him for a ride."

"Yeah. Tony is a guy who operates on principle. There's the good guys. There's the bad guys. It's black and white. You do the right thing—even if that means breaking the rules. Or you do the wrong thing. It's all very simple to Tony. Diana operated in moral shades of gray. He's different. He's really just the most decent man I know."

Tessa nodded. "I could see that."

"Well, just because Tony Flynn operates that way doesn't mean the rest of the world does. So, in the case of Diana, he could have handled the fact that the marriage wasn't working out. When you've got a woman who wants to dine at Gracie Mansion and you've got a guy who thinks gourmet is found in cardboard take-out, maybe it's not such a good match. But what killed him, what really killed him, was she started sleeping around on him. Had an affair with a judge—someone she worked with. And then came this doctor dude, whom she eventually left Tony for and married. Ink wasn't even dry on their divorce decree."

"He must have been devastated."

"Not so much over her. I mean over the principle of the thing. He wondered how he could have been so wrong about her character."

"Poor Flynn."

"That's not the half of it. I mean, look around the world, Tessa. We deal with creeps and perverts, dealers, murderers, rapists—and that's all before breakfast, if you know what I mean. So he's this good guy swimming in a sea of bad guys. Me, I just accept that's the way it is. Him? I think it really bothers him that the good guys don't always win."

"You know, Alex, I'm not all good."

"I saw you at the warehouse, Tessa. I was passed out for a lot of the gunfight, and it's not in my report that you were there, but I know you were there. And I know if you were there, you may be mixed up in some stuff. But if Tony trusts you, then we're cool."

"I'm on the good side. It's just a little bit complicated."

He nodded. "Yeah. I hear you. Real life tends to be complicated. But you've proven yourself to me by caring about him. We're cool."

Tessa leaned over to Alex and kissed him on the cheek. "Thank you."

"Now, don't be all kissing me and stuff. I'll have to tell Tony. Maybe that'll pull him out of his coma. Make him all jealous."

Tessa laughed. "I have to go, Alex. But I'll see you tomorrow."

"You got it, Tessa."

Tessa rose, and with a glance backward at the ICU, walked down the hall and out of the hospital. Maybe the NYPD thought the score was even, having caught the manufacturers of Shanghai Red. But Lily was still missing, and Marco was loose in Manhattan.

It wasn't even at all.

Chapter 18

Tessa was in a long, dark tunnel leading to King's lair when she was jumped. Two men, one with a dull-edged, rusty knife to her throat, pulled her to the ground. They were filthy, and both of them reeked of alcohol. One started unfastening her pants as she struggled.

She knew, especially since they were drunk, that she could kill them both, feed on them and be done. But killing two of King's followers wasn't a move that would endear her to King, so she tried to reason with them.

"Let me go," she told them, struggling against their hands and arms. "I'm here to see King. I'm a friend. Don't do this. You don't want to do this."

"Shut the fuck up, whore. Don't you tell us what we want to do. Right, Mickey? We know what we want to do." And with that, the man with the knife howled like he was insane and held the knife to her throat again. She felt a tiny trickle of blood. This asshole was so drunk he might just slice her jugular by accident. And she wasn't going to let that happen.

She felt the other one's hands reaching into her pants, and Tessa decided she had had enough.

"Remember, boys. I offered to be friends." With lightning speed she reached up with her hand and snapped the wrist of the man who held the knife to her throat. He shrieked in pain, fell to the ground and curled into a fetal position, nursing his broken wrist. She jerked her knee upward, finding her target—the nose of her would-be rapist—and then grabbed him by the hair and smashed his face into her knee a second time. Blood poured down his face, and she guessed he was going into shock.

"You really should play nice," she said, and stood up. From down the tunnel, she could make out the figure of King. "Damn," she muttered under her breath.

King walked more quickly, and soon he was standing with her between the two wounded men.

"What is the meaning of this?" he asked, fury registering on his face. "In my domain. In my haven!"

"King…I—" Tessa started to explain.

"Silence." He cut her off. "I was talking to them. I saw them attack you. That's not what we're about down here, gentlemen. Just because we live below the ground doesn't mean we become no better than sewer rats." He kicked at one of them. "Get up and get out of here."

"I can't," the man with the broken nose wailed.

"Get up," King commanded, kicking the man even harder with his boot. "Before I add to your injuries."

Both men recoiled and rolled away, finally standing and backing off down the tunnel toward the light of a distant station.

King turned to Tessa in the darkness. "What brings you back here?"

"I think you know."

"Yes. I heard through the grapevine. Your lover is near death in the hospital, but before that happened you took the law into your own hands and dispatched many undead to their own destruction."

Tessa nodded, cringing as she thought of Tony being "near death."

"Don't you have something to add, Tessa? We had a bargain, a deal."

She knew there was no withholding. "I saw Marco. He is alive. And he has Lily."

"How did he look?"

"Exceedingly healthy, unfortunately. And as evil as ever."

"I like to reward truthfulness."

"Thank you, King."

"I've heard a rumor—unsubstantiated, mind you—about your friend Lily."

Tessa played it cool, but her heartbeat quickened. "Oh?"

"St. Margaret's Church. Beneath it are catacombs. Lily is being held there. For safekeeping. Until Marco can get his hands on you—his real trophy."

"Well, King, I don't intend to let that happen."

"He will never give up. He has to be destroyed, you realize."

She nodded.

"Can you do that? He was your husband, after all."

"He was also the bastard that turned me."

"Indeed. Of course, if I reach him first, I will be only too happy to drive a stake through his heart. Be on your way, then. And I'm sorry about those two."

"You can't control everyone in your kingdom."

"Just as you cannot control who you are. The truce remains."

Tessa bowed to him, then turned and ran down the tunnel toward the light, determined to rescue her friend, and thankful Manhattan's vampire hunter was still on her side.

Tony Flynn's eyes fluttered. Foggy on morphine, the first face he saw was Gus's. Then he felt panic. He couldn't talk. He was in a hospital. A machine was filling his lungs with air. His eyes fluttered closed.

"Nurse!" he heard Gus call out. "Nurse! He was awake!"

Three nurses scurried into the room, moving Gus aside. One called for a doctor.

"You're sure he was awake?"

"Yes. I'm positive."

One of the nurses said to Flynn, "If you can hear us, open your eyes."

From the recesses of his drug-induced state, Tony Flynn forced his eyelids open for a moment. He saw a blond nurse. He heard Gus's voice. He couldn't talk with the breathing tube in, so he moved his lips, mouthing, *Tessa.*

The doctor came in. "Detective Flynn, can you hear us? Open your eyes, if you can, or move your index finger."

Flynn opened his eyes. He searched for Gus, locking his eyes finally on his old friend and mouthing *Tessa* again.

"Relax there. You've been shot. You've lost a lot of blood, but you're in the hospital, and you're going to be okay." The doctor turned to Gus. "Do you know what he's mouthing?"

Gus leaned over the bed. Tony again moved his lips.

"He's asking about his girlfriend, Tessa." Gus moved a lock of hair off Flynn's forehead. "She's fine, Tony. She's fine. She's been here every day. Every night, actually. She sits out there in the waiting room with Alex for hours and hours and hours, just to come in here for five lousy minutes every hour or so. You picked a good one, Tony. She cares for you very much."

Tony Flynn couldn't recall everything that had happened. In flashes of memory, he recalled Tessa and guns and people who seemed subhuman. He didn't understand, but it was enough, for now, to know she was okay…and that she had been by his side.

Chapter 19

Technofreak: I worked as fast as I could, Nightlady. Attached R the plans for St. Margaret's Church.
Nightlady: Thanks, Hack.
Technofreak: U sure U want to do this alone?
Nightlady: I have to. Let me open the files. Just a minute. Oh, these R perfect. Look at all those catacombs. Kind of creepy.
Technofreak: Not for the claustrophobic, that's for sure. Just thinking about being stuck down there makes me freak out!
Nightlady: I'm not exactly looking forward to it, but I've got to find her. Thanks, Hack. Wish me luck.
Technofreak: U know I always do. Fight the good fight. And Nightlady?

Nightlady: Yeah?
*Technofreak: I read about your detective in the
paper. I'm sorry. Is he going to be okay?*
Nightlady: I'm not sure. Do you believe in prayer?
Technofreak: In my own way.
Nightlady: Pray for him.
Technofreak: I will. Amen.

Tessa printed out the architectural plans for St.
Margaret's Church and studied them. The catacombs
fanned out in a circular pattern from a central chamber under the altar of the church. Individual rooms
and long tunnels crisscrossed and wandered beneath
the surface of the earth. And somewhere in that lab-
yrinth, Lily was being held.

Tessa dressed in black leather. A gun would be
useless down there; bullets would ricochet off walls,
and add danger. But she would take her daggers, and
a flashlight. She could see well in the dark, but she
couldn't be sure what she'd find.

She braided her hair and was about to leave her
apartment, when the phone rang.

"Hello?"

"Tessa? It's Alex."

She sat down in a chair, half expecting him to tell
her that Flynn was dead.

"Yes?" The panic in her voice was palpable.

"He woke up."

"Oh my God." Relieved tears flooded her eyes. "Is
he going to be okay?"

"It's a long road, but yeah. The doctor says this is

the first step. And…I took a bullet for the guy, but guess what?"

"Hmm?"

"You were his first waking thought. He can't talk yet. They're going to try to take him off the respirator. See if he breathes on his own. But he can mouth words. And 'Tessa' is the only word that stubborn son of a bitch is interested in."

"Are you at the hospital now?"

"Uh-huh. I'm going to stay here for the night. You going to come over?"

Tessa felt torn in two. "I have to help another friend who's in a world of shit, Alex. But I'll try to get by as soon as I can."

"You need any help?"

"No. I'll let you know if I do. For now, I think I can handle it. Do me a favor though?"

"Sure thing." ·

"Tell him I love him."

"Oh God…gotta get all sentimental with him." He laughed. "Good thing you're so beautiful. I can never resist a plea from a lovely lady."

"Thanks, Alex. He's lucky to have you as his partner."

"Well, don't tell him this or anything, but I'm the lucky one."

Tessa hung up the phone. She was energized, knowing Flynn was going to make it. Now she needed to get to Lily.

St. Margaret's Church, the size of a small cathedral, was down by Wall Street. Tessa stood on the rooftop of an office building opposite the church, the wind at this tip of the island of Manhattan battering her as it blew in off the water. A small graveyard with headstones circa 1900 stood out back, surrounded by a wrought-iron fence. The spires of the stone church itself rose toward the heavens, which looked surprisingly barren since 9/11. From the Wall Street building, she could gaze down into the well-lit pit of the site of the former World Trade Center, a scarred graveyard of a different sort.

Descending through a rooftop door she had jimmied open, she took an elevator to the ground floor and walked through a hollow-sounding lobby, a revolving door and then out to the street. Half a block up stood Saint Margaret's, one of the city's oldest churches. Tessa gazed at the stained-glass windows, which depicted the passion of Christ. On the front of St. Margaret's was a rose-shaped stained-glass window, a replica of Notre Dame's.

The streets were empty. Most of the young Turks of Wall Street were long gone. Looking up at nearby buildings, only the odd light or two were lit, likely cleaning crews making their way through the offices. The streets were abandoned. It seemed like a ghost town, and the bitter chill made it seem even more so. Tessa slipped over the fence of the graveyard and crept to a back door that was locked and that led, according to Hack's architectural plans, to storage facilities. She took a knife and pried off the doorknob and then finagled the door open.

Stepping inside the storage area, she allowed her eyes the second they needed to adjust to the darkness. She smelled earth. This part of the storage was for gardening tools. She looked around, memorizing the room, then moved forward, past hedge clippers and shovels, on to another door. According to the plans, this door led to the catacombs.

Wary of making a noise that might tip off any vampires guarding Lily, Tessa silently picked the lock, grateful she had once made the acquaintance of a cat burglar in Monaco who had taught her a few tricks of his trade. Slipping into the dank stone corridor, she worked from the plans she had memorized and headed to the center chamber beneath the altar. Her instinct told her this is where they would keep Lily.

She walked for a few minutes, pressing herself against the wall. She could hear the scuffling of rats, and occasionally one brushed her leg or ran over her foot. She steeled herself against reacting with a squeal. She hated rodents. Back in her attic apartment in Paris, they used to come out at night, and she thought they were repulsive. She shivered. Then she inwardly chuckled at herself. She could face down a phalanx of zombies, fight other vampires to the death, and it was rats that made her want to run away.

When she was about thirty paces from the chamber, she heard whispering. Straining, she could hear two distinct voices—neither of them Lily's.

Tessa inched closer, drawing her dagger. She knew she had to use the element of surprise to her advantage. It was two against one.

In one smooth and fluid motion, she threw her dagger at the taller vampire. She aimed for his throat and found her target, hearing a scream echo in the underground tunnel. While he clutched at the blade and reacted in panic, she moved on to the other vampire with a series of roundhouse kicks. This one blocked each kick with his arms. He had martial arts experience.

The corridor was narrow. She had no room to maneuver, and her ears were filled with the unnerving sound of the gurgling gasps of the vampire she'd stabbed.

Suddenly, she was knocked off balance by the second vampire. She could see he wore a long braid down his back. Reaching out, she grabbed his hair before she hit the ground, causing him to yelp and lose his balance. Then she took her leg and kicked straight up at his crotch. He doubled over in pain, but was furious enough to reach down and grab her face, smashing it against the stone wall of the corridor. Her cheek scraped the wall, and she fought against him, drawing a second, longer dagger and driving it into his heart when his face was inches from hers.

She needed to hurry. There was no telling if more vampires lurked beneath St. Margaret's. Moving toward the chamber, she was terrified of what she might find. Lily had been held captive for days now. Sad experience told her these fiends were capable of anything.

When Tessa arrived at the chamber, she saw Lily sprawled on the floor, arms and legs akimbo. Kneeling beside her, Tessa could see her best friend was barely breathing.

"Lily, darling, it's Tessa." She stroked her friend's cheek, trying to orient her to the gentle sound of her voice.

"You came for me," Lily whispered, her lips cracked and bleeding.

"That's what sisters do."

"I haven't fed in days. I'm dying."

"Shh." Tessa put her fingers to Lily's lips. "We've got to get you out of here. They're down…" She looked at the fallen bodies of the two vampires. "But I don't think they're out."

Tessa put one arm beneath Lily's shoulders and tried to get her to sit up. Lily could barely move. Tessa now had to think quickly. As a vampire, she had the strength of many mortals and was strong enough to carry Lily all the way to safety but only if they weren't attacked. Her only choice would be to offer Lily her own blood. Tessa would be weakened by the feeding, but Lily would gain enough strength to make it out of the catacombs. It was their only chance.

Putting out her wrist, Tessa urged Lily, "Feed. Just do it, Lily, and get it over with. We've got to get out of here."

"I can't. You're my best friend. It will weaken you."

"If you don't…we both die."

Lily and Tessa stared at each other in the dark chamber. After decades together and all they had been through, their level of communication was almost telepathic. Lily nodded in resignation and sank her teeth into Tessa's wrist.

The pain, for Tessa, was excruciating. And as blood left her and entered Lily, it was as if lead weights had suddenly been tied to Tessa's legs. Every muscle hurt. Her eyes couldn't see as well in the dark. Her hearing grew muffled, as if she were listening to things under water.

Lily fed fiercely—the undead had that animalistic reaction when they went too long without feeding. But there was still enough of the true Lily left that she stopped feeding before draining too much of Tessa's life force.

"I can walk now," Lily said, her voice stronger. "Though I still feel like…well, like a woman who's been kept in a tomb for a week."

"Let's go."

The two of them struggled to their feet and moved along the opposite wall from where the two wounded vampires lay. They walked as quickly as they could past them, and then Tessa, filled with a sense of foreboding, urged Lily on faster.

"I think they're stirring."

They had reached the door leading to the storage area when Tessa heard something moving behind them.

"Damn," she muttered frantically as she opened the door. "Come on." They burst through the door and were now amongst the lawn tools. Lily slammed the door behind them, but suddenly the tall vampire, the one she'd struck in the throat, burst through the door, splintering wood. Lily screamed.

"Leaving us so soon, my pets?"

"Sorry, buddy, but we don't have time to play," Tessa snapped as she looked around her. Training in Shanghai had taught her the value of decisions made in an instant. She grabbed and then hoisted a heavy shovel and smashed it with all her might over his head, sending him toppling to the earthen floor. Grabbing the hedge clippers she'd spotted when she first broke in the door, she drove them through his heart. The groundskeeper would be plenty surprised tomorrow.

Spinning around, Tessa and Lily escaped into the graveyard. Hugging Tessa, Lily breathed in the night air. "I thought I would die there, alone. Never breathing fresh air again. Look at my arms." She held them out. Small red marks covered them. "Rat bites."

Tessa shuddered. "I was going to find you and get you out of there, one way or another, Lily. Come on, baby."

"You know we're not safe—not truly safe—until we destroy Marco."

"I know. A lot's happened this week. Let's go to the club. You're safer there than in your apartment." Tessa cringed.

"What?"

"There's a little blood spatter in your apartment."

"What's a little blood spatter between friends?"

Tessa laughed at her friend's unending spunk and sense of humor. "God, I've missed you."

The two of them stumbled from the cemetery and then, in their weakened state, hailed a yellow cab rather than taking their usual rooftop route.

Arriving at the Night Flight Club, they used the back entrance. Tessa rang Jorge's cell phone. "I have her."

"Lily?"

"The one and only."

"Where are you?"

"Back stairwell."

"Wait there."

In five minutes, Jorge and Cool had Lily and Tessa in a giant group hug.

"You both look like shit," Cool said.

"Thanks, Cool. You know how to welcome home a lady."

Cool winked at her. "You know you're my girl, Lily."

Tessa did a double take. The look between them sizzled. Had she somehow missed a little love affair between Lily and Cool? They both looked exceedingly happy to see each other. If it wasn't an affair, it was at least an infatuation.

"Let me get her up to a shower. Jorge, she's going to stay here for the night. Tomorrow night, too, I'm sure. She needs to get on her feet. Just keep an extra eye out."

"You got it."

The two men went back into the club, and Lily and Tessa made their way up to the loft. It was shortly after midnight.

"Lily, baby, I've got to get over to the hospital."

"Hospital?"

"Long story. God, we have some catching up to do. Detective Flynn was shot. It happed at a factory where they were making Shanghai Red. Marco's slaves. It was crazy."

"I thought they were going to haul me out and stake me to the ground to wait for the sunlight. One night they talked about a battle at a factory. Marco was plenty pissed."

"Yeah, I figured as much. King was the one who found out where they were keeping you."

"I still can't believe I'm safe."

"I have to clean up and go see Flynn. You take a shower in the guest bathroom. Then settle into my bed. I'll tell you all about it tomorrow night."

Tessa showered hurriedly, still weak, but grateful to wash off the grime and bloodstains. She dressed in a simple turtleneck sweater and blue jeans, and then, after kissing her friend goodbye, set off for the hospital.

Tessa walked the near-abandoned corridors, with their antiseptic hospital smell, at two in the morning. She had found two pints of blood awaiting a transfusion as she walked purposefully through the ER. She slipped them in her purse and then took the elevator to the ICU. She found the ever-faithful Alex Williams in the waiting room, dressed in street clothes.

After embracing, she asked him, "Discharged? You're not in your sexy blue hospital gown."

He nodded.

"Is he alert?"

"Off and on, but he needs another operation."

"Why?"

"A buildup of some blood in his belly. Some internal bleeding."

"When are they doing the surgery?"

"Tomorrow morning at six."

"Alex…he's going to make it, right?"

"Let me tell you something about Tony Flynn."

"Hmm?"

"That man has more will and heart than anyone I know. He'll pull through. One time—God, it was just after he and I partnered up—we were investigating a murder that we figured was related to someone dealing dope at a junior high school playground. Seemed to be a territory thing."

"Do these dealers have no shame? Junior high?"

"I know. Sick bastards. Anyway, we ended up bursting into an apartment where we thought it was just going to be one guy measuring out drugs. Our informant had told us the guy would be high as a kite. No big deal."

"Let me guess—it was a big deal."

"Shit, Tessa, we walked into a firestorm. I got shot in the shoulder. Flynn and I were trapped, bullets were flying. But that man in there never got scared. He never lost heart. Even with me down, he ended up arresting two of the shooters, killing one dude, and then our backup caught three others as they tried to get out via the fire escape. He'll pull through, I'm telling you."

Tessa nodded and sat down in an orange plastic chair. "They could use an interior decorator around this place."

"You could say that again."

Tired from the rescue of Lily and the exchange of blood, Tessa found she could barely keep her eyes open. Soon, she had nodded off, her head resting on Alex's shoulder.

A half hour later, a nurse, six feet tall with a weightlifter's physique, entered the waiting room and told Alex and Tessa they could have their allotted visit with Flynn. Alex had told her the medical staff tolerated their late-night visits—outside scheduled visiting hours—for the fallen hero cop. The local New York stations still ran updates on his condition nightly.

Tessa stretched, her head pounding, anxious to see Flynn.

Alex gave her a pat on the back. "You go in, Tessa. Alone. Have some time with him."

She kissed Alex's cheek, then followed the nurse back behind the double doors to the world of beeping machines and lives hanging in a balance. The first night, she had been too in shock to look at the other patients as she passed. Now, she peered into the softly lit alcoves and saw crumbled bodies of other accident victims. Occasionally, she saw family members weeping softly, clutching hands, some kneeling at the bedsides of their loved ones. The grief behind the doors of the ICU was almost unbearable. It was a world of crisis.

Walking into the alcove, Tessa immediately saw that Tony was now breathing on his own, though tubes still protruded from his side and his nose. He looked like he was sleeping.

The nurse grasped her shoulder tightly, giving her a boost of strength, then he left her as she moved to the bedside.

She didn't want to wake her lover. Instead, she looked down at his sleeping face. He had the beginnings of a beard, and his coloring was still very pale, but his face was peaceful. She reached for one of his curls and wrapped it around her pinky, marveling at its dark sheen, longing to take him back to her loft and put him in a warm tub, nursing his wounds, healing him.

Tony Flynn stirred and moaned.

"Flynn? Tony?" Tessa leaned down and whispered in his ear. "It's me. Tessa."

Flynn's eyes fluttered open. He squinted, concentrating on her face. She could tell drugs were making that difficult. His eyelids would flutter down or his eyes would roll back.

"It's me…. God, I've been so worried about you. Please hang on." She tried to orient him to her touch, taking her index finger and gently stroking his cheek. He looked as if he was struggling to speak, and she urged him to rest. "Sleep, darling. Keep up your strength."

But still he struggled. Soon, machines were beeping and two nurses appeared at Flynn's bedside.

"His heartbeat is erratic. We need to call the doctor. Why don't you return to the waiting room?"

"What's wrong?" Panic crept into Tessa's voice.

"We don't know. He's been through so much. He may just be overexcited to see you right now. He needs to rest. He's got surgery tomorrow."

Tessa leaned down and kissed his forehead. "I love you," she whispered.

Exiting the ICU, she tearfully bade farewell to Alex Williams and left the hospital, bursting from its corridors and medicine smells to the streets of New York. Ambulances pulled up to the doors of the ER, and she could hear the sirens of cop cars and more ambulances wailing in the streets.

If this were Shanghai, she would have gone to her gardens and prayed. If this were Germany, she would have knelt at her small shrine and said prayers. But suddenly Tessa was filled with a thought. Buddhism was *her* belief system. But Tony Flynn was an Irish Catholic—no matter what he said about not going to church. She would go pray before the altar of *his* God. She would pray for his recovery. For the doctors to heal him.

Tessa walked the streets of New York, thinking of Flynn and heading toward St. Patrick's Cathedral. Some vampires were reduced to squealing, quivering mutants by the sight of crucifixes and holy water. They wouldn't walk on hallowed ground. They would never darken the door of a church. It was belief, of course. They believed, as the undead, that they lived in the shadow of God, forever separated from him, and so the sight of the cross sent them into a panic.

Marco's followers were not intimidated by the cross. The reason was that they were so far down the path of evil, and he so hated the concept of a single Christian God, that he spat on all things associated with a church and had no fear. She, on the other hand, respected all faiths. She felt that there was room beneath the heavens for her and her faith, and for Tony Flynn and his faith. For it all.

She entered the cathedral doors, dipped her finger in holy water and kissed it to her lips. "Praise you, for Tony's sake," she whispered.

Walking along the outer corridor of St. Patrick's, Tessa passed small altars and shrines to Christian saints and martyrs. She could barely remember the days when she, like her family, had been part of the Anglican Church in England. Her uncle Henry had had a small chapel on his property and a country vicar to attend to it. They had worshiped there every Sunday, and decorated the tiny country chapel with pine boughs at Christmastime.

When she traveled to Shanghai, she became intrigued by Buddhism. As she studied that, as well as the words of Confucius, she found that Buddhism resonated within her. It made her wonder if in another life she had lived in Buddha's time. Been a follower. Whatever the reason, she embraced her new beliefs. But she was here, in St. Patrick's Cathedral, for Flynn.

Glancing into the pews she saw praying figures and sleeping homeless. She walked farther and found a small altar to the Blessed Virgin. She felt this mother of Jesus was as good a religious figure to pray to as any. Kneeling, she slipped a few dollars into the poor box and then lit a candle by taking a long thin matchstick, about a foot in length, lighting it in the flame of an existing candle and then lighting another candle.

"Blessed Mother," Tessa whispered. "Watch over Tony Flynn. I know I have no right to ask you for mercy, but he is a good man. Please help him."

Tessa didn't know how long she knelt in the candlelight. Eventually, she heard the shuffle of footsteps behind her, and a priest in clerical robes came and stood behind her.

"The blessed Virgin," he said in a whisper. "She brings such comfort."

She nodded.

He knelt beside her. "I don't mean to intrude. Are you praying for yourself? For a friend?"

She looked at him quizzically, wondering why he was questioning her.

"Tears. You're in pain, my child."

She nodded. "A friend. A policeman who's been shot in the line of duty."

"The one in the papers?"

She nodded. "I'm not a Catholic, Father. I'm a Buddhist. And I have committed many sins, even as I struggle to do good works. But my friend…he helps people. So I thought perhaps his God might hear me."

"He's your God, too."

In the marble alcove, they kept their voices to a whisper, aware the acoustics of St. Patrick's carried their spoken words, bouncing them off the marble ceilings and walls.

"That doesn't sound like the party line, Father. A Buddhist and a Catholic sharing the same God in heaven."

"The fact that you are here, praying for a friend…I

believe God recognizes that. I believe the Blessed Mother recognizes that. Would you like me to say a prayer with you for your friend?"

The priest was young, about thirty, with brown hair and beard. Small wire-rimmed glasses framed his eyes, giving him the appearance of an owl. He had a gentle, trusting expression on his face.

"I would, Father."

"What is his name?"

"Tony Flynn."

"Blessed Mother, we ask you to intervene on the behalf of this fallen hero, a man who wears a badge and places his life on the line for the people of this city, for the unspoken poor, for the disenfranchised, for those who cannot fight for themselves. He was wounded in the line of duty, and now he needs the healing touch of Jesus Christ and God the Father. We also ask that you guide his doctors, nurses and all the people involved in his medical care. Help them to make the right decisions, to bring this man back to health…and finally, we pray for his friend here. She claims she is not a good person, Mary, Mother of God, but she is here in the wee hours before dawn, to pray for this man. We ask that you bless her. In His name we pray. Amen."

Tessa's head was bowed. She looked up. "Thank you, Father."

"You're welcome. I will pray for your friend in my personal intercessions."

With that he stood and walked down to the next alcove. Tessa remained kneeling. Eventually, she rose stiffly and caught a lonely cab back to the Night Flight Club. It was four in the morning and the club was still rocking. She rode up to her loft and woke Lily to urge her to feed on the blood from the hospital until they could both go hunting and feed properly. Then she locked and bolted her door and fell into a restless and fretful sleep.

Chapter 20

"Things are looking better, Tessa." Alex Williams told her on his cell phone. "The operation today repaired something in his spleen that was causing some internal bleeding. He's not out of the woods, but if I know Tony Flynn, he's on the road to recovery. He's talking. They're going to let him eat a little something, finally. He said he's hungry, so that's a good sign, though I don't know if they'll let him chow down on a foot-long hot dog with sauerkraut and onions just yet."

"That's great news, Alex. I'm still helping my friend. Give him my love and I'll get there as soon as I can."

Tessa, sometimes superstitious by nature, couldn't help but wonder whether it was the prayers of the priest, Buddha, Flynn's willfulness, fate, or medical miracles. Not that it mattered. Even if it was all of the above, she was just relieved that he was doing better.

Lily had woken and was in the shower, relishing the small miracles of freedom: hot showers, good wine, the company of friends. When she emerged, the two friends sat at Tessa's dining room table with a printout Tessa had of Hack's concentric circles.

"This is the most recent circle, and it's tightening like a noose," Tessa explained to Lily, pointing out the rings closing around the Night Flight Club. "Tony Flynn, Alex Williams, Jorge, Delorean…you…Cool—you're all in danger. It's me he wants. And you are all just pawns in this giant chess game he's playing. He was devious and clever over a hundred years ago. I'm sure he's grown more so with time."

"He wants his wife back. He said as much to me. He believes you are soul mates."

Tessa nodded. "I'm not sure how that's possible when he has no soul. And speaking of soul mates…what about Cool? Do my eyes deceive me or do I detect something going on between the two of you?"

Lily grinned mischievously. "We kissed one night, late, when I was getting ready to go home. In the CD storage room. It was hot."

"Doesn't he date an actress right now?"

Lily shrugged. "And don't I feed on blood? You and your morality, Tess. I liked you better before you went to Shanghai. Before you were a Buddhist."

"It's what keeps me from becoming like Marco."

"You'll never be like him."

"You say that, but the appetites of a vampire don't know morality. Haven't you ever been feeding and felt a frenzy come on? You cease to be aware of past and future, and all you care about is the present—and drinking until you've had your fill."

Lily nodded.

"Maybe you're okay with that, Lily, but I feel a sense of self-loathing afterward. That's why I struggle to stay in control."

"And how much control do you feel when you're around Detective Flynn?"

"It's been a very long time since I felt anything like this. It frightens me. But you know me." She looked slyly at her friend. "I'll find a way to stay in control."

"Handcuff him to the bed, perhaps?" Lily asked, laughing.

"I see you're recovering your wicked sense of humor."

"Yes. But I *will* get even, have no doubts about that."

Later that night, Tessa contacted Hack.

Technofreak: Hey there, lady of the night.
Nightlady: Hey there. I got Lily back.
Technofreak: Fantastic.
Nightlady: Now I have another question for U. U said U were going to do something with algorithms. Do U have any idea when those circles R going to reach the club?

Technofreak: By my calculations, U have a week, tops.

Nightlady: And then?

Technofreak: My guess is whatever these Shanghai Red people have been doing all over town PALES in comparison to what they're going to do at your club. Not to worry U or anything.

Nightlady: I'm long past worrying and into frantic mode. It's not me, of course. It's my friends. I've tangled them all up in my problems, my life, my past.

Technofreak: But did U ever stop to think that's what friendship is all about?

Nightlady: Friendship shouldn't be about giving up your life.

Technofreak: There R some things worth fighting for. If U don't think I would have given up my life in an instant to save my mother. Or my brother.

Nightlady: I know U would have.

Technofreak: Of course I would. Sometimes, U have to take a stand. U have to sacrifice. Do U want me to e-mail you my files on the algorithm?

Nightlady: Yeah. And the map.

Technofreak: Will do. Fight the good fight.

Nightlady. I'm in it with U. To the end.

He sent her a zip file, which Tessa stored on her hard drive. Then she dressed and took a cab to the hospital.

"Hey, handsome," she said when she walked into Tony Flynn's room. It was a private patient room—

no longer the ICU. Alex Williams had gone home to shower and shave.

"Tessa…" Flynn's voice was raspy from the tubes that had been down his throat.

She moved to his bedside and gingerly sat on the edge, taking his hand in hers, entwining their fingers.

"It's so good to see you off those machines."

"It's good to *be* off those machines. Alex told me you were here every night. I remember some of it, but other things…" He furrowed his brow.

"We don't have to talk about it now."

"I remember the warehouse…"

"Shh." She took his hand and kissed his fingertips.

"You sure are a sight for sore eyes."

"So are you. If you think, Detective Flynn, that making me worry about you is going to change how things are between us from this point forward…you're right."

"I still may haul your ass downtown to ask you a few questions." He grinned.

"Will handcuffs be involved?"

"I think that can be arranged."

"In the meantime, do you need a sponge bath?"

"Yeah. And a private-duty nurse."

Tessa laid her head down in the crook of his arm, avoiding his IV lines, and kissed him tenderly on the neck, slipping her hand inside the folds of his hospital gown.

"You keep doing that," he growled, "and I just may be outta here tomorrow."

"Well, we'll see about making you feel all better," she purred.

Tessa returned to her loft at three-thirty in the morning. Lily was still down in the club partying like a fifteen-year-old club kid, her first time behind the velvet rope. She was enjoying herself for all it was worth.

Tessa smiled to herself, but couldn't help thinking about the algorithm. One week. One week to…what? What was Marco planning?

Her laptop was where she had left it, and the screensaver was on, a picture of Shanghai, of a garden just like her own. Of course, she had never seen her own garden in daylight. She had never seen the glint of the sun reflected off the back fin of a koi. But the picture she had found on the Internet soothed her and made her feel a little less homesick.

She decided to check her e-mail. Hack was the only person to e-mail her. Actually, that wasn't true. Cool sometimes sent her MP3 files. Delorean sent pictures of her daughter, and now her new son. And Lily, wired to infinity, e-mailed her just for the hell of it. She especially liked to pass along vampire jokes. That was Lily—always irreverent.

Today, she had only one e-mail. The subject line was "No one is safe."

Tessa felt a chill pass over her. Quaking inside, she sat down. The sender was not a name she was familiar with. Hack had given her program after program—identity encoders, encryption programs and spam blockers. She never got messages from anyone she wasn't expecting. Never.

Her finger poised over the arrow key.

"Please…" she whispered into the air, speaking to no one, to Buddha, to God, to the silence.

The e-mail opened to reveal an attachment. She ran a virus check. It was okay, so she clicked and the file opened to a Flash movie. First the words

YOU ARE MINE

They flew across her screen, the letters in random order, dancing in a way, and then reassembling to form the words correctly.

Then:

YOU HAVE BEEN MINE FROM THE MOMENT I SAW YOU

Then:

YOU CANNOT ESCAPE ME

Then:

AND NEITHER CAN ANYONE YOU LOVE

Finally, there was a video clip. Of an apartment. It wasn't an apartment she had ever been to, but she leaned in close. There, on a table, stood a bottle of Manhattan Special soda. This was Hack's place.

A shadow passed across the screen.

And then Tessa stared in cold horror at a strung-up body. A handsome man. A boy, really. She knew he had to be Hack. His eyes dead. His neck snapped and unnaturally bent to one side.

A sound escaped from Tessa's lips. A wail so primal she didn't recognize the voice as her own.

Chapter 21

Instead of sleeping during daylight, Tessa and Lily stayed up all day, behind the locked and bolted door of Tessa's bedroom, talking. Tessa went through a cascade of emotions in one twelve-hour period. Horror, dread, anger, grief, rage, sadness, and back to anger again. She reminisced to Lily about Hack, and Lily listened with patience and sadness as Tessa repeated tales over and over again in the ramblings of grief.

"We used to talk on the telephone all the time…he was such a gentle soul in so many ways. I know he was in his late twenties, but I think, after all he had been through, in some ways he was still a little boy. And then at other times I detected the weariness of an old man."

"I'm so sorry, Tessa. Marco has taken this fight to a whole new level."

"It's not a fight anymore. This is war."

When night fell, she knew she had to go to Hack's apartment and tend to the body. Hack had told her once that there was no one left—no living relatives. His world consisted of the four walls of his apartment and the world of cyberspace with its dizzying freedom. And Tessa, his lone personal contact with the outside world. Tessa knew he considered her his best friend. And he had once made her promise that when he died, she would have his body cremated and scatter the ashes in the Hudson River by tossing them from the *Circle Line,* a sight-seeing boat that encircled Manhattan. Hack had an attorney, she knew, an Adam Stern. Tessa had a copy of Hack's DNR order, his living will, his regular will, and a letter detailing his wishes. She was the executor of his estate. Hack had told her all his equipment, all the hacking he had done for profit, meant a sizable bank account. He wanted all the money to go a charity for victims of domestic violence.

Tessa called Alex Williams's cell phone.

"Williams here."

"Alex?" Her voice came out as a choked-off sob.

"Tessa? What's the matter? Flynn's okay, you know. They may discharge him before the weekend."

"It's not that. I need you to meet me at a friend's apartment. I think he's been murdered."

"Holy shit… I'm sorry, Tessa. Give me the address."

She gave him Hack's building address and apartment number and then asked, "Can you just come? Just you. I need to say goodbye to him. Please, just come alone."

"It's a crime scene, Tessa."

"But you don't know that yet. Pretend I just called you and asked you to check on my friend. I'm begging you, Alex."

"For you, I'll break the rules. How soon can you get there?"

"Give me a half hour," Tessa said, and hung up.

Lily told her to be careful as Tessa dressed. "Maybe you should bring a dagger."

"No. For all Alex Williams knows, I'm just a regular nightclub owner."

"I don't know about that. If that warehouse wasn't enough to clue in those two cops…"

"Yeah, but Alex hasn't pulled it all together yet. If I show up looking like the Trinity character from *The Matrix,* that's another story, Lily."

"Do you want me to come?"

"No, I want to say goodbye. Alone."

Ordinarily, Tessa and Lily would have bantered. But Tessa felt only a numbness, but beneath that was a desire for revenge so powerful that she knew it would take all of her spirituality to conquer.

Making her promise not to touch anything, Williams allowed her to say goodbye to Hack.

She stood next to his body as Williams called for backup. "Hello, baby," she whispered, staring into

Hack's unseeing, blank eyes. They were blue. She hadn't known that. She had once read that the human retina captures a person's last moments on its lens. She wondered what Hack's eyes had seen.

"You're with your mother and brother now. At peace. And I promise you, whoever did this to you will pay."

Though she had promised Williams she would not touch anything, Tessa fingered one of Hack's blond curls. Blood had seeped near his temples, turning the hairline a crimson color. Beyond that, much of his blood seemed to be drained, but any bite marks would be obscured by the ligature of red marks, now mottled, from the coarse rope tied around his neck.

Williams came over to her. "The ME will be here soon. They'll photograph him, dust for prints. Do you want to answer a few questions, now, before there are cops swarming this place?"

"Sure."

"You say you know this guy as Hack."

She nodded. "His real name is Brett Jameson. We met on the Internet."

Williams raised an eyebrow.

"It's not like that. Get your mind out of the gutter, Detective. I mean we were friends. Good friends. Best—" she choked on the words "—friends."

"And do you have any idea who would want him dead? Was he mixed up in anything that you know of? Drugs? Gangs?"

"Caffeine."

"What?"

"His drug of choice was caffeine—and lots of it. He's a techie. A hacker. His world was cyberspace."

"Maybe he pissed off someone whose site he hacked into."

Tessa shook her head. "I don't know. I don't think so."

"What about his family? Do you know them? How we can reach them?"

"He has no family, Williams. He spent all his time in this apartment. The Internet was his drug, his portal to the world."

"So he stayed here all the time? Didn't he go out? Go to the grocery store?"

"You live in Manhattan. It's the city that never sleeps. Delivery. He had everything delivered."

"What about doctors' appointments?"

"He didn't have any—appointments, that is. He was agoraphobic. He couldn't even step in the hallway."

"You're kidding. I've read about people like that."

"He even paid the man across the hall to pick up his packages downstairs and to run the occasional errand for him."

"Paid somebody? With what? How'd he earn a living if he never left his house?"

"Programming. Software. He is—was—a genius."

"How did you come across him? I mean today. You know…how'd you know something happened to him?"

"Off or on the record?"

"I'm not a journalist, Tessa. It doesn't work that way. But I can stop taking notes for a minute if you want. Between us friends."

"On the record, I just came by for a visit with an old friend. But between you and me, someone sent me an e-mail with a video clip of the apartment, poor Hack hanging there."

"You still have the clip on your computer?"

Tessa nodded.

Williams rubbed his eyes in a gesture of world weariness. "Then…I've got to say that whoever has this beef has it with you, not your friend. Someone was obviously sending *you* a message."

Tessa nodded.

"Do you know who?"

Tessa nodded again. "A drug dealer named Marco. He and I have been enemies for a long time. He's a former lover. And suffice to say, I don't like his chosen profession."

"You know where we can find this Marco guy?"

"No."

"Got a last name? An address?"

"No. Williams, have you ever settled a case, solved it, by bending the rules?"

"Honestly? My partner is Tony Flynn. And he has some strange way of looking at the world. He thinks we work for good."

"What's so strange about that?"

"I guess I didn't explain it right. He thinks we work for Good with a capital *G.* And we fight against Evil with a capital *E.* Like there's some battle going on we can't see, can't name, can't touch, can't fathom. But it's there. Like a war. And we're on the front lines. So yeah…we bend the rules. We're smart enough to not get caught. Smart enough to do it only when it counts, like if a kid's involved…or we're running out of time and someone's gonna die."

"Well, to solve this case, you're going to have to bend the rules. You're going to have to trust me. And you're going to have to shut your notebook and not write most of this shit up."

Williams stared at Tessa. She knew he was sizing her up. Like Flynn, he was going to use his instincts to tell him if this was a good idea. Thankfully, Tessa passed some intuitive litmus test. After a few moments, he nodded his okay.

"All right. I'm going to assume there's some weird shit going on here."

"My friend Hack had helped me track down the origins of Shanghai Red."

"Goddamn. I thought by taking down that warehouse—and nearly costing Flynn his life—we were through with that shit."

"Not quite. Not yet."

"You watch yourself. Tony'd kill me if I let anything happen to you while he's laid up."

"I'm a big girl, Detective."

"I can see that."

"And I can take care of myself."

"I don't doubt that, either. But be careful anyway."

Tessa nodded. "I'm the executor of his estate. He wants to be cremated. The details are with his attorney. Adam Stern. Has an office down in Greenwich Village. They went to college together."

"His body won't be released until we do an autopsy."

The fury in her belly turned icy cold. First they desecrated his body by killing him. Next the ME would rip him open from chest to pelvis to figure out how he died. They'd take his brain out and weigh it. Poor Hack. She gave Williams a hug goodbye and, with one backward glance at Hack, Tessa turned and left the apartment.

Stepping out into the night air, she looked up at the rooftops. Somewhere, out there, was Marco. And this time, either he would die…or she would.

Two nights later, Hack's body was released from the medical examiner's office and transported to a crematorium. The official cause of death was multiple stab wounds on the neck—he had bled to death. They had gotten his jugular vein. The hanging had just been an extra bit of theatrical flair.

Tessa tortured herself by looking at the video clip on her laptop over and over again. She sent a copy to Williams. Eventually, she knew the only peace would be found at the altar. She chanted and prayed, and she tried to find solace in her belief that Hack was in a better place. Not so much a place, but a state of being where there was no pain.

She had visited Flynn, who tried to console her, but she felt a need to be alone. Jorge, Cool and Lily were solicitous. They left her to her own thoughts. And to her preparations. For the next two nights, she trained relentlessly.

Tessa's loft had once been barren, without living space, like most converted lofts in Manhattan. Archi-

tects and designers had worked to construct walls and
living space, dividing up the massive floor plan into
a living room area, a kitchen, three bedrooms, a dining room and bathrooms—plus her royal-size closet.
But in back of one living room wall, accessible only
through a door recessed into paneling, was Tessa's
do jang, her training room.

There, samurai swords she'd brought with her
from Shanghai were mounted to the walls, gleaming
displays of metal that were literally priceless. Most
of them had engravings, said to bring the samurai
power, strength or honor.

The wooden floors were polished to a sheen, allowing her to practice her lightning-fast moves again
and again, until she and her sword or dagger moved
as one. She would go to this room every day, anxious
to maintain her prowess.

She was well fed. Though she hated thinking
about that part of her power, in truth, she had to feed
in order to be strong. And strength she needed, as
well as her decision making, her reflexes, her completely honed instincts.

Tessa took one of her swords from its holder on
the wall, and then from its sheath. Beheading Marco
was one way to kill him. Then she'd strike him
through the heart.

She had researched vampires, but had found so
much fiction mixed with fact. Sunlight, for sure,
could kill them. But silver bullets were questionable.
Garlic—she ate garlic all the time. Crosses to ward
them off? Again, it was belief. She had once faced

down a vampire and hurled a cross at him, only to watch him shrink in horror as it touched him. Over time, Tessa came to discover there were bloodlines of vampires sired from different parts of Europe, and even one line originating in what was now Moscow. She believed genetics—or sire lines—accounted for the variations in strengths of vampires.

Tessa moved with her sword, slicing through the air until the weapon was a blur. She moved tirelessly, her muscles taut. She practiced until she was sweating and exhausted. Then she returned the sword to its place on the wall. She exited her secret room and went and took a shower. As she washed her face, she shut her eyes, and the vision of Hack returned to her mind. She scrubbed hard at her skin, as if trying to wash away the ugliness of all she had seen in the last two weeks. In her long lifetime.

Stepping out of the shower, she dried her hair and pulled on silk pajamas. It was only eleven p.m., but she couldn't bring herself to descend the elevator to the club. She couldn't see all the life going on as Hack's body awaited burning.

She poured herself a glass of red wine, and she was about to settle in to watch television when she heard someone knock on her door. Instantly wary, she leaped up from the couch and peered through the peephole.

Excitedly, she flung open the door. "Welcome home, Flynn," she whispered.

"Tess," he said hoarsely.

"Should I be angry with you? What are you doing out of the hospital?"

He pulled out a small bottle of pills. "Amazing what a few painkillers can do. Now don't go being all worried. They were gonna let me out in a day or so anyway. So I just did an AMA."

"AMA?"

"Against Medical Advice. I signed myself out. You gonna let me in, or does a wounded man have to stand on your doorstep all night?"

"Oh my God, come in!" She wrapped her arms around his neck and hugged him tenderly. "Where does it hurt?"

"Everywhere. Let me get over to the couch."

She ushered him in and settled him on the couch, even taking a soft velvet throw and putting it on his lap, fluffing the pillow behind him.

"A man could get used to this treatment!"

"Yeah, well, it's only because you're wounded, Flynn," she teased. "Can I get you something to drink? Some water? Something to eat?"

"No, Tess. I'm okay."

His eyes were glassy from the painkillers, and he was still very pale, but it was such a relief to see him out of the hospital bed, out of the stupid plain blue gown, freed from IVs and tubes.

She kissed him softly on the lips. He kissed her back, hard.

"I can see the hospital didn't take everything out of you," she said softly, leaning back in to kiss him again.

Then Flynn put his hands up. "I have to talk to you, Tessa. It's a good thing I'm on painkillers or I'm sure I wouldn't. I'd just let sleeping dogs lie."

She had known, in her gut, that this conversation was coming. It had been coming since they had their first kiss, because there was no way they could move on in their relationship otherwise.

"Williams…he was knocked to the ground, shot. But before I was hit, I know what I saw."

"Flynn, it was crazy in that warehouse. So much was happening all at once. You can't be sure of anything. Add to that, you've been on morphine for a week."

"Don't try to gaslight me, Tessa."

"What does that mean?"

"It's an old movie term. It means don't try to convince me I'm crazy."

"I wouldn't do that to you."

"Yes, you would. Doesn't that mess with your karma?"

He reached into his jacket pocket and pulled out the photo from Gus. He set it on the table, wincing as he leaned forward.

"I've already seen that photo."

"So tell me the truth about it. I thought vampires couldn't be photographed."

Tessa exhaled slowly, quietly. "You're high on painkillers."

"I know what I saw, Tess. I'm a detective. One of the reasons I'm good at what I do is my power of observation. I saw you fighting those guys. I saw you flying through the air. I saw those things—whatever the hell they were. I saw it all, Tessa. That woman in the picture is *you.*"

Tessa fought the urge to run from the room, to dash

out on the fire escape to the roof and leap to another building, feeling free in the moonlight. There was a full two minutes of silence between them. She stared down at her hands while she gathered the inner courage to see this conversation through to its conclusion.

"Some of us can be photographed," she finally said quietly.

He grabbed her hand, as if urging her on.

"I was born in London in 1880…." She glanced at him, but he wasn't looking at her with disbelief. His eyes said, Go on. Tell me.

"Marco was my husband. I met him when I was a young widow. I was lonely, bored, hated my social role. He ingratiated himself with my family, with all of London. I was swept away by the talk of a deceiver, a snake. By the time I understood who and what he was, it was too late for me. I had been turned, completely and irrevocably, into what I am. I hate even the word…vampire."

"It's a good thing I'm medicated. Tessa, I want to know everything, and at the same time, part of me doesn't want to know everything. Jesus…you're immortal. You'll live forever. Just as you are now."

She nodded.

"You can't grow old."

She nodded.

"Can't go near crosses?"

She shook her head. "That one's a myth. Some of us can't. None of us can go in sunlight. We live in the world of the dead. Darkness."

Flynn winced and leaned forward, sinking his

head into his hands. "I finally find the woman of my dreams and she's...not mortal."

"Technically, that's true." Tessa tried to make him laugh. "But I was mortal at one time. Completely."

"Well, why couldn't I have met you then?"

"Because your great-grandfather wasn't even born. You weren't so much as a twinkle in your father's eye."

"All kidding aside, this means you—"

She nodded. "Yes." Her voice was now barely audible. "I kill people."

"I don't know if I want to know any more."

"Look...the Buddhism. The unadorned office. I try to stay connected to my humanity. I know this all sounds crazy—"

"You don't know the half of it. I *saw* those workers. They weren't human. What were they? Are you like them? How can you seem so fucking normal?"

"They aren't fully turned. They're slaves to Marco. Slaves to the drug trade. I'd rather die myself than end up like that."

"Then how can you do what you do?"

Tessa thought back to the girl she once was, a girl who ran in the fields of Willow Pond, devoted to her father and mother. The question Flynn asked resonated inside her.

"Haven't you ever taken the law into your own hands?"

Flynn nodded. "Charles Moreno."

"Who's that?"

"Guy who kidnapped a girl and buried her alive

in a bunker beneath his house. Tortured her while his wife was off shopping, at work. Tortured her every chance he had to get down there. A motherfucker in every sense of the word. I could smell the guilt on him. I hurt him. And I'm not sorry I did."

"What happened to the little girl?"

"She got a lot of therapy. Her name was Annie. She saw a shrink twenty-four/seven for over a year. Lived in a hospital. Then she saw somebody three times a week. Moved back home. But I didn't hold out much hope she'd ever be sane. Then she sent me an invitation to her high school graduation. She's going to go to St. John's. Wants to be a lawyer. Defending kids. That's what she wants to do. I have to hand it to her...she made it."

"And what made Charles Moreno different from some of your other busts? The ones where you didn't take the law into your own hands?"

"His eyes."

"What about them?"

"They were hollow. Dead. He could have cut that little girl's heart out and eaten it for breakfast as if it were no different from brushing his teeth. He didn't feel guilty about it."

"Remorseless."

Flynn nodded. "I remember watching him on the witness stand. How he said he was actually trying to *help* the little girl. He knew she was being abused at home, he said. He was offering her refuge. Lies would trip off this guy's tongue like he was Satan himself."

"Maybe he was."

"I thought Buddhists didn't have a Satan."

"We don't. We don't have a heaven and a hell either. But we believe in evil acts. And the man you describe was evil."

"Through and through."

"And the people I kill are, too."

"How do you know?"

"After a hundred years…I can just tell. I can smell the deceit on them, the lies. I can see it in their eyes. I go after dealers, pimps, batterers, rapists. But fighting drugs remains my focus. I have a code, Flynn. Not unlike a cop's code."

"So the dealers who've disappeared from the Night Flight Club—can I assume they're…?"

Tessa nodded. "Yes, you can. And I don't think I've looked back for a moment. Maybe a moment, but not for much longer. If I have to be who I am, then I'm going to make sure I take with me those who deserve to die."

"And how is this guy Hack that Williams told me about…how is he all mixed up in this?"

"Hack didn't deserve to die. Hack's brother was a meth addict. He and I met on a drug Web site and soon found we had a common interest—fighting the drug war."

"And your interest in this war?"

She pulled the locket out from beneath her sweater. Opening it, she showed Flynn the lock of hair from Hsu. "I loved a man once. He was young…in some ways a boy. But I was there, in

Shanghai. I saw the opium addicts—we called them ghost people—shuffling, confused. Hsu died of an opium overdose. Sometimes, when I think about it, I think he may have committed suicide just to be free of the burden."

"Did you kill the person who gave him the opium?"

She shook her head. "No. But I burned down his poppy fields. And I knew then that drugs had the power to ruin humankind."

Flynn let out a long sigh.

"What?"

He didn't answer.

"What, Flynn?"

"How many vampires are out there?"

"A lot. I think New York draws them. They can be anonymous here."

"And most of them aren't like you."

"Right. Most are so consumed by bloodlust, so hungry for blood, that they'll fly into a frenzy, kill anything that moves. They see themselves as undead, and it tortures them. Then, when they can no longer live with what they have become, they give in to that soullessness. They kill more easily, more hungrily. They lose any sense of their old humanity."

"Part of me wants to say this whole conversation, this whole night, is a morphine dream…. But I *know* what I saw. I also know I've run into a vampire before."

"When?"

"Years ago. I was first partnered up with Alex. We were investigating a homicide. Two hookers found dead, blood drained from them. They'd been tortured first. No one cared. They were found in a loading dock. City went on the next day... 'just two hookers' is what everyone must have thought."

"But you thought different."

"Yeah. First off, I thought maybe it was done by someone who *thought* he was a vampire. So that was one theory I had. But there were surprisingly few clues, and I was half tempted to just figure...two hookers. Until the mother of one of them came to the precinct."

"And what did she say?"

"She had a picture of the one hooker before she came to the Big Apple. Pretty, pretty girl. Cheer-leader. Long blond hair, apple-round cheeks. She'd gotten into the life to support the drug habit of her boyfriend, the mom said. First, she was a high-priced call girl."

"So how'd she end up in the loading dock?"

"It was at the height of the AIDS crisis. She went from high-priced call girl to emaciated hooker, turning tricks in cars down by the waterfront. I felt like I had to solve the case to give that mother peace of mind."

"Did you solve it?"

He shut his eyes and shook his head. "No. But one night, Alex and I were checking out the scene of the crime. A lot of the time killers return to the scene. A compulsion makes them do it. We see some hookers. The usual traffic...johns pulling over to negotiate blowjobs.... And then I see this guy. Dressed all in black, standing on the roof of the building opposite from where the two hookers were killed. So Alex and I get out of the car and start looking for a fire escape that will get us up on the roof. We climb up there and the guy just vanishes."

"What do you mean 'vanishes'?"

"It was like, one minute he was there, and the next he was shrouded in fog…and then gone."

"What did you think?"

"If Alex hadn't been there, I would have thought I was losing it. Burnout. Or the aftereffects of too much beer the night before."

"What did Alex think?"

"We didn't really talk about it. I mean, we stood there and kept scratching our heads. We couldn't figure it out. But we're guys. We're not touchy-feely. Without even discussing it between us, we both sort of figured it was one of those things. But in the meantime, I had this little voice inside me, this gut instinct, that wondered if the guy was…you know, a vampire. Or else a really good magician."

"I wish I wasn't what I am."

"I don't."

"How could you not?"

"Because if you weren't immortal, we never would have met. You would have died a long time ago, and I would still be wondering why I can't seem to make a relationship work."

"Because you were waiting for me."

"That's right. I told myself on the way over here

that I couldn't have been wrong about you. We're both on the same side."

"We are. It's just you do it within the confines of the law, and I handle justice within the parameters of my own code of justice."

"So now what?"

"Now we go to bed."

Flynn leaned in to kiss her. "So one day I'll be old and you'll still be young and beautiful."

"Yes."

"Doesn't sound like a bad deal to me," he whispered in her ear, kissing her neck and nuzzling into her hair. "You smell so fantastic."

She smiled at him, feeling both happy and melancholy. One day, she would be young, still beautiful—if she survived Marco—and Flynn would be old. She would watch him slip from her, to illness or senility or just plain age. As she led him to her bedroom, she realized that being a vampire, for her, was about mourning. She mourned for the sun she could never see, and for the people she had lost over the years: her parents, John, Hsu, Shen...even silly George Ashton, the diplomat.

In her bedroom, Tessa bolted the doors, explaining how the room kept her safe. Then she undressed seductively, standing naked before him.

"I forgot how perfect you were."

"Your turn. Are you going to show off your scars?"

"Sure. Sympathy points."

Flynn unbuttoned his shirt. He was still bandaged

at his incision sites. Tessa moved over to the bed, turning down the luxurious comforter. She lay down and patted the bed next to her.

Flynn slid into the bed next to her, rolling with difficulty onto his side. They were stomach to stomach, chest to chest.

"Just hold me, Flynn." Having someone in bed with her felt strangely new. Tessa snuggled into Flynn.

A short time later, she heard his breathing grow rhythmic and heavy. She leaned up on one elbow. "Guess those painkillers caught up with you," she whispered, moving his thick, curly hair from his brow. In his sleep, he looked innocent, peaceful. Tessa watched him for some time, hoping and wishing the peace they had behind closed doors could somehow continue into their waking lives.

"I think I may have turned into a vampire, too," Flynn said to her at dusk of the following night. They had both slept through the rest of the previous night and most of the day.

"No, I think the painkillers had something to do with it. At the tail end of our conversation last night, you were pretty glassy-eyed."

"I know. That's always what amazes me about people who do drugs. They actually want to feel fucked up."

"I'll take my reality straight up."

"Me too. Though a little less reality today wouldn't be too bad. Jesus, I'm sore as all hell."

Tessa looked at first one clock, then another, then

a third. The sun had set, thanks to encroaching winter. The moon, a crescent moon according to the *Farmer's Almanac,* had risen. She rolled over and slid into the crook of Flynn's arm.

"I need to handle Marco alone, Flynn." He clenched his jaw, and immediately she reached her fingertips up and stroked his cheek. "Don't get so tense, Flynn. I'm not watching you get shot again. Or worse."

"Look, you expect me to handle this vampire crap. Well, I'm a cop. It's like I have internal radar that lets me know where and when to get involved."

"Uh-huh. Like Spider-Man?"

"Kind of like that."

"Well, in this case, when you get that 'vibe,' keep away from my club."

"I can't believe you're serious."

"Of course I'm serious. Just how would you kill a vampire?"

"I haven't had to deal with that in the line of duty before. I suppose I'd shoot him through the heart."

"Ordinary bullets won't work."

"Stake through the heart?"

"And how would you get him to hold still long enough to do that?"

"Get him while he's sleeping."

"Uh-huh. You saw the security system on my door, the locks I have. The twenty-first century is a vampire's friend. High-tech security, light sensors."

"I'd cover him in garlic powder."

"Uh-huh. Like some kind of culinary challenge? Murder by garlic?"

"Won't work?"

"Some vampires have a violent reaction to the ingestion of garlic—but some don't."

"Lemme guess. Marco doesn't."

"Gosh, you're a bright boy," she teased.

"What, then? How do I kill him?"

"You don't. You leave that to me. In general, if you chop off their heads and destroy the head by burning it or burying it separately from the body, that usually does it. Fire…trap them in a raging fire. Or expose them to sunlight."

"So I can tie him up and take him out in the sun? And that would kill him?"

"Yes. But you forget the strength of a vampire is twenty times that of a mortal. He'd hardly come willingly, and you'd be unable to tie him up."

"Fine. Head chopping it is."

"Flynn…just stay away."

"Can't do that."

"Why?"

"I just can't. It goes against every code I follow, every belief I have. My father ran into a burning building to save an infant on the third floor, knowing full well it was probably futile and he'd leave his own son without a father."

"What happened?"

"Saved the baby by lowering her down in a makeshift setup with blankets. He got out just before the building collapsed. Died of smoke inhalation."

"So you grew up without a father."

"Yes and no. He wasn't there in the sense that I

had him around to play catch with, go to a Yankees game with. But he was always there, this presence. I was the son of a hero, and it has colored everything I've ever done the rest of my life."

Tessa listened to Flynn and then laid her head on his chest, avoiding the bandaged area. "All right. But promise to be careful."

"Careful's my middle name."

"No, it's Salvatore."

"What? How'd you find out? I *hate* my middle name."

"Hospital bracelet."

"No fair." He squeezed her tight, making her laugh.

"You know, I could stay here all night, but I've been AWOL from my own club quite a bit lately. I better go downstairs tonight."

"I'll go home. Shower, shave. I'll come back later or in the morning."

"Not morning."

"Right. Tomorrow night."

They both climbed out of bed. Flynn fished something out of his pocket. "Here." He handed it to her. It was a small electronic device on the end of a nylon necklace.

"This won't go with my outfit," Tessa deadpanned.

"Very funny, wise guy. Do you even know what it is?"

She turned it over in the palm of her hand. "No."

"It's something detectives use. You press this." He showed her a button. "And it's like a call alert. I have a beeper and it will go off as an SOS. A 9-1-1.

Meaning you're in trouble. I'll be the only one who gets the message, and I'll come right away."

"That's very sweet of you."

"Well, I've gotta keep tabs on you. This is some serious shit."

Tessa walked him to the door of her loft, kissed him goodbye, then went back in her bedroom. She placed the electronic gadget on her dresser. All these years, she'd managed to defend herself just fine alone. She wasn't about to use Flynn's device. And if she had her way, Marco would be dead long before Flynn ever returned to her club.

Chapter 22

Tessa watched her rack of designer clothes spin around and decided vintage, perhaps, was not the best choice—just in case. She was jumpy. Around every corner she half expected to confront Marco or Jules or some half-turned freak.

She dressed in leather pants and low-heeled black boots, topping them with a black cashmere sweater. She twisted her hair on top of her head in a ballerina's topknot and went to her dining room table. There, she replayed the torturous scene of Hack's death. The fleeting shadow was Marco; she was sure of it.

She tried to imagine Hack alive, but couldn't. The first time she had viewed the clip, she had felt a rush of insanity and fevered anguish. Now, she had gone to a place inside herself that was cold. Hack would be avenged. She went into her *do jang* and took two swords. She'd hang them on the wall of her office, ready and waiting should she need them.

Staying in that mind-set, she descended the elevator to the club and went into her office. She leaned the swords against the wall, settled into her desk chair and turned on her computer. A short time later Jorge knocked on the door.

"Come in."

Jorge greeted her warmly, but his eyes were wary.

"What is it, Jorge?"

"Nothing. I just wanted to say welcome back."

"I see it in your eyes. I know you want to say something."

Jorge inhaled deeply, as if trying to choose the right words.

"Come on. Tell me."

"I know you're in some kind of trouble."

That's an understatement, Tessa thought. "Maybe."

"I come to you with my problems all the time. When I wanted to adopt—even though I was exonerated, we were having a tough time—I came and talked to you about it. When Delorean had a lump in her breast, I came and talked to you about it. And Cool…"

"What about Cool?"

"When his mom died, he came and talked to you about it. When he broke up with that girl—the one who had the drug problem, who overdosed over him—he came and talked to you about it."

"I know. You know I care about all of you. I don't have any family. The Night Flight is my family."

"But you don't talk to us."

Tessa pushed her chair back from the desk and looked straight at Jorge. "I've been so accustomed to my solitude, Jorge, that I'm not used to relying on other people. There's a score I have to settle—and I don't want anyone else I love getting hurt. When I can tell you about it, I will. And that may be soon."

"Promise?"

"Buddhists vow not to speak untruths, Jorge. I'm learning to rely on my mortal family."

"Your what?"

"Nothing." She waved her hand. "I promise if I need your help, you'll be the first to know."

"Okay," Jorge said hesitantly.

"I *promise*."

"You know I was in prison."

"Yes. I was aware that made it onto your job application."

"Yeah, well, I hung tough. So don't you be worrying that I can't handle whatever action comes this way."

"I never doubt that. I just want you all to be safe."

Jorge left her office, and Tessa looked at her watch. She gave it five minutes before Cool came and handed her some variation of Jorge's speech. She smiled to herself. The two men were as different as two people could be. Cool was a ladies' man, a white kid from a rough neighborhood who found an escape from his alcoholic parents in music. Jorge was a Puerto Rican from Spanish Harlem. His family was intact and loving and never missed a court hearing when he was unjustly accused. He was deeply religious, devoted to one woman, and a dedicated family man. He worked at the Night Flight Club because of his size and his keen eye—not for the music. He hated what Cool played. But they had become friends.

True to form, Cool arrived within ten minutes.

"You got a minute, Tess?"

She leaned back, bemused. "Don't you have to man the turntables?"

He smiled. "Listen…" He moved over to a speaker in her office with volume control. He turned up the sound from the club. "That's an extended play Moby song. I've got eleven minutes."

He lowered the volume again and crossed his arms over his chest.

"Let me guess, Cool…you're worried about me."

"You could say that. You've been outta sight, boss lady. We've been worried."

"I'm fine."

"Bullshit. You in some kind of trouble? You…you having some trouble with the mob?"

Tessa burst out laughing. In New York City she was used to dealing with shakedowns from everyone from the sanitation union to the Teamsters to the mob. But she never caved. "No, darling. I am not in trouble with the mob."

"Okay. 'cause whatever it is, Jorge and I got your back."

"I appreciate that," she said sincerely. She had underestimated their devotion. "And I promise if I need your help, I'll let you know."

"Cool."

"Cool."

"I better go before Moby runs out."

"Dead air would not be a good thing."

"I hear you."

"Yeah, well just make sure I hear *you*."

"Good one."

Cool left her office, and Tessa looked at the plasma television on the far wall. She picked up her remote and tuned it to channel 99. Immediately, the club's dance floor came into view. Plugging in channels 100, 101 and 102, she was afforded views of the hallway by the bathrooms, the area by the DJ booth, and the velvet rope.

By clicking on a button in the lower left of the remote, she could zero in on any area of the picture on the plasma screen and zoom. Suddenly a couple grinding on the floor was the focus, or, with another click of the button, she could see the upclose, glassy eyes of someone high outside the velvet rope.

Tessa saw a shadow pass the dance floor. After a century, she knew better than to doubt her instinct and vision. She thought of Hack's analogy. "Bull's-eye," she whispered.

Using the plasma screen and the remote, she tried to capture different views of her club using picture-in-picture technology. Soon, her screen was divided into four views, each one a different perspective. But she could never focus on that shadow. It was always a blur. A flash.

She remembered, before she ever met Marco, her eyes occasionally playing tricks on her. As a mortal, she would convince herself that the blur on the corner of her vision field was tiredness. Her eyes playing tricks. But now she knew it was something far more sinister— the shadows of evil at play amongst humanity.

Tonight was the night. She could feel it. The shadows had gathered at Night Flight. And she was ready.

Tony Flynn looked around his apartment. After a night in Tessa's place, it was truly depressing. It wasn't just that he had bad taste—all right, perhaps his taste was bad, he conceded to himself—but he had so little. It was barren. No pictures on the wall. A single couch, a television on a makeshift table made from plywood and concrete blocks. A small card table and chairs for the occasional poker night. It wasn't a home. And most of all, Tessa wasn't here.

When he had arrived back at his apartment, he'd showered and shaved, put on some fresh clothes. He then settled on his couch and mindlessly flipped through channels on television, eventually settling on a basketball game. But his mind kept going back to Tessa and the unbelievable, yet undeniable truth that she was a vampire.

For a minute, Flynn thought he was going crazy.

"Next thing I know, I'll be seeing Spider-Man," he muttered to himself. But then he would remember the guy on the roof and the two dead hookers.

He and, he assumed, Alex, had convinced themselves they'd been seeing things. They didn't even report the guy on the roof who disappeared into a cloud of fog. For one thing, they'd both probably be sent to the departmental shrink. For another, they just found a way to forget it. The human mind worked in mysterious ways. Somehow the guy on the roof was too difficult to comprehend, so he and Williams blamed the whole thing on fatigue. It was the same thing with Tessa. Part of his brain wanted to shut down. There was no *way* what she said was true. But then, he *knew* what he saw at that warehouse.

Flynn was nothing if not pragmatic. Why, he finally asked himself, was a vampire impossible to believe? Why was it any harder to believe in a vampire than it was to believe in a man who would lie next to his sleeping, pregnant wife each night while underneath his yard lay a kidnapped girl, his sexual plaything?

And the Charles Moreno case hadn't been the worst. It had just been the first case to really test his faith in a God, in humanity.

Over the years, he'd seen a lot of things he preferred to forget. Most of his waking hours, he did forget. But then he'd come back to his apartment and try to sleep, and the images haunted him. A little girl raped. A mother who drowned her infant while high on crack. A wife-beater who knocked all the teeth out of the mother of his children. Kids on crack as young as eleven. Hookers dying of AIDS. Young men selling blowjobs, homeless when their families threw them out for being gay. Mentally ill sleeping on the streets. Children murdered in their beds.

Was a vampire any more unreal than the depravity of man?

Flynn rubbed his eyes. He picked up the phone and dialed Tessa's cell.

"Hello?"

"It's me. And I miss you."

"I miss you, too. But stay put and get some rest."

"You wearing your calling device?"

"Uh-huh."

"Well, let's test it out. Beep me."

"Beep you?"

"Yeah. I want to make sure it works."

"Well…the funny thing is, I actually left it upstairs."

Flynn leaned forward. "Tell me I'm not hearing you correctly! Tessa, I told you to wear it."

"Flynn…"

"I'm coming down there."

"Don't."

"Fuck that."

"Flynn, I'm not wearing it because you have no idea of the power of the vampire who's coming for me. This is my battle, and it's over a hundred years old."

"Let's talk about this."

"Flynn…talk to Alex. Look at the medical examiner's report on Hack."

Click. She had hung up on him.

Flynn rubbed his hand over his face. She made his blood pressure go up. Goddamn but she was stubborn. He called Williams.

"Hey, it's Flynn."

"How you feeling?"

"Like a fucking Hummer ran over me, backed up, and ran over me again."

"That good?"

"Yeah. That good. Listen…you have the ME report on Tessa's friend? The kid who was strung up?"

"Ye-ah…"

"What?"

"Well, it's funny you should ask about it. This case is just strange, Flynn."

"Can you make a copy and bring your file over?"

"Aren't you supposed to be resting?"

"Aren't you supposed to be my friend?"

"Fuck you."

"Just like old times."

An hour later, Alex and Flynn were sitting at Flynn's card table looking at the file.

"I forgot how nicely decorated your place is," Alex deadpanned. At the look on Flynn's face, he added, "I would have thought having a girlfriend would put you in a better mood. If it's possible, you're worse."

"Well, this particular girlfriend comes with excess baggage."

"Oh, and like you're a piece of cake. Does the name Diana ring a bell? Or how 'bout the all-nighters when you just stay in the apartment and pace because you can't turn off a case in your mind? Yeah…you're a regular teddy bear."

"Cut the psychological analysis. Or shall we bring up your womanizing?"

"All right. But I did take a bullet for you."

"After the warehouse, I say we're even."

"No. We'll never be even. I have to put up with you. Whereas you get wonderful, well-mannered me."

Flynn rolled his eyes. "Just read the files."

The two detectives looked at the medical examiner's findings. Most of the blood had been drained from Hack's body—but there was little blood found in the apartment. Where was it? Alex Williams posited that the killer was familiar with embalming techniques.

"Think about it. A funeral worker. Knows how to drain the body…made incisions on the neck… which were obscured by the ligature marks from the rope. Drains the blood by…I don't know…guess we have to go interview some funeral directors. But I think that's where we'll find the killer. This is some seriously fucked-up killer. Could even be a serial killer, you ask me."

"I'm not so sure of that. Let me ask you something, Alex."

"Hmm?"

"Remember the two hookers killed down by the Hudson?"

"Few years ago?"

"Yeah."

"Sure I remember them. That one girl's mother came and visited us, begging us to find her daughter's killer. Bothered me we never solved it."

"But what about the other thing?"

"What other thing?"

"Alex…we never talked about it. What about the guy—the guy up on the roof?"

"Some nut."

"Who just happened to disappear into thin air?"

"Well, there's that. But we were tired."

"That's what I told myself, too. But I know what I saw."

"You don't know nothing. We were tired. I was hungry. It was dark."

"What if there was another explanation?"

"What?"

"A vampire."

Alex stared at Flynn for a full minute before he howled with laughter. "Yeah…and you know, Flynn…Frankenstein and the wolfman were out there that night, too." He laughed some more and wiped a tear from his eye. "Vampire. That's a good one."

"Do I look like I'm laughing?"

"No. But you *sound* like you're crazy."

"You've known me a long time, Alex. Ever think I was crazy before?"

"Besides when you walked down the aisle with Diana…no."

"Look at this file. What's not to say it wasn't a vampire. That and the other cases we've worked on with victims who had blood drained. And what about those crack dealers who bought it down in Alphabet City? The junkies were screaming about vampires."

"Look…I can buy—maybe—that there's some freak roaming this city who *thinks* he's a vampire.

But that's as far as I'm willing to go. It wasn't a vampire because there's no such fucking thing. And I think you've been knocked on the head or had too much anesthesia."

"I need to go to Tessa's tonight."

"Why? You think someone's gonna try to suck her blood," Alex said, affecting a Transylvanian accent straight out of central casting.

"Yes."

"What kind of drugs did they give you at the hospital?"

"Alex, I'm serious. I need you to come with me."

"You *are* serious."

"Serious as a heart attack. So are you coming with me?"

"If only to prove to you this shit is crazy."

"Good." Flynn stood and tossed Alex his jacket. "And another thing?"

"What?"

"Ordinary bullets won't kill them. You have to chop off their head or drag them out in sunlight."

"Sure you do," Alex said. "Sure you do."

Flynn walked to the door of his apartment. "And the garlic thing won't work either. Not with this bloodline."

"Damn," Alex said. "And I was just thinking we'd eat some Italian food and breathe on them."

"Keep laughing. *Keep* laughing. But don't say I didn't warn you," Flynn said as he locked the door to his apartment.

Chapter 23

Tessa hurriedly went up to her martial arts studio and brought down more samurai swords. As she carried down the last of her swords and looked at them lined up in her office, she shook her head and wondered— just how was she going to be a one-woman army?

Then she had an idea.

Dialing her ultra-wired friend, she got Lily on the first ring.

"Hey, girlfriend."

"Hey, Lily. Where have you been?"

"Ohh, Cool and I have a little thing going. Spending time with him, while you, my dear, are ensconced in your bedroom with that sexy detective. I'm behind locked doors at his place."

"Lily, I need you to listen to me." Tessa adored Lily, but reliability was not one of her friend's strong suits. If you told Lily you'd meet her at midnight, she might be there around two a.m. Unless it was to go hunting, in which case Lily's predator instincts kept her on time.

"Sure thing."

"Remember I showed you the concentric circles…and sooner or later we would hit bull's-eye?"

"Yeah."

"Well, the time is now, honey. And I need a favor. I need you to go down to Grand Central Station, to King. And I need to you tell him I sent you…and that Marco and his friends have arrived. If he wants a war, he's got one. At the Night Flight. Tonight."

"I hate going down there. In fact, if I never enter an underground tunnel again, it will be too soon."

"I know. And I wouldn't ask you if it wasn't—"

"Tess…I would do *anything* to get Marco. I'd eat a rat if I had to. I'm leaving now."

"Good luck."

"Luck has nothing to do with it. Whoever's stronger tonight will survive."

Lily stood at the entrance to King's lair. She fought, for a moment, a queasy feeling in her stomach. Of course, it was a similar queasy feeling to the one she'd felt the first time she awoke in Marco's chambers, so long ago….

"Where am I?" she had asked.

"With me, child."

"Sir Constantine?"

Lily looked around her. It was 1870, and she was in his private chambers, but she had no recollection of how she had gotten there, and she was acutely aware of a buzzing in her head.

"Sit down, Lily. Sit down," he soothed.

Lily looked over at the sitting area where a dead body was slumped over in a chair. A trail of blood trickled down from the woman's neck to her bosom, to the floor. Lily fought the urge to throw up.

"What's happened?" She heard the panic in her own voice. She stared down at her clothes. Her breasts were practically pouring out of her undergarments.

Suddenly, the soothing voice of Marco Constantine was replaced by a cruel one. "Don't you remember?" he sneered.

"Remember what?" The room spun around and around.

"Your dear, oafish father came. With an offer of marriage from a neighboring farmer. A widower with ten wailing, screaming, insufferable brats. You would be nothing more than a pathetic slave. A workhorse, until that life killed you just as it killed his second wife—you would be the *third* maiden he'd worked like a dog."

In a flash, Lily recalled her father yelling at her that this was her only chance at marriage. That she had to obey him. Then darkness. She squinted and held her head and tried to remember, but nothing came to her.

"And then, my precious Lily, you came crawling

and crying and begging to me not to send you away. You have it pretty good here, do you not? You have a comfortable room, luxurious linens, all the food you wish, and a Master who only wants to be left alone all day. You *begged* me to help you. So I did."

"But why can I not remember?"

"You can, you sniveling brat. You can. You just refuse to remember. Well, let me refresh your memory…."

He strode over to the dead body and lifted her head up by the roots of her hair. "You and I fed on this creature together. You now have two choices— come with me permanently…or die."

Lily panicked. She began breathing shallowly and clutching around her for something to steady herself.

"I'll leave you to your decision, then," Marco spat at her. Then he walked out of his chambers, locking her in, leaving her with the dead body of a woman she didn't recognize.

Lily started to have flashes. The memories were fragments, each more horrifying than the next, and none of them made sense. She didn't know if they were pieces of a nightmare, or reality. Each time she blinked, she saw something, like momentary flashes of the countryside when lightning lights up the night sky.

Her father. Twisting her arm and shouting at her.

Marco striding into the room.

Begging Marco to save her…to not send her away. Clutching at his boots, sobbing.

Marco ordering her father to leave, then soothing her, speaking softly as one might speak to a child.

Then…later that night, wine. Too much wine. Then pain. Horrible pain on her neck. Then feeding on Marco in return. He called it a blood wedding.

Lily raced over to the small mirror on the Master's dresser. She lifted it up, trembling, and there, unmistakably, were two bite marks on her neck. They looked infected…festering.

More memories.

A woman from a tavern…invited back by Marco…then…but it couldn't be…him offering her neck to Lily.

One word.

"Drink."

Now, remembering, Lily collapsed to the floor and threw up. She clutched at her sides in agony.

And then, darkness.

Lily didn't know if she woke up that night or a week later. She only knew she felt searing pain.

It was pain unlike any she had ever felt. Every bit of her, from her hair to her eyelashes, to her joints and bones, to her skin, cried out in agony. The touch of the fabric of her dress against her skin pained her. When she blinked it was as if someone were piercing her eyes with needles.

She screamed. And the scream made her head hurt more. Struggling, her legs like lead, she half crawled to the door of Marco's chambers and pounded. Then she collapsed again from the exertion and lay on the floor unable to move, sure she would die at any moment.

But she didn't die.

Soon, she would only wish for death.

She gasped for air. She clawed at her face, leaving scratches. She felt agony. She called out for God, for her long-dead mother, for mercy.

And finally, mercy arrived.

But it was not the mercy she wanted.

Sir Marco Constantine arrived and unlocked the door. He pointed at the dead woman. The woman's neck had bite marks identical to Lily's.

"Your choice is simple. Death or eternal life."

Lily, in that moment, understood. She rolled over and threw up again. But Sir Marco Constantine had chosen his victim wisely. Because in the servant girl Lily Duvall, he had seen a spark of life, a girl who wanted more than to end up the caretaker of ten brats, uselessly pawed by her husband each night in an old, stained bed on a farm, used like a goat or a cow.

And so Lily chose eternal life. And sealed her fate.

Now Lily felt unfamiliar tears gather at the corners of her eyes. She swallowed hard. It had been so long since she was that girl in agony on that floor, offered a choice she barely comprehended. But she knew her revenge against Marco would all come down to this night.

She strode with confidence down the tunnel. Twice men in rags made a lunge for her, and each time she kicked them hard with her boots and walked on until she stood before King's throne.

"Tessa sent me."

"I saw you once before."

"It happens tonight. At her club."

"And how do I know this isn't a trap? Why shouldn't I take a stake and drive it through your heart now?" He stood, raising himself up to his full six-foot height, his face threatening.

"One, I would kick your testicles up into your throat before you were two steps my way. Two, you know Tessa. She has some kind of code about these things. Marco is coming for her, and you can either be there or not. I personally don't give a damn, because either way, I'm taking down as many of his fiends as possible tonight."

"You speak pretty ballsy for a woman."

"Yeah, well, you're not the only one with a grudge against him."

"I'll think about what you've said. Now get out of here before I change my mind about driving a stake through your heart. My truce is with Tessa, not you."

Lily turned on her heel and walked away. Whether King and his followers came to the Night Flight or not, she was going to make sure Marco faced sunrise.

Chapter 24

Tessa buzzed for Jorge around one a.m.

"Yeah?" He poked his head into her office.

"I need you to close early tonight. I want everyone out of here within an hour. That includes all the dishwashers, bartenders…. Tell them there'll be a bonus in their paychecks this week to compensate for the lost tips and wages. Tell them I'm shutting for a private party that just came up."

She saw Jorge's eyes wander to the swords.

"Your private party have anything to do with those?"

"Maybe. Just do it, Jorge. Send everyone home."

Fifteen minutes later, she clicked on the plasma screen and saw the house lights go up. Lily arrived at her office door.

"Come in, Lil, hon."

"I told King."

"And?"

"He was hostile."

"How unusual."

"I know. And noncommittal."

Tessa ignored Lily's last words and waved to the swords. "Choose your weapon. I suggest we make a few heads roll tonight."

"You sure it's tonight?"

"Well, sweetheart, look at this." Tessa flicked on different views from the club, all showing shadowy blurs moving amongst the lingering crowd. The house music had stopped.

"Oh yeah, definitely trouble."

"And then I looked at my calendar."

"What about it?"

"It's my wedding anniversary."

"Your what?"

"My wedding anniversary. It's not like I celebrate it. To me, it's like any other day. But when I happened to look at my calendar, it just jumped out at me. This is all synchronized for maximum effect."

"You must be exceedingly good in bed."

"What?"

"Marco Constantine gathers all his dark forces to converge on you in the twenty-first century—more than a hundred years after he marries you and sleeps with you. I'd say that's codependent behavior, wouldn't you?"

Tessa couldn't help laughing.

"I'm serious! What's your secret?"

"Shut up, Lily. I swear with each passing decade you get more…feisty."

"Well, I just want to make sure I'm never deceived or taken advantage of again!"

Tessa used the remote to click on a view of the club. It was finally empty. She called Jorge's cell phone.

"Yeah, Tess?"

"Go on home. I'll lock up."

"Okay, be careful."

"Always."

"Well, Lily, pick a weapon."

Lily chose a sword made in Eastern China circa 1880, Tessa chose a sword from Japan. Together they left the office for the cavernous club, to wait.

Jorge and Cool stood half a block down from the Night Flight Club.

"I ain't buying this private party shit," Jorge said. "She's in trouble."

"You think the mob is leaning on her?"

"Honestly? No. I think it's something big."

"Like what?"

"Something supernatural."

"What? Like aliens?"

Jorge shrugged his massive shoulders. "No. Not aliens. But something. In the club tonight…I got a bad feeling."

"A bad feeling?"

"Yup. Like Satan was there."

"You believe in Satan?"

"The things I saw in prison, my man, I surely do."

Cool stared off down the street. "Bro, I got to tell you something."

"Shoot."

"I broke up with Holly."

Jorge's eyes twinkled. "You did, huh?"

"Yeah. I got a thing going with Lily, man. I think I'm in love."

"Really?" Jorge exaggerated the question—as if the word were five syllables long.

"What? You knew?"

"Please, Cool. I'm in charge of *security*, man. I'm paid to know everything that goes on inside that club. Which is why we're going in the back way and sticking around in case Tessa needs help."

"Lily's the real deal to me."

"I know, Cool. I saw it in your eyes. When she was missing, I knew you were a goner."

"You think she's in there with Tess?"

"I know it. They're as tight as you and me."

"What do we do once we get inside again?"

"Tessa's got a bunch of kick-ass swords in her office. Whoever she's expecting, she's planning on slicing 'em to pieces. So I say we grab two swords and get ready for whatever happens."

Cool nodded, and the two of them started walking toward the club.

"I ever tell you I was in a gang when I was a kid?" Cool asked.

"Yeah, white boy."

"Just so you know—I can be tough when I have to be."

The two of them knocked fists together in a gesture of solidarity. "I never doubted it, bro. I never doubted it."

Flynn and Alex sat in an unmarked car across the street and down the block from the club. They had a pair of binoculars between them and were watching the activities outside the Night Flight.

"They closed the club awfully early," Alex commented.

"And now her head of security and DJ are walking back."

"You think something's going down, don't you?"

"Yeah."

"With vampires."

"Alex, my friend, I do."

"Flynn…you realize you sound like you've lost it?"

"Yes, I do. But if they're not vampires—how do you explain *that?*"

Flynn handed his partner the binoculars and pointed in the direction of the roof of the Night Flight Club, where, like a flock of crows perched on a telephone wire, seven black-garbed figures stood.

Chapter 25

Tessa and Lily stayed in the center of the room, waiting for whatever came through the door.

They didn't have to wait long.

Two vampires slammed open the front door and flew into the room and over the bar, knocking glassware down and landing on their feet in front of Tessa and Lily.

"Hello, boys," Lily taunted, thrusting out her sword.

"Is this Marco's idea of an anniversary present?" Tessa asked, her sword drawn, too.

"His idea of an anniversary present is to punish you," one of them sneered. "First he'll kill anyone you care about, then he'll make you suffer. Eternally."

Tessa was aware of lore in the vampire community. Suicide was only possible, for the most part, by walking into blinding sunlight. Swallowing pills, swallowing the barrel of a gun, were not enough to commit suicide—healing would follow. So she had heard of creatures like Marco holding vampires prisoner and torturing them night after agonizing night, for decades on end, never enough to kill them. Bringing them to the brink of death, and then letting them have just the taste of blood—sometimes in the form of a farm animal—enough to heal them so they could be tortured again the next night. She wouldn't put it past Marco to envision such suffering for her.

Without further warning, the first vampire leaped at Tessa, fangs drawn. She waved her sword, and a dance of death ensued. He would come at her, occasionally levitating, always hissing and making bloodthirsty noises; she would slice through the air with her sword.

To Tessa's left, Lily also attempted to fight off her opponent. Lily was not as practiced with her sword, and Tessa was fearful she would falter—but she had underestimated how badly Lily wanted revenge.

Tessa feinted to the left, then whipped around and, with a single perfect stroke, beheaded the vampire she was fighting. His head sailed through the air, and his body stood erect for a moment before toppling, blood spilling in pulsing rivulets.

That act was enough to momentarily shock the vampire facing off with Lily. Then, as if the fates intervened, he slipped for a moment in the blood of his companion. That slip cost him his head, as Lily's sword sliced his neck clean through.

For safe measure, Tessa moved to each body and stabbed both through the heart.

"This is going to be a hell of a mess to clean up," Lily commented.

"I don't even want to think about it."

"Now what?"

"Now we wait. He's got an army, Lily. He's been amassing them since I left him. This is only the beginning."

"Now what?" Flynn asked Alex.

The two men had just watched all seven whatever-they-were leap down from the top of the building, a distance that would kill a mortal. They landed on their feet, and two of them entered the building. Then the other five went in.

"Think we should go check it out?" Williams asked.

"Yeah. But now do you believe me?"

"I'm not saying I *don't* believe you, but you realize whatever we see tonight stays with us or we'll be sent packing on a psychiatric leave. Man, leave it to you—you *finally* get a woman and she's a fucking vampire."

As the two men prepared to exit their vehicle, they saw a veritable horde of what appeared to be homeless people marching up the street.

"Will you look at that?" Williams asked.

"This is going down as the weirdest night of my life."

"Me too."

When the ragtag band of people got to the Night

Flight, Flynn and Williams could see one of them, a man with flowing white locks and an expression of grim determination, was clearly the leader.

"I wish I could read lips," Williams said, staring through the binoculars.

The man appeared to be shouting orders to the other people, who all carried makeshift weapons—shovels, pickaxes, two-by-fours.

"Friends or foes of Tessa's?" Flynn asked.

Williams shook his head. "I have no idea."

"All right. We go check it out."

"Should we call for backup?"

"Not yet. Not with those flying vampires around. This is too crazy even for New York City in the middle of the night."

As they got out of their car, Flynn remembered what Tessa had said about ordinary guns being useless, but he took out his gun anyway. Just in case.

From Jorge's and Cool's vantage point, they had now seen five vampires beheaded. But every time the front door opened, another one flew in looking for battle. The two men were watching the entire scene unfold from Tessa's office on her plasma screen.

With the arrival of King and his followers, the club was getting pretty crowded.

"Who are *those* cats?" Cool asked.

"I have no fucking idea, but I say we go in there."

They each grabbed a sword.

"Whatever those things are," Jorge said, "seems like you have to cut off their head to stop 'em."

"What do you think they are?"

"I have no idea, but whatever they are, they're not human, and they want to kill. So I say, let's go."

"I'm in. What about these new guys?"

They watched King's disciples swarm into the building. Tessa appeared to talk to their leader, and he gave her a thumbs-up sign.

"Seem to be on our side," said Jorge.

"All right, then. Here we go."

Tessa's two friends left her office and then entered the fray inside the club. The floors were slippery with blood. No sooner had they entered that the front door opened and a solid wall of black seemed to block the light from the streetlamps outside.

"Fuck," Cool said. "We just got a *whole* lot more company."

Tessa was at Jorge's side in a minute. "What the hell are you doing here?"

"I'm not letting the godmother of my son fight whatever the hell these things are alone."

"You're picking me to be godmother?"

"Yes, but can we focus on those heads over there? What the hell are they?"

"They're vampires. Ever use a sword before?"

"No."

"You?" She gestured at Cool.

"Lady, I'm from the projects. Samurai swords aren't too common. Ask me about switchblades."

"Look, guys." Tessa raised her voice above the keening of the vampires. "Switchblades, guns, they might halt them for a minute or two, but it won't stop them. They're bloodthirsty, and they're powerful. Taking off their heads is the only defense right now. But be careful when you swing that sword—bring it too far back, you'll slice your own shoulder open."

"Got it," Jorge said.

Tessa spun around. "No time to talk now, boys. Watch your backs."

As she moved into the commotion, she could hear Cool's incredulous voice. "Did she say *vampires?*" But Tessa had no time to focus on what her friends thought of the scattered heads around the building. There was a battle to be waged.

The vampires seemed to multiply before her eyes. She understood, in an instant, why Marco had planned to fight her this way. First he had sent them in singly, to wear her down, make her fight longer— then he would crush her with the sheer number of his soldiers. But she had one weapon he hadn't counted on: the drive for vengeance.

She moved through the fighting, swinging her sword and carefully avoiding hitting any of King's foot soldiers. She saw two of them get bitten and fall to the ground, but all around her, with ferocity, they struck at the vampires with bats and axes. They weren't killing them, but they were halting them for fractions of moments, time enough for her or Lily, and soon Jorge and Cool, to strike with their swords.

She looked over her shoulder. Cool was perilously close to being bitten as he fell down on one knee in a morass of blood. Tessa leaped over two headless bodies and sliced the vampire in half. He still opened his mouth, baring his fangs. Cool sliced off his head. It went rolling with a final hiss.

Tessa moved on, trying to stay alert to her friends, while keeping her wits about her to fight the oncoming horde of vampires. Ever present in her mind was the fact that Marco would arrive in all his strength and glory—he would be her final battle. And he would have been feeding on virgins or whatever else he believed gave him strength. He would be powerful, and he would be brutal.

She struggled with all this as she saw the front doors open again.

"Flynn!" she shouted. "Damn him!"

She made her way toward him through the chaos of violence. She heard the sounds of bodies being beaten, the wails of victims, the hisses of vampires. They were the sounds of her nightmares.

"What are you two doing here?"

"Apparently walking into something no one would believe," Williams shouted. He had his gun drawn but was obviously dumbfounded, unsure who was friend and who was foe, and still trying to fathom that New York City was apparently a vampire haven.

"Williams, your gun can only stun them. I have swords in my office. Watch your backs—beheading them is your best bet."

Moving away from them, she struck down a female vampire with flaming red hair. She whirled and faced her old nemesis, Jules.

"We meet again," he snarled.

"Yes. Only this time, you'll be losing your head."

She struck him with her sword, slicing into his side. But he was ready for her, lifting his leg up and kicking her full in the face. Tessa fell to the ground, and he was over her with a dagger drawn. Rolling over a body and into a crouching position, she took her sword and aimed it up through his belly, piercing his heart. Blood spurted out of his mouth, and she withdrew her sword and chopped off his head.

"Life's a bitch…and then you die," she muttered, and moved on.

The carnage was massive. The smells and sounds were enough to drive a person to insanity, and she hoped her friends would all be able to cope…if they won against the darkness.

She battled on, feeling weary, but then using her powers of concentration, her thirst to avenge Hsu and Hack's deaths to spur her on. She looked around to ensure her comrades were okay. She spied Jorge and Cool, Lily, and Williams and Flynn. Then the door opened again. He was flanked by fresh vampire soldiers.

Marco.

And now the real battle would begin.

Chapter 26

She watched how he operated. Immediately his vampires scattered to the four corners of the room. Fresh fighters against her weary troops.

Marco exchanged a look with her, taunting her, and he moved in fast strides across the bloody night-club to the back stairwell. He was going to the roof.

King saw him, too, and he hacked off the arm of the vampire he was fighting and then gave chase.

"King, don't!" Tessa shouted, but he didn't turn back. "Damn him," she muttered. King and his pickax were no match for Marco. But she knew King's thirst to avenge his wife and child was so great, there was nothing she could do to stop his suicide mission. She ran across the room, sword striking left and right, and then down the hallway. She would at least back him up; maybe together they stood a chance.

She could hear the clanging of boots on the metallic staircase above her as she charged up. Then she heard King's howl. It was as if all his pent-up grief was emerging into a war cry. She rushed through the door to the roof to find Marco and King confronting each other.

"You killed my wife and child," King said, his voice strong yet choked with emotion.

"Old man, I'm going to kill you, too."

"Do you remember? A desert. New Mexico. You plucked them from my van and killed them, and left me to wander this earth, waiting for my revenge."

"I kill so many… No, I don't remember," Marco said casually. "Oh, wait. A little girl with brown hair?"

"Yes…" King's resolve seemed to crumble, and Tessa didn't know if Marco really remembered or just wanted to torment poor King.

"She cried for her daddy over and over again as I sucked the life out of her. Children only enhance my strength. I love plucking little flowers."

It was more than King could stand. He charged at Marco with his ax, swinging wildly, his emotions getting the better of him. Tessa moved closer to the pair, her sword drawn.

"Wife, I'll settle with you in a moment. First, I'm going to make him suffer—"

"Don't, Marco. This is all about me and you. Not any of these people."

"Always feeling sorry for mortals. You've let it cloud your judgment, Tessa darling."

As Marco spoke, he used the element of surprise, taking three long strides and stopping King as the older man raised his ax. Tessa heard the snap of bone and King's pained cry, then Marco took him into his jaws and killed him, pulling his mouth back, full of blood, reveling.

He dropped King's body to the rooftop.

"Now, my darling wife, it's time for us to dance."

Down in the club, only five vampires were left. Climbing over human and vampire limbs, covered in blood themselves, Flynn and Williams were beyond exhausted. Flynn looked down at his shirt.

"I think I reopened some stitches."

"You've got to rest, Flynn."

"Are you crazy? With all this going on?"

As the last of the fighting wound down, Flynn realized Tessa was not in the room.

"Anyone see Tessa?" Flynn shouted out to Jorge, Cool and Lily.

"Roof," Lily said. "She followed Marco."

Flynn raced toward the back hallway. A lone vampire blocked the entrance to the stairwell.

"Move out of my way, pal," Flynn instructed.

The vampire just laughed at him. Flynn took out his weapon, fired three rounds into him, stunning him for a moment, then took the sword he was using and chopped off his head. He kicked the body out of his way and tore up the staircase.

On the roof, Tessa glared with hatred at her husband.

"Why?" she asked. "Just tell me why. Over a hundred years, thousands of miles, multiple continents…why still chase me? Why all the carnage? It's a bloody battlefield down there."

"Because you are my one."

"Marco, you deceived me about what you were. We took our vows under a veil of lies and darkness."

"But from the moment I saw you, I knew I had to tame you, own you. You were my one across time and place."

"But you were not *my* one, Marco."

"So who is your one? This *detective* you've been seeing?"

The question made Tessa uneasy. She held out her sword. "You should have stayed away, Marco. Either I die tonight, or you die."

"Or I capture you for my own."

He flew at her, and she swung her sword but sliced at air. He was fast, even faster than she remembered him. He levitated and kicked her in the stomach, temporarily knocking the breath out of her. When she leaned forward, he reached down for the pickax that had fallen near King's body and, using the handle, struck her in the head. Tessa crumpled, her sword falling to her side. In one swift motion, he kicked it out of her reach. Then he descended on her, unzipping his pants, pressing himself against her.

"Don't you miss me, darling?" He took her face

in his hands. She fought him with her fists, striking at him, but this just seemed to amuse him.

"I don't miss *you!*"

"But do you not remember how we used to make love all night long?"

Up close, she saw time had not dimmed the intensity of his eyes. He was as youthful and dashing—and evil—as the last time she saw him.

He kissed her mouth, even as she bit his lip. "See," he teased, "you still like the taste of my blood."

"Don't flatter yourself, Marco."

His eyes grew fiery, and he reached down with one hand and ripped open the zipper on her pants. "You *will* be mine. I will break you until you are begging for me."

Tessa felt the cold night air on her pelvis as he started pulling down her pants. She fought against him with all her strength, but she was weak from the fighting. Her arms were sore from swinging her sword, from the tension and the exertion.

Suddenly, they both heard a clatter as Flynn slammed open the door and burst onto the roof.

Raising his gun, he seemed to gauge whether he had a clear shot at Marco. Tessa could see his cop's mind calculating the odds. He lowered his gun. He wasn't going to chance it. But the distraction gave her just the edge she needed. She pulled her knee up and jammed it into Marco's testicles. He groaned momentarily, and she took her fingers and rammed them into his eye sockets. As he reacted with pain, she rolled with all her might and grabbed at her sword, then swung it sideways and sliced his back. In fury, he rose, preparing to fight her. Tessa scrambled to her feet and swung her sword again. She missed him but, swinging the other way, caught his neck, slicing a vein. As the blood sprayed her, he moved his hands to his throat. She then lunged with the sword in a classic fencing move, piercing him straight through the heart and out his back.

He could still speak, but she knew he was dying.

"Did you ever love me?"

She nodded. "But it was based on shadows and darkness. You were my prince. My prince of darkness, just as Flynn is my prince of light."

She yanked out her sword, watching the color drain from his face, and then, with all the strength she could muster, she pulled back and swung her sword for what she hoped was her final time.

"It is ended, my love."

She sliced, and his head rolled off to the side, his body poised for a second before it folded to its knees and then fell forward.

Flynn rushed to her side. "I didn't know what to do."

"It's okay—it's over."

The two of them clung to each other. Flynn was bleeding.

"Were you stabbed?" she asked.

He shook his head. "My stitches ripped. I'll have to tell the doctors my girlfriend did it to me while we were making love."

"Yeah, I don't know if they would believe it happened in a vampire war."

"So, what do you think this has done to the vampire population of New York City?"

"It's lowered it considerably—but there will be more. But we also made a dent in the drug trade. No more Shanghai Red." She kissed him. "Let's go downstairs before the sun rises."

"You know, Tess…I think I'd rather stay here while the sun comes up and make sure that head and body over there don't figure out some way to get reunited."

Jorge, Cool and Alex Williams surveyed the club's interior with its sloshing puddles of blood and piles of bodies.

"Now what?" Jorge asked.

"We get this cleaned up. My God, can you imagine what would happen if this was sprayed with Luminol?" Williams asked.

"What's that?" Cool asked.

"A chemical. When it comes in contact with blood, even months later, it will, with special lighting, glow, revealing evidence of past crimes. This would light up like the tree at Rockefeller Center."

"I think I'm numb," Jorge said. "I mean, we got vampire heads all over the place and I'm not even flinching."

"Good thing, 'cause now we've got to get them all into trashbags. I suggest we take a boat out on the Hudson and then out to deep water, and *dump*," said Williams.

"What happens if they ever rise to the top again?"

"If they're vampires, they're probably so old that

they're long forgotten. No missing persons reports. No DNA matches. But we weigh 'em down to make sure they *don't* rise."

"And you? You're a cop," Cool said warily. "How do we know we can trust you?"

"My friend, there isn't any way on God's green earth that I could file a report that told one fraction of what went on here tonight and hope to keep my job and stay out of Bellevue," Williams said.

Tessa waited in her bedroom. She had given Flynn the keys to all the locks—including, she supposed, the one to her heart. She waited as she looked at the clock. After sunrise, she heard the sound of the keys, and he came through the door.

"Well?"

"Fried like a sunny-side-up egg."

"Tired?"

"Exhausted."

"Need a bath?"

"Desperately." He smiled crookedly and followed her into the bathroom while she drew a steamy bath.

She stripped and climbed in, spreading her legs seductively and waiting for him to climb into the space between them.

"You know what this relationship means, don't you?"

She shook her head.

"I'm going to have to learn to live in the night."

With that he leaned down and kissed her as he slid into the tub.

Epilogue

Tessa, Flynn, Alex, Jorge, Cool and Lily took the *Circle Line* around Manhattan. The boat was nearly empty as the bitter December night kept away all but the most stouthearted. The lower outside deck was abandoned except for the six of them. Each held a glass of champagne.

"To my friend Hack, who bravely fought with me. Brave to the end, a dear and gentle soul who is in a better place."

Everyone lifted a glass. "To Hack."

With that, Tessa furtively opened the urn. Flynn had told her she would need a permit to scatter the ashes legally—but who would be out on such a cold winter night? She turned over the urn and the ashes flew out on the wind, then down into the black waters of the Hudson.

"Peace, my friend," Tessa whispered.

The six of them were silent.

After a respectful length of time, Cool and Lily, and Jorge and Alex went inside to the warmth. Tessa and Flynn remained outside, the wind causing tears to roll down their faces.

"Do you think differently about me, love, now that you've seen what vampires are capable of?"

"No. Do you think differently of me knowing I can shoot a man?"

"I don't think it's the same, Flynn."

"It is."

"How can you say that?"

"Because…we're here, saying goodbye to your friend Hack. And I know, as well as I know anything, that you, my dear Tessa, fight the good fight."

"Always," she said, and with Flynn's arms around her, she turned to face the lights of Manhattan.

About the Author

Erica Orloff is the author of *Spanish Disco, Diary of a Blues Goddess,* and *Divas Don't Fake It,* all published by Red Dress Ink. She is also the author of *The Roofer,* published by MIRA Books, as well as the upcoming *Mafia Chic* (Red Dress Ink). Erica lives in Florida, where she enjoys her close-knit circle of family and friends, playing poker and tending to her large menagerie of pets. Her next book for Bombshell, *Knockout,* will be released in November.

She may be reached at her Web site at www.ericaorloff.com.

**In November 2004, don't miss *KNOCKOUT*,
Erica's next action-packed Silhouette Bombshell book.**

ATHENA FORCE

Chosen for their talents.
Trained to be the best.

Expected to change the world.

The women of Athena Academy
share an unforgettable experience
and an unbreakable bond—until
one of their own is murdered.

The adventure begins with these six books:

PROOF by Justine Davis, July 2004

ALIAS by Amy J. Fetzer, August 2004

EXPOSED by Katherine Garbera,
September 2004

DOUBLE-CROSS by Meredith Fletcher,
October 2004

PURSUED by Catherine Mann, November 2004

JUSTICE by Debra Webb, December 2004

**And look for six more Athena Force stories
January to June 2005.**

Available at your favorite retail outlet.

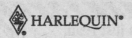

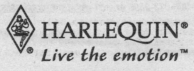

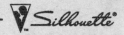

SPECIAL EDITION™

A Texas Tale

by

JUDITH LYONS

(Silhouette Special Edition #1637)

Crissy Albreit was a bona fide risk taker
as part of the daredevil troupe the
Alpine Angels. But Tate McCade was
offering a risk even Crissy wasn't sure
she wanted to take: move to Texas and
run the ranch her good-for-nothing
father left behind after his death. Crissy
long ago said goodbye to her past.
Now this McCade guy came bearing
a key to it? And maybe even one to
her future as well....

Available September 2004
at your favorite retail outlet.

Visit Silhouette Books at www.eHarlequin.com   SSEATT

Silhouette® BOMBSHELL

BODY DOUBLE

The first in award-winning author Vicki Hinze's thrilling new three-book trilogy, War Games, featuring the agents of S.A.S.S.

Captured. Tortured. Buried alive. Special Forces captain Amanda West survived it all and escaped her early grave only to discover a mysterious IV wound in her arm...and three months missing from her life. The hunt for information leads her to Mark Cross, another secret agent seeking answers to the same questions—and an ingeniously terrifying plot that means the one man she trusts might not be who she thinks he is....

War Games: When the enemy is everywhere, she's the one you want on your side.

Available at your favorite retail outlet.